DWELLERS OF THE DEEP

Izzinius Fox is a particularly avid collector of *Tremendous Science Fiction* magazine. He is also in regular contact with the Rhelm, who repeatedly zap him instantaneously up to their ship and try to convince him to part with a highly collectible edition of *Tremendous*, the May 1950 issue to be exact. This issue has a non-fiction article by Cupboard called "Engineering and Science of the Mind" and the aliens need it. But Fox is a stubborn man. He knows that as reasonable as the Arch-Leader is, the aliens' ultimate plan is to take over mankind, and he simply won't be a party to that. Can a science fiction collector really save mankind? Well, maybe…

GATHER IN THE HALL OF THE PLANETS

The aliens have disguised one of themselves and will be at the world science fiction convention in New York. All Kvass has to do to prevent the destruction of mankind is locate the alien—who will look just like someone he knows—and shout "Unmask!" And humanity will be saved. Kvass, a science fiction writer currently suffering writer's block, feel like he's encountered this plot before. But he figures, "If a group of aliens comes into your room in the strange hours of the night and talks to you about large issues seriously, it makes sense to deal with them on their own terms." Which is precisely what he does.

DWELLERS OF THE DEEP

GATHER IN THE HALL OF THE PLANETS

BARRY N. MALZBERG

Stark House Press • Eureka California

Contents

DWELLERS OF THE DEEP

BARRY N. MALZBERG

Writing as K. M. O'Donnell

"The attempt to collate, the instinctive urge for possession may strike the run of men as monstrous or insane ... but who is to say what power may not reside in these objects; what pity and terror in an artifact?"

—H. H. Brenner *The Last Possessor*

"You have the August 1947? Wow! Now that I've got it at last I've completed my file back to 1941 with the exception, of course, of the September 1953."

Dialogue at a magazine seller's table: New York World Science Fiction Convention, 1967.

For HARRY M. HARRISON

▮

Introduction to a collector, July 3, 1951.

Izzinius Fox comes out of the Astor Place station of the Lexington Avenue IRT blinking, slightly bedazzled by the sun, choking apprehensively on fumes which trucks exude as they stagger up lower Park Avenue. He takes a brief orientational stare at John Wanamaker's, then strikes out purposefully for the Book Stall; his stride twinkling powerfully against the routine background. Still shaken by his encounter on the South Ferry local with the Rhelm people, he tries to now put it out of his mind, concentrate on the goods he expects shortly to find; but the last words of the Arch-Leader himself ring in his mind, overtaking the thinner and more familiar thread of the Izzinius Fox stream-of-consciousness.

"Be reasonable," the Arch-Leader is saying. "Come on now, it's not only for our sake but for the sake of all the peoples of your planet we only want to liberate. We're going through this too often already, Fox. Now the time has come for stronger measures. Will you or will you not give us the article?"

"No," Fox had said with all the firmness he could manage, choking meanwhile on the fumes within the spacecraft. "No I won't; you see, I still don't believe you."

"Don't believe us, eh?" the Arch-Leader had said in a terrible voice while the surrounding and lesser aliens mumbled. And Fox had felt a thrill of terror go through him at the sudden force in the monster's tone. "Can't believe us after all we've done for you? Well, we'll have to take severe measures then, Fox; severe measures indeed."

And then Fox had been out of the ship, spiraling gracefully back to Earth again to find himself in the clattering subway as it eased into the Astor Place stop. It had been a numbing experience; surely the most threatening since the aliens had somehow seized his mind two weeks ago. And he resolved to himself right then that if it didn't stop soon he would have to, against all his principles, probably seek professional help. Now, however, it is already somewhat pushed away: he is concentrating on the Book Stall. And as he goes into the musty interior, and toward the small alcove in the back where Stuart Wiseman maintains his science-fiction collection, Fox gives way to the earlier mood of the day which had been bright: Stuart had phoned him to say that a February 1948 *Tremendous* had come in.

"Is it there?" Fox asks, as he comes into the alcove to find Stuart sitting perched calmly on his chair, reading an old issue of *Terrific Terran Stories* under a reading lamp. "No one took it did they?"

Stuart gives him a long easy smile—really a great guy for all his small nastiness—takes off his glasses, rubs his hands, and say: "I promised it to you, Fox; isn't that good enough? It's right here." He takes from beneath him a mint edition of the precious Feb. '48 *Tremendous*, the famous Balsch Adorer glowing blue at him; the familiar logotype clear and plain.

"Came in last night," he says. "Some guy over in Bensonhurst sold out his collection; he's getting married. Few months later he's going to buy the whole thing back but he doesn't want his wife to get the wrong ideas about him."

Fox takes the magazine from Stuart's hands, his own fingers trembling slightly as he runs them over the glistening cover, the slightly raised impression coming through to him; then turns it over to find that the back cover has a rip. Nothing very serious, but a clear deadly indentation running down the middle of the Audell Auto Manual advertisement. "How did this happen?" he says. "I thought you said *mint*."

"It's mint. Back cover means nothing. You can't even *see* that tear. Besides, I can't be responsible for what happens to a magazine when a guy packs it. Do you want it or not?" Stuart says and half stands from the stool, adjusts the string on the dim overhead lamp which provides the only faint illumination back here and then sits, closing his copy of *Terrific*. "I mean, I gave you first offer because I know you needed that one to fill, but there are plenty other guys who I could have called, any one of whom—"

"Oh," Fox says, "oh, I'll *take* it." The possibility that the issue might be taken from him fills him with dread. Rip or no, he needs this one desperately to clear his files of *Tremendous* through 1948; with it he can go clear back to June 1947. (May 1947 is another rare issue.) "Is it a dollar, right, the usual price?"

"No," Stuart says, "it's got to be a little more for this one. I paid double my usual to get it because of the condition and the guy didn't want to give this copy away anyway." Stuart winks at Fox, says, "He said he knew it was a rare issue, and he wanted to hold onto it for starting a new collection which he says he is going to do just as soon as his wife gets used to his way. This one's gotta be three dollars."

"Three dollars?" Fox says. It will be the most he has ever paid for a magazine, excepting always the ten dollars he paid Stuart six weeks ago for vol. 1, no. 1 of *Thoughtful-Stories,* mint condition, just as it came out of the plant. But vol. 1, no. 1, as Stuart himself had told him, was always an investment: fully guaranteed to go up immediately in value from the very day you bought it, hardly a magazine at all in that sense. But three dollars for a routine, barely three-year-old issue of *Tremendous* is something else again.

Fox takes out his wallet, considers the thing carefully. He is due, of course, to sign for another unemployment check this afternoon and in the bargain he is still five dollars below his weekly budget. But there is the question of extra rent coming up because his landlord installed a window in his furnished room and also he has the feeling more and more now of disappearing margins—edges being approached. He has been out of work for three months.

"Look," he says, "can I pay you two dollars today and the other dollar next week? I'm a little bit short."

"I'm sorry," Stuart says—to show that he is hardly sorry at all. He is a nice guy but there is simply little give in him.

"It's not that I don't trust you, Izzie. It's just that I've got a very solid item here; you don't get many of those around and for anyone else the price would be *five* dollars. I only gave you first crack, you know, because you're such a customer and I happened to know that you had a special need for this one and had the request in ... but it's not fair to others to give you a break on a low price. Not when they're all waiting. I got three calls this week from customers saying 'Got the Feb. '48 *Tremendous* in?' Matter of fact, I could kind of use this baby myself, you know, for my personal files; it being a rare issue and all that. It's okay, Izzie, you can pass it up, even after my making a special point of calling you this morning and holding it on reserve and so on. I don't care. I take a lot of trouble for certain customers only to get disappointed."

"No!" Fox says and realizes with some embarrassment that he has screamed; three old ladies prowling in the outer bookstore's Marriage & Childbirth section look at him with bright and victimized loathing. He lowers his voice and says, "Stuart, please Stuart, I'll take it."

Removing three dollars from his wallet, he puts the money the Stuart's palm and then snatches the magazine away before Stuart can think better of the deal. The thought of actually losing it after agonizingly having searched out this issue for months appalls him; he holds it lovingly. A strange heat seems to curl up from it as it slides so easily, so inevitably into his palms: a beautiful melding. He knows that he and this particular issue were made for one another, and he opens the contents page, looks at the familiar names and stories, and feels himself tingling with narrow anticipation. It was really an excellent issue; and in particular he can hardly wait to read Cupboard's "The

Green Death": the first and (reportedly) the best of the Space-Surgeon-in-exile series under Cupboard's pseudonym of Ronnie Lafebvre.

"Thanks Stuart," he says hoarsely. "I really appreciate this."

"Oh, it's my pleasure, Izzie. Want to look over the stock? We just got some new *Thoughtfuls* in."

"No thanks," Fox says. *Thoughtful* and *Thrilling* are the two newer science-fiction magazines, both started only a year or so ago. Although they have more "prestige" than *Tremendous*, as well as most of the old *Tremendous* contributors, Fox has for them only a dull kind of loathing, a feeling of disconcerted loyalty to *Tremendous* itself which for a decade or more was the jewel of all the science-fiction magazines and which will endure forever. He thinks vaguely for a moment of talking to Stuart about the Rhelm people, what they are doing to him, the strange events of the last couple of weeks. But Fox decides against it: Stuart could probably not understand this and in the bargain might take him for being insane—risky business when you are trying to live a normal twenty-three-year-old life in New York City,

"Well thanks," he says. "I guess I'll be in again toward the end of the week you know. Call me if the May '47 *Tremendous* comes in."

"Sure," Stuart says. "Incidentally, there's a meeting of the Solarians next Thursday. If you'd like to make it I'd be happy to take you over. They're going to discuss the early work of Teck Jones and I think you'd enjoy it"

"Stuart," Fox says. "Stuart, I told you about those things, I don't want to go. I'm not a fan, I'm a collector." Fox is dimly aware, of course, that there exists a whole substructure of people who not only accumulate the magazines but gather to talk about them *socially* and that these people are called "fans." But beyond a kind of puzzled revulsion he has no other feelings, certainly no curiosity. "Not that I don't appreciate the offer," he says.

"Well, it's up to you, Izzie. There's a whole wonderful group of people who feel just the way we do and like to get together to talk about it. But, hell, I can't force you." Stuart winks. "Bet you can't wait to go home and put that thing on the shelf, right?"

Fox gulps, nods in embarrassment, looks down at the floor feeling quite discombobulated. Stuart is the only one who really understands him—that is a truth.

"Right," he says. "But I'll want to read it first, of course."

"Well, good luck then," says Stuart "Enjoy it, it's a nice issue anyway," and returns to the issue of *Terrific,* belching slightly.

Disconcerted as always by the strange and rapid way which Stuart has of terminating conversations—it is as if Stuart loses interest in the whole thing the moment a deal is made—Fox backs out of the alcove smiling, dodges the old ladies who have now somehow drifted into the Medical Text book section, and goes out into the street. The slight, thin warmth of the magazine in his armpit fills him with a feeling of elevation which, were it not for his other problems, would pass for euphoria. It really has been a good morning, an extraordinary piece of luck and decent weather in the bargain.

On the street he plows toward the subway again. But before he reaches it the Rhelm people—goddamn those sons of bitches anyway—snatch him up again and take him far away from there. It is all he can do in his rage and surprise to hold tightly onto the precious magazine so that that at least the ungrateful bastards will never be able to take away from him. It is really too much. This thing has been going on too long. And if there were a way that he knew to stop it he certainly would. Unfortunately, events are far outside of his control—something having to do not only with the Rhelm people but with other happenings long before he met them, which tends to make them, in one particular sense anyway, almost corollary.

II

*Menacing dialogue with the aliens; Fox understands
that the fate of the world hangs in
balance.*

He finds himself sitting neatly in the interrogation chair; a cluster of aliens again around him; the Arch-Leader sitting opposite in one of those strange, tentacled contrivances which are the only means by which they can sit normally. He is passed a pack of cigarettes, takes one, has it lit courteously by a nodding alien who seems, somehow, to be smiling. Of course it is difficult to tell. The thing about the aliens is that they are so irretrievably *distant* from any normal point of reference that what he considers courtesy may be, for all he knows, an expression of murderous impulse.

"Now you listen to me, Fox," the Arch-Leader says. "You are not being reasonable. You know that I hate to keep on summoning you this way, but we really have to bring this to some kind of resolution—and quickly."

"No," Fox says stubbornly, biting his lips and shaking his head. He is a limited man, he knows; but he has a certain streak of courage. If they tortured him, of course, that would put things into a different context—then he would do anything for them. But he found out early in the game that the aliens have no power other than to bring him into the spaceship and make threats; they cannot even, for some reason, retain him for more than ten minutes at a spell due to some kind of psychic energy loss or the equivalent. Helpless against his refusals then, they can only try to persuade; but he must admit that the persuasions have been getting on his nerves. He does not know if his capacity to resist is strictly unlimited.

"I told you, it's hopeless to argue with me, I won't do it."

"To recapitulate …" the Arch-Leader says.

He has a peculiar habit, this one, of doing this almost every time Fox is summoned: going back to the reasons for the aliens' presence and their goals and motives and progress and so on. Perhaps it is only part of their civil service procedure: the Arch-Leader having let drop early on that the entire invading crew were composed of middle-level technocrats on the home planet, who carried on their assignment in terms of certain routine procedural and directives, and had to petition Headquarters for any prospective change.

Then, too, Fox is aware this habit of the Arch-Leader is very similar to the plotting of many stories he has read in Tremendous—in which people were always sitting over desks and bringing each other up to date for the reader's convenience: "… forty years ago, the Hobbs Projector had been introduced and had made transmission to distant worlds immediately within everybody's range" Patrick said. He went on to remind Donovan that there had been enormous feuds, fires and famine in the early days of the Hobbs Process but…

"To recapitulate, Izzinius Fox, twenty-three year old of the planet Earth, we have come from our home star of Guelph to inaugurate a new era of peace and progress among the peoples of your planet and to educate you into joining the Great Galactic Federation—which will free you forever from the ravages of war, starvation, misery, depression, and loneliness. We have contacted you since we can approach Earth only through a single intermediary and felt you likely. According to the policies and procedures, you must bring to us one copy of the important written materials we request—materials which are the keyword, so to speak, for our making peaceful contact with your race.

"You have refused and refused us, probably because you feel that we do not have the best interests of your planet at heart and are really destructive in intent. We have tried to plead with you, reason, persuade, cajole—all to no effect. And now our time is almost gone. We must complete our mission or return in disgrace. I am happy to say that we have now received directive 4-122B from Headquarters in answer to our own petition form 14XZ, which enables us to take more direct action if necessary. Now think this over, Izzinius Fox, because time for all the parties is running extremely short."

"I just don't believe you," Fox says, struggling to rise and then settling back with a sigh. "I mean, it's nothing personal, but I can't get away from the feeling that you're just being very cunning and intend to take us over somehow. Probably you're a group of mercenaries doing this on a flat rate."

"We must have the writings shortly," the Arch-Leader says, ignoring this. "We give you one cycle of your own time to present them to us. If you do not, we will then have to take stringent and coercive measures. Are there any questions?"

"Why me?" Fox says, which is an old response. "There are two billion of us down there."

"Because we believed that your love for science fiction would make you tolerant and we felt that your devotion to this mind-broadening kind of adventure fiction would make you a knowledgeable contact. Oh, boy, were we ever wrong!" the Arch-Leader says with what Fox takes to be a bitter twist of his eating cavity, and then raises a tentacle. "Nevertheless, our time is running short. Have you decided to be reasonable or not?"

"I don't know," Fox says sullenly. His initial panic has long since been given over to resignation, monotony, and a dull, pervasive feeling of entrapment, which is really so little different from what he has gone through during other, more mundane periods of his life. "You've never made your position very clear to me, you know. Besides, I've always had the feeling that I might be dreaming this; in which event, of course, I'm completely insane and nothing I'm saying to you applies any meaning whatsoever. But I don't *think* I'm insane."

"Oh, you are not. You are definitely not: you of all people, a far-ranging, wide-reading man in your popular field of science fiction should be able to accept the unknown without doubting yourself. You are totally rational. Anyway," the Arch-Leader says sadly, "this is really getting us nowhere and is just working into the dry, deadly repetition of our previous conferences. We cannot hold you any longer and the next time we expect that you will be more cooperative. Would you like me to introduce you to my daughter who is on shipboard through special dispensation of Headquarters? She's really attractive, for one of the Rhelm people that is, and if I thought it would do us any good at all, I'd try to have her seduce you. You know the way it is."

"No thanks," Fox says, feeling his ears redden. "I don't think that we look attractive to you, either. Besides, I've never had too much to do with girls; you know, girls on Earth, I mean, or like that."

"Well, then," the Arch-Leader says and presses a button.

Fox feels himself whisked away with enormous speed and force and then reassembles on the East Side local uptown now huffing into the Fifty-ninth Street station. Two high-school girls stare at him uneasily as he shifts on the seat and tries to draw slow, even breaths to reorient himself. He draws out from his armpit slowly the precious issue of *Tremendous*, which he studies carefully, trying to steady his hands.

The thing is that the business with the Rhelm people is really beginning to get a bit out of control and the issue of threats—he had never been previously threatened—takes it to a new level. Perhaps he is in a bit deep. The thing to do at the moment, however, is to concentrate, hold onto himself, try to get back to normal. He knows that he will not give up the Cupboard article to them if he can help it, whether Earth is at stake or not. Anyway Cupboard's "A New Engineering of the Mind" is available in the May 1950 issue of *Tremendous*, copies of which are still easily available with Stuart. Fox is sure that if the aliens care that much for the transcripts, they will simply come down and take it or call Stuart to them or some such.

The girls wink at one another, giggle, slide on the seats to converse in finger code; they seem to be talking about him. It is no matter: if only they knew what manner of man was sitting across from them! What consequences, what causality, what enormous balance wheel revolves about him! It reduces to triviality anything that they could do to deprive him of their bodies.

He plunges into the Feb. '48 *Tremendous*, delighting as always in the fine Oliver cover, the diverting book review section by Nassler, the superb editorial by the venerable K. M. Conrad, editor of *Tremendous* for as far back as most readers can remember. It is an uneven issue but a pleasure to possess. Reminding himself not to miss the Eighty-sixth Street stop, Fox gives himself over to the magazine and, for the moment, absorbed as he is in this rare issue, the Rhelm people mean nothing to him. He hopes that this is not escapism. He has always believed, passionately, in facing reality.

|||

A short flashback in deference to the
novelistic code; investigation of the Fox drives.

Fox quit his job several months before in order to devote full time to the collection of science fiction. He had been an investigator in the Bureau of Resolution and Retreat, visiting dispossessed or evicted welfare recipients in hotels to which they had been relocated, trying to find out—for a massive study which the government had financed—how their social dislocation had affected their psychology.

"Do you feel that in leaving your home you have now left yourself?" he would ask people as individuals or groups. "And what were your precise emotions when you realized they were going to throw you out?"

They would look at him with a kind of dull muddled hatred until Fox, by finger signals or winks, would be able to convey to them that it didn't matter a damn: he was just putting in time like the rest of them; all he wanted was some colorful answers. The job paid $74.82 net a week after pension plan and medical deductions, and this was pretty good pay for a liberal arts graduate.

But somewhere along the way he had fallen into the accretion of science-fiction magazines, beginning to understand that there was something going on out there far more interesting than anything the bureau could offer him. And, at a certain point, he had simply handed in his form 31B, notice of resignation, and had quit. He had figured out that the unemployment compensation would cover his rent and food nicely and leave him almost twenty dollars a week for science-fiction magazines; it would do this for at least twenty-six and possibly fifty-two weeks, and that was as far as he cared to look into the future. Life, after all, was a blind lottery.

Then he figured that if he could expand his collection of *Tremendous* to completion he would probably be able to use it as collateral for a bank loan and then get into something really interesting, maybe a dealership of his own. The fact was that Fox had not figured things out too carefully. But then, on the basis of almost anything he had learned, there was really no reason to. There was another lousy war going on—thank God he had asthma and bad eyesight—and all through the field of science fiction things seemed to be breaking down. *Thrilling* and *Thoughtful* were offering competition to *Tremendous* and stealing all of Conrad's best writers, making insulting comments about *Tremendous* in their editorials. And then too many of the writers seemed to have fallen on bad days. Sometimes he had found himself thinking that he was not reading new science fiction but was instead reading three or four basic stories being rewritten endlessly: the field had fallen out of energy.

Also his social life had gone to pieces; not that he had ever gotten along particularly with girls in the first place. But he simply had never had any luck with them at all, and at twenty had given up the whole thing with a sigh. They just weren't worth the kind of self-destruction caring about it would have involved.

The people he had associated with in the bureau had all kind of drifted away after his resignation, even though his quitting had been regarded as a great act, the first blow for freedom among his acquaintances. At the farewell party they had given him in the bar across the street all of them had said that they wanted to keep in close touch with Fox: maybe he could lend them a little of his courage. He had never gotten around to quite explaining that it was not courage which had dictated his resignation but a simple failure of involvement. He did not care anymore. The bureau no longer served his psychological needs. And he did not need the money.

Fortunately Stuart had taken an interest in him and that was an important contact even though Stuart was perhaps a little too money-oriented. There were a few people in the rooming house whom he could have talked to, but none of them, with one exception, cared about science fiction. That exception, Susan Forsythe, who lived across the hall from him, looked at it in an entirely different way: always wanting to involve him in social events and meetings and conventions and the like.

So, when you thought the whole thing over carefully, it was almost ominous. He was getting practically nowhere with his collection, having run up against a stubborn handful of rare issues which he could not for the life of him acquire; and the field did not seem to have the energy that it did when he fell into it a couple of years ago. Then, too, there was the confusing matter of the Rhelm people. That was why finally picking up the Feb. '48 had been a genuine breakthrough. But even that the bastard aliens wouldn't let him truly enjoy. Besides, they were after his files, wanted the Cupboard transcripts which he could not possibly turn over without breaking up his collection.

It was a lousy situation, there was no question about it. Sometimes Fox had the feeling that he was at a crossroads; that he would have to make a decision shortly on which way his life was going to go because twenty-three was no longer so young. On the other hand, he also occasionally had the feeling that he knew exactly what he was going to do, had found his life's purpose, and that if they would only get off his back—the Rhelm people and Susan Forsythe, that is—he could simply go ahead and put together painlessly the most complete file of science fiction in all of West Side Manhattan. It was hard to figure. The war didn't help. The Rhelm people didn't help. And sometimes, he had to admit, Stuart didn't help particularly either—what with his eternally putting a price on the nameless, a value on the imponderable.

IV

Susan Forsythe is introduced;
basic questions again emerge.

Fox enters the rooming house, climbs the four flights, gasping, and staggers into his room. For a moment he is blinded by the dazzle: someone has put the shades up and in the glare he can barely see the familiar outlines of the bed, the chair, the table, and the stacks and stacks of carefully piled magazines placed in all corners of the apartment—as well as residing in a glorious heap at the very center.

For a frantic instant he believes that he has been robbed; that some fan or lunatic has gotten in by bribing the landlord and has cleaned him out. But then he hears a giggle on the bed and meanwhile his vision clears a trifle and he comes to understand that it is only Susan who has come into the room during his absence, opened the shades, and is now sitting on his bed with an early issue of *Thoughtful*.

Otherwise the room is as he last remembered it. Furniture is lined up against all of the walls in various states of disrepair—all of it several decades old. It was placed there by his landlord, Mr. Browning, several weeks ago for "safekeeping." Burglars had been into the heirlooms which he keeps secreted in the cellar and Browning had felt he would stand a better chance, all things being equal, by scattering his possessions into the rooms of the various tenants—none of whom objected to this maneuver very strongly.

"You got to remember," the man had told him, "that I'm the landlord and that means that the property is mine and I can make any use of it I see fit. These are my rooms and you are merely my tenants. Like, if I own a slave and the slave owns a book, then I own the book, right?"

This logic had struck Izzinius as somewhat tortuous. But immersed as he had been at that time in the job of stacking up his *Thoughtfuls* into a neat unshelved row beside his bed, he had let the question go without argument. Now he has learned that some discomfited tenants have passed around memoranda concerning a tenants' meeting of protest to Browning's appropriation of their "private lives." It hardly seems to matter.

Susan takes off her glasses and says hello without any emotion at all, looking with curiosity at the *Tremendous* which Fox has removed from his armpit. She is a slender about twenty-three or twenty-four year old, with a fairly good figure. Her eyes reflect a look of hard aggression, which the glasses strangely manage to soften, and of a wondering, blank confusion, which he has always found puzzling and somewhat attractive.

Fox gathers she is some kind of production assistant in a minor advertising agency, concentrating on paste-ups of variously illumined whiskey bottles and occasional modeling of footwear. But her hours at the agency are rather loose and she tends to be in the rooming house more often than she is not, explaining that she is basically a free-lancer. He suspects that she is really unemployed but has never seen her at the unemployment offices; this may only indicate that they have different reporting dates, of course. More importantly, she is a science-fiction fan—the only science-fiction fan that he has ever known other than Stuart, and that is a professional relationship. Since he found this out by purest coincidence months ago, when she dropped into his rooms to borrow a dollar and ended up kneeling over his collection for several hours, he has never gotten over thinking that life is, after all, a rather enclosed phenomenon. The delimitation of circumstances, for all the possibilities inherent, is strictly remarkable and is the kind of thing which might be worth an essay at some time. But they have no social or sexual relationship whatsoever—Fox cannot truly regard her as a girl, which is the only reason that he has been able to get along with her in the first place. Although Susan has been trying to persuade him for several months now to become involved in a fan organization of which she is corresponding secretary and has told him more than once that his collection-instinct without social outlet is a very dangerous thing which can only lead to loneliness, parsimony and insanity if he pushes it to its logical conclusion.

"What do you have there?" she says, blinking at the magazine. "Oh, I see, it's a *Tremendous!*" She gets up from the bed, takes it from him, and begins to look at it with close interest while Fox goes to the refrigerator, takes out a coke bottle and sips from it idly, trying, as he always seems to be doing with Susan, to regain control of the situation.

"Listen," he says. "I mean, we're good friends and all that, and we have the same interests, but do you have to just come into my room without letting me know or behind my back or something like that?" Trying to come on quickly and forcefully with her, he finds himself once again trailing off into obscurantism and gloom, and says pettishly, "I mean, this is very dangerous, just going into people's rooms like that: you could be hurt or something."

"Oh, crap, Izzie," she says. "You know that Browning's crazy; he won't give anybody a key or let us lock our rooms because he believes it would be an insult and we're all just a good big family here. This is a lousy cover. Who is this guy? J. C. Oliver? All of his people look like bears and his aliens look just like people. And the color is lousy."

"It's a rare issue," Fox says. "I paid three dollars to Stuart for it so handle it carefully."

"Oh come on, Izzie, really! It's not a rare issue at all; Teddy Wilkes has five of these in his files, I happen to know. And as for Stuart, you've really got to get away from that man; I'd think that you would have seen into him by now. He probably picked that up from Teddy for ten cents and pushed it on you for thirty times the cost. He's probably trying to corner the whole market so that he can slip them all into you like rare issues. I've warned you about him, Izzie, he isn't to be trusted. I see that they have a Zeiler novelette here; that was probably the sequel to *The Tones of Timuriad.* I don't like it. That was a lousy year anyway.

"What you've got to do, Izzie," she says, tossing the magazine on the bed with a pretty gesture of contempt, making it appear somewhat ridiculous and Fox's own joy in its possession seem merely the craven ravings of a lunatic. She has always been able to do things like this to him. "What you've got to do is to get yourself away from all of this stuff, begin to associate with people who *really know* science fiction and then you'd begin to understand that Stuart Wiseman isn't your friend at all. He doesn't even know science fiction. The truth is that Stuart Wiseman couldn't tell a *Tremendous* from a *Smashing Satellite Stories* with the cover off. He's just a little cheap businessman who makes off ignorant people like you. If you'd come out with me to the Solarians—"

"Stuart invited me," Fox interrupts. "He said that there's a meeting coming up and *he* invited me."

"Oh, he just did that to impress you and because he knows you'd never come. The fact is that Stuart Wiseman couldn't show his *face* in the Solarians; since that time in 1949, when he said what he did about David Martinson, there's no one there who would *touch* him. Izzy, you've got to learn to get around and face things like this. It's a whole big world out there; it isn't only just putting together a file of *Thoughtful Stories.*"

"I don't collect Thoughtfuls. I collect Tremendous and Thrilling."

"Tremendous, Thrilling, it's all the same thing, Izzie. What's the whole point of it unless you relate to people who have the same interests that you do? Well, I can see that this is getting nowhere; you never listen to me."

Only part of this is true, Fox knows. But almost every discussion he has had recently with Susan has gone in this direction. For reasons which he cannot understand, she seems to have an almost missionary impulse to convert him to "fandom" and which she says is the key to a happier existence—not only for Fox but for any serious reader of science fiction since "fandom" operates to get a person out of his "shell."

It is possible that if she was a little less positive, a little less determined, a wee bit more tolerant of his nature, he might have told her all about the Rhelm people some days ago. Because the fact is that he needs very badly to have someone to talk to. He is not sure what is happening to him but has had the intimation that his sanity is crumpling, and it would be a good thing to at least share his apprehensions if not the madness itself with another person of similar interests. On the other hand, Fox is sophisticated enough to concede that if his relationship with Susan was deep enough to embrace any concept of confidence she might terrify him so much that there would have been no relationship at all. The thing is that he simply cannot regard her in that fashion. It is for that reason, as much as any other, that Fox finally lets himself go after weeks of resentment and says:

"Listen, Susan, I've really had enough of this. You don't like my collection. You don't like my magazine. You don't even like *me* that much; everything which I do is somehow wrong for you. All you want to do is to push me onto your friends. If I'm so bad why don't you just stay with your friends and leave me out of it?"

This speech, given with the intent of being a smashing and final retort to everything which she has done to him somehow seems to go right past her. She merely sighs and rumples the sheets on the bed and says:

"Oh, Izzie, you take everything so *personally.* No wonder Stuart Wiseman can rob you blind."

And he is left absolutely speechless, suspended somewhere between rage and grief. There will never be an end to it until Susan moves out of the rooming house, which, she has indicated, she will not be doing for a long time since she finds the rent cheap and Browning "a real crazy and interesting character."

"I'm a collector, Susan," he says irrelevantly, trying not to whine, which is almost always his tendency under pressure. "I'm just interested in the magazines and the writers. I don't really feel like making a social thing of it."

"Yes," she says. "Yes, Izzie, but you're all, all wrong, you see." But she seems to have lost interest in the topic and her attention, as usual, when she no longer wants to deal with a subject, seems to have drifted somewhere below and slightly to the left of him; her eyes fixated on some crack near the ceiling into which Browning, some months ago, inserted the corpses of two roaches, apparently not only for safekeeping but for aesthetic reasons.

"How many *Tremendouses* do you have now, Izzie?" she asks. She is obviously less interested in his answer than in creating some kind of a mood. Still it is the kind of cue which Fox finds irresistible.

"It isn't how many you *have*, Susan," he says. "I mean, anybody can have a lot of issues. The point is how far back the collection is complete."

"If you're that kind of collector."

"Well is there any other kind of collector to be? Now the thing is that you want to have an unbroken line of a magazine going back of course to vol. 1, no. 1. But it's also important that you keep your gaps filled in. That is you wouldn't want to have a lot from 1949, say, and a lot from 1942 and nothing in between. That way you'd have a seven years gap whereas if you scattered the *same twenty-four issues* through the years you could have three issues from every year and then fill in around them. Lots of people make mistakes like that: they think that they should pick up a complete '48 or a total '46 and then they lose everything in between because the issues they passed up while they were going for separate years can get kind of lost in the shuffle and turn out to be *rare* and then where are you when you try to fill in, when you want to back up toward completion, well, Susan, you're in the *soup*. That's all there is to it, straight in the *soup*. But I want not only completion but a good *scatter, if* you follow what I'm saying, and I try to scout out the rare issues. Now, in my case—"

"All right, Izzie," she says, "all right, calm *down*." Fox realizes that he has been pacing and gesticulating rather wildly and sits down on the bed next to her. She absently strokes his palm and seems to slide her hips against his: a peculiar movement.

"In my *case*," he goes on, "I've tried to have it both ways: good scatter and then bulking around certain months. But now I'm complete back to June 1947 and, skipping the May 1947, I'm complete again back to December of '45 and then I only gap until July. I've got them in every year. I have—I figured this out now—I have an 85% complete collection with a modal variation of missed months of only *two* and then—"

"Well," she says, "that must be very exciting, Izzie, but you're sweating," and puts a hand on his forehead. He can feel the cool, flat dampness of her palm working against his skin, the hint of circles around the hairline. She moves in to look at him closely and he sees the open blandness of her eyes, small curves of her neck. It is suddenly a peculiar moment, unlike any he has previously known with Susan, and he feels frightened. There is a strangeness to it, but then something seems to slip into gear.

He puts a hand on her waist and with a small groan she slides against him, her mouth parting toward him, and he comes down on her. There is a feeling of clanging in his limbs and a strange sensation, which can only be described as *curiosity,* and he is immersed—immersed as he really never has been in this way in his life. Something seems about to happen and something *is* happening and just when Fox feels himself on the verge of something enormous—either catastrophic or beneficent, he does not know which—at that very moment the Rhelm people—the dirty sons of bitches, the lousy stinking miserable bastards—the Rhelm people snatch him up again and there is a feeling of dislocation. Wow, is there a feeling of *dislocation!* And she goes away and everything goes away and he is back in the goddamned ship again with the aliens bobbing and leering over him and here we go again all right and Fox is not sure, at this juncture, that he can stand any of it. Invasion is one thing but meddling with a man's private life should certainly be called another.

V

*Further dialogue with the Arch-Leader; a threat
is made; Fox feels that the situation is slowly
getting out of hand; feeling of rushing stardriven
in the endless universal night.*

"Well, then, Fox," the Arch-Leader says, bending over him with something which seems vaguely like compassion twinkling in his deep-set eyes. "Well here we are again. Have you thought things over? May we have your decision?"

Fox struggles against the bindings, feeling himself fill with rage. It is really the first time he has gotten *mad* at the Rhelm people.

"Listen," he says, "are you aware of what I was *doing?*"

"Of course we were aware," the Leader says sadly. "We're aware of everything; we just can't intervene much. The thing is that we have to take you back when it's necessary, not when it's convenient. Besides, I don't really think much of that fellow human of yours; she has a very shallow consciousness."

"No she doesn't and in any event it's none of your business! Do I give opinions on your crew?"

"Why should you?" says the Arch-Leader. "It wouldn't make a bit of difference to any of us. We all have full certification. I'm afraid that our standards of judgment would not apply to you or, of course, vice-versa. Nevertheless, that is a very silly girl you've got there, Fox. She's dangerous because she's so stupid. And, furthermore, she doesn't appreciate you."

"I don't give a goddamn what you think." Fox roars, trying hopelessly to twist free of the bindings. "And in the bargain she's not my girl, and in the last place I really can't take any more of this. Now if you want to conquer the universe that's your business and good luck to you, but I'll be damned if you can interfere with my private life!"

"Oh nonsense," the Arch-Leader says with an almost benevolent calm. "Nonsense. You realize that there's no lag at all, our discussions take place in neotime, in a couple of milliseconds between respirations. And when you go back you won't have missed a beat. Your silly social affairs have never been meddled with. And in the second place you're the one causing all the trouble for yourself; we're just trying to be utterly reasonable. Have you made your decision?"

The insufferable arrogance of the Arch-Leader is the final straw. Fox says, "Yes, I *have* made my decision. I won't turn over the article to you. Why should I? If you're so omnipotent you can just go down and *get* it, then you won't have to wheedle it out of me."

The Arch-Leader sighs a massive sigh which seems to inflate his being into different proportions.

"All of you get out of here," he says to the other aliens. Scurrying, they hasten to obey. They leave the room very quickly and there is the sound of bolts and tumblers clicking into place. The Leader floats away for a moment, comes back, sighs again and kneels down to a point where he regards Fox's knees.

"Oh, come on," he says, "be reasonable. I thought we'd have one last private discussion and maybe try to bring you to your senses, Fox. The trouble with most of this crew is that they have no sensitivity, no patience, no awareness of the intricacies of diplomacy; they are a bit more eager to take direct action than perhaps I might be. After all, they're only putting their time in, they want to complete the mission and get home. A man like me, with certain social and technological advantages, can take a somewhat longer view. But I tell you the truth: I don't know how much longer we can keep up our mild little discussions and expect me to retain control. There are certain strong, dissident groups here who are in favor of torture or worse. So I'll try to be reasonable this one more time, Izzinius, and then things will really have to get moving along. Why are you so stubborn?"

Not thinking for the moment, Fox answers with the simple truth of it. "You see, the thing is that I think I'm insane," he says. "I feel that I'm probably dreaming the whole thing anyway or that I've gone into one of those schizoid breaks with reality. So nothing that I do can possibly matter and I might as well retain my self-respect."

"That's common," the Leader says, "I mean, it would be expectable in the normal population; but you're a supernormal, Izzinius: an exceptional man, an intellectual, a collector and a science-fiction reader. You are someone whose involvement in this field of special extrapolation should, by any reasonable expectation, prepare you to be open-minded, to accept, without question, things that the rigid, narrow, limited hierarchical types up there couldn't. I just can't understand why we're having so much trouble with you. Surely you've read enough stories of alien invasion and so on to be able to accept this kind of thing as a real possibility."

"But you see," Fox says, "you see, that's the thing. I've gotten really hooked on science fiction in the last year or so, I admit that. But maybe I couldn't put up with the strain, all of this stuff taking over my mind and so on, really getting involved with it. So I've had a breakdown and from time to time I hallucinate. Of course I don't *want* to be insane, it's just the way that it looks to me. Probably it's nervous fatigue, but I can't afford to get the kind of rest I'd need."

It is really surprising, now that he and the Arch-Leader have finally gotten to talking things over quietly alone, how reasonable, calm and sensible a discussion they can have. The creature is not really unreasonable. As a matter of fact it has a point—at least as much of a point as Fox does. Of course this cannot change the outcome, but for a moment he has a feeling of regret: it would be nice if it could. It would be nice if he could work the situation out on a rational basis, accept it for the insanity it is, but still follow it through to a reasonable point. Of course this is impossible under the circumstances; but it is the kind of thing, at least once during a situation, that you might want to think about.

"Now you see," the Arch-Leader says, "the point is this: we very badly need Cupboard's 'Engineering and the Science of the Mind.' Those transcripts are far more crucial than you might possibly imagine to our plans and goals and until we have them we cannot proceed. But we can't get them ourselves as you suggest, it just isn't that easy."

"Well, why not?"

"Because," the Arch-Leader says with infinite patience, "those transcripts are in the May 1950 issue of *Tremendous Science Fiction* and that happens to be a rare issue. There are very, very few copies around: just a few with specialized dealers who hardly want to sell anyway and would be loath to let go of it for almost any price. The articles created quite a storm, we're aware of that. Now, we just can't appear in a bookstore or at one of your conventions and try to pick up issue of that magazine. It would create a sensation."

"Why?"

"Can you imagine us, one of us that is, coming in and to buy a May 1950 *Tremendous* and being treated as ordinary customers. No, Fox, it wouldn't work: it would create a sensation and we'd never get it anyway. What we have to do is to approach someone—someone like you—who happens to already have a copy of that issue on hand and with whom we can negotiate. Besides, where did you get the idea we're omnipotent? The fact is that we're very limited in what we can do and we function in terms of a very structured situation. We're just the civil service. That's ultimately why you have nothing to fear from us. We couldn't possibly 'take over' your foul little planet; all that we could do would be to kind of, um, *guide* and *instruct* it a bit while leaving it as always in the hands of leaders, who, I might say, seem to have far more of their interest at heart than yours. Leaders, who, I might add, further seem to represent far more of a danger to you than any one of us. You might want to think about that some to add to your other series of considerations: *who really cares about Izzinius Fox?*"

"I've never been a political person. I mean, I just never was interested in that kind of thing. It isn't that bad as far as I can see. We have a lot of problems, but things seem to be getting better. And, anyway, what the hell does it have to do with me?"

"Well," the Arch-Leader says a bit grimly, "you just wait, Fox; you just wait. We've had experience after experience with systems like yours, and I tell you that the trends are nothing that would make you particularly happy. The whole thing is beginning to go under with such shocking speed and force that twenty years from now, if you people are not diverted from the course you are following, twenty of your years from now the nature of the lives led by most of you will be simply insupportable. And all through the right, left, and center the society will be absolutely riven, literally toppling about you: tremendous repression, anarchy, dislocation, drift.

"Well, why talk about it, Fox. It's just depressing and anyway it has nothing to do with the situation at hand. I can't persuade you that way. The trouble with you creatures is that you *like* the nature of your lives; you think that the system is somehow *inherent* to your nature and then you tie it up with religious determinism and destiny and so on and there you are. This kind of culture lag is shocking, simply shocking. Why you people are *post*-technological, Fox, and you don't even realize that yet; you're still trying to work with an armory of emotions and social devices which were outmoded over a century ago. But I'm tending to wander, I took a few sociology credits in the training school and perhaps tend to think about it more than is really necessary in my job.

"We want those transcripts, Fox, and we want them now."

It is one of the most interesting discussions Fox has ever had with anyone. One of the lacks in his life has always been vigorous intellectual discourse to the level of his potential. The Arch-Leader, no matter how much a figment of his imagination on the one hand or how malevolent on the other, is a fascinating conversationalist—there is no doubt about that at all.

"What's so important about 'Engineering and Science of the Mind'?"

The alien's eyes seem to gleam and he gives a short, hysterical bark, then settles back, curling around Fox's knees and says, "He discovered the *secret*, Fox. The veritable *secret* of relations among creatures on your planet, the behavioristic tendencies, the nature of the repressions and blocks which so saddle you under. With those materials to work from we can instantly deduce the best way in which we can grant you the mass therapy you will need to join our union; without them we have to struggle in the dark! Profound wisdom, Fox! Profound, inert mysticism interlarded with the holiest of truths! In any culture, at some stage like this, there comes along a man to yield you the best, truest, most concise and deadliest picture of yourselves and that is what Cupboard did in his 'Engineering and Science of the Mind.'

"Of course it's a pity he had to do it in one of your pulp magazines as opposed to what you would call the, uh, the *slicks*. But the nature of genius and the final insight is that it is almost inevitably going to be cast aside in its own time. It only finds its truest identity, causation, meaning, and relevance later; and the important thing is that he was able to publish it. Now, we must have those articles, Fox, in order to proceed."

"I see," Fox says. "I never thought that Cupboard was much of anything really except a science-fiction writer. I never liked his stuff particularly. If you want to know the truth, I never even *read* the article. I never read the articles in *Tremendous*. They're really sort of dull, if you want to know the truth, and I don't like the editorials too much either. I used to like them, but now I don't understand most of them. And I don't even like the letter section too much; something seemed to happen to it late last year—the letter section, I mean—and now it has nothing to do with the stories. And when you come right down to it, I don't even read the *stories* too much anymore."

"Well," the alien says crisply, "that's just one of those things, Izzinius. Perhaps the trouble is that you're growing up and your energies can no longer be contained by this particular obsession. At least that's what one of our psychologists might say about you if you were one of our people; my understanding of the psychology of the people of your planet is hardly so excellent. I really would enjoy going on and on, talking these things over with you, but I'm afraid that the gap is spreading and we really must wind things up now. I've tried to be reasonable, you know, and really hear you out and explain our point of view as well. Will you give us those transcripts?"

The alien leans forward, his strange eyes seeming to narrow. At that moment Fox realizes that it has all been a pose and that the creature, no less than at any other time, has simply been out to get him, to manipulate him against his will into a kind of betrayal. Whatever else can be said about Izzinius Fox, this one thing is sure: he is not of the stuff that would betray mankind. Not ever. Mankind is all he has. It is, so to speak, his Home Race—he has begun to think this way only since the coming of the Rhelm people, but it is still very stimulating way to feel—and there is nothing he would ever do to turn his back on the genus that has given him life.

All these thoughts and more go through his mind in the instant. He is aware that the alien is regarding him coldly, but at this moment the alien itself does not exist. All that there is is conscience, choice and memory. Seizing on to the three together, Fox knows what the answer will be.

"No," he says.

The creature's face seems to congeal. The doors are instantly torn open as a flood of aliens come through, all of them with expressions as disconcerted as the Arch-Leader's.

"All right, Fox," the creature says quietly. "Well and done. Our time now is unfortunately up and we will have to resume our discussions on a different level when we begin again. I thought that it was possible to reason with you. I thought that an approach which dealt with sense and justice would be satisfactory. But naiveté, as you see, is not a trait restricted only to members of your race. Next time, Fox, there will be no discussions. There will be no dialogue. There will be no persuasion. You do not really expect us to try to be reasonable forever. Not in the presence of a representative of a race so stubborn, so vindictive, so deeply rooted in its projective neuroses that it is unable to deal with simple universal *truths*.

"We'll get you Fox!" the alien screams. "We'll fix you for what you've done to us. You're not dealing with a pack of your extrapolatory monsters here you understand; we happen to be official representatives of the galactic union."

The Arch-Leader bends down once again, rubs his face against Fox's foot. And for the first time Fox senses respiration, ingestion; comes to understand that the aliens, like most sentient beings, probably have bodily processes and that those processes in the case of the Arch-Leader have been momentarily impeded.

"Next time the whips!" the alien screams, while the figures behind him seem to mumble in dispassionate agreement. "Next time the irons, the spikes, the nails, the thumbtack. The small, excruciating marks left upon the flesh. The kicks, the humiliations, the barbarism, the degradation, the realization of every one of your silly archetypal nightmares! That's it, Fox!" the alien bellows.

The scene, thankfully, begins to dissolve. There is once again the feeling of implosion coming upon Fox and he submits to it gracefully this time, trying to speed his removal.

"The irons, Fox!" he hears in the background and opens his mouth to scream defiance. Something sufficiently terran and heroic like: "You mean nothing to me, I'm just dreaming!" or "I'll never betray the green hills of Earth!" or "Mankind is clean and vigorous and growing and we will never settle for your corruption!" Something that would put the wraps on the interview, so to speak, and show these filthy aliens where he, Izzinius Fox, will always and truly reside.

But it is too late and thank God for all of that because the fact is that he is terrified and he is back on Earth, in his furnished room on the West Side, in Susan's arms. No dissolution here as he stiffens against her, in the interval of no-time, giving one small, barking screech to punctuate his adventure as she gasps in response and tries to fold her large breasts around his helpless head.

VI

*Retrospection in the heart of darkness; two
kinds of deprivation collaborate; the
first examination of this.*

Susan has taken his fear for passion—which may be an old problem with her anyway for all he knows—and her response is both acute and surprising. What she is trying to do, with enormous concentration and intensity, is to work Fox into some kind of implementation of his sounds, trying to bring forth from him some concrete testimony of necessity. And there is no way for the moment, of course, that he can explain to her that she has got him wrong. It also would be an unseemly thing to do since Susan, except for Stuart, is his one contact with humanity and certainly his only contact at this difficult moment. So Fox, trying desperately to thrust himself into a mood and purpose he has never known, does what he can, fumbles with her, tries to lay her bare, encourages himself with twitches and moans to rise beneath her.

She mumbles into his ear, "It's all right, Izzie. I'm here; I'm here," as if she could be anywhere else.

For the moment his terror of breaking away from Susan outweighs the terror of staying with her. So the fact is that for the first time in his life Fox finds himself truly on the verge of Getting It. *Its* qualities, *its* implications hover within his very grasp and it is nothing like he imagined it would be. He is not in the least terrified; it is only a matter of flesh against flesh or perhaps one could call it a question of matching bruises, breath, sobs sigh for sigh in this close, unwieldy space.

But his preoccupation is too enormous. He is thinking of the Rhelm people (perhaps this is the reason why he is not terrified: he has other and more important things on his mind). Shortly his movements start to become mechanical; he becomes aware that he is forcing himself rather than moving spontaneously. There is a feeling of slow, vanishing retreat from all the edges and then he has backed away from her.

She is holding him at arm's length and looking at him with some intenseness while she says, "Izzie, you've got to be more *patient*. You're *forcing* yourself."

This is the final straw. He cannot control himself any longer. The irony of all ironies is that after twenty-three years of deprivation he has found himself in the act of Getting It precisely at that moment of time when nothing could interest him less. Small chuckles and gasps move gracelessly inside him.

Susan looks at him out of a kind of deep bright pain and says, "Why are you laughing?"

He comes to understand in the instant—he is a man of unusual sensitivity no matter what the Rhelm people or Stuart Wiseman think of him—that she feels that he is laughing at *her*. A moment of absent tenderness flicks through him, thrusting him to a moment of emotional perception, perhaps as "mature" as any he has ever known, because in that instant he sees her pain and he comes to understand that in a difficult, more qualified way, it is more profound than that bleak pain of his own which he has carried around for so many years.

How could they do this to him? How could this be the joker at the end of all those years of loss? ... that women felt as profoundly as men and suffered as much. He understands that he is in a position to hurt her very deeply and the thing is that he does not want to. He does not know what he owes to her, probably nothing, certainly very little, but he certainly has no right to bring this look into her eyes; and in any event he is too shaken, too shaken. Too much has happened to him now, even if the Arch-Leader is correct in saying that his particular interrelations occur in no-time. He cannot control himself anymore. He feels it all coming out. What he does is to tell her all about the Rhelm people.

He does so by leaning back on the bed and beginning to talk, after a while when she is listening intently (at first she had thought he was crazy but in a few moments he was able to wipe that suspicion along with all remnants of pain from her face; Susan, he comes to understand, could more easily apprehend, understand and accommodate herself to the destruction of all human life on the planet than she could a sexual rejection), he leans forward to gesticulate, when he has her totally involved, at every conceivable level, he leans back again and finishes it off.

It takes about thirty minutes, maybe a little more or less, he is not keeping time. He tells her about the First Interception which occurred while he was lying on his cot equably reading the January '49 *Tremendous: Parking Ticket,* a novelette by Damon Tyson, has been the Tek Room winner for that month and he had looked forward for a long time to catching up with it (but it turned out to be pretty lousy) and the Second, longer Interception which occurred while he was rushing for the uptown bus on Fourth Avenue and which had seized him midway between stumbling over a fat old lady and coming into the enormous hilarity of a patrolman's hug, the Third Interception which fortunately had occurred to him in his very own rooms, this very place, a few days later and then the famous Fourth Interception itself at which time the Arch-Leader had finally gotten to the point and made the request for the Cupboard Transcripts.

Susan listens to the entire story with strange intentness, fitting a cigarette repeatedly into her golden holder without ever quite lighting it. She sighs to herself; mutters and mumbles; once reaches out and strokes his forehead when he describes a particularly chilling gesture of the Arch-Leader. Finally she kindles into horror and outright concern when he explains what has just happened to him at the very moment he was in Susan's arms on the very lip of finally having an experience he had never had before and which, thanks to the cruel and stubborn Arch-Leader, had been permanently wrecked for him.

"Oh, I wouldn't say *that"* she hums.

But Fox is not quite finished yet. There are implications to be discussed, and his theory of Alien Behavior. "I think it's all a blind," he says. "I mean, I don't think they want the Cupboard transcripts at all. That's all crap and nonsense. After all, who could take Cupboard seriously? No, if you want my theory, they want one artifact, one physical *thing* from Earth which they can keep; they can't *keep* anything, you see, unless it is willingly given over to them by a human being. That's my theory. And once they have these transcripts then they'll have power over us. So they cooked up this whole story about needing the article because they thought that I, as a science-fiction collector, would be gullible and willing to believe it; but they could have asked for *anything*. I mean, that is my theory, anyway, Susan, and that's about the whole thing now.

"I've been living under a great deal of strain as you know, but I'm glad I finally was able to talk it out with someone like you who might understand. But if you think I'm crazy, well, then I'm crazy and that's all there is to it. You don't think I'm crazy, do you, Susan?"

She ponders the point for a moment before answering, curling her lips together, and finally lighting the cigarette; watching the smoke drift up to the odorous corners and surfaces of the room while she makes him wait. He realizes that she is enjoying this, but on the other hand perhaps she is entitled; he has, after all, given her a rather rough time and she has been very courteous about listening to the whole thing. At last she says:

"No, Izzie, I don't think you're *crazy*. I mean, I don't know quite what there *is* to think. It's a highly unusual thing, of course, and the average person might think that you were crazy, but who am I to think so? Besides, my judgment doesn't mean anything. I do think that you've been reading too much science fiction, though."

There is a bland calmness to her voice; a kind of careful, gentle, overreaching sentiment which utterly masters him *and* her own implications. He comes to understand that Susan is so grateful to have had any kind of explanation, no matter how peculiar, for his withdrawal that she feels that the situation, in any event, has returned to her.

"It has nothing to do with science fiction!" he says rather loudly. "*You* read a lot of science fiction! All your friends in the social club read a lot of science fiction!"

"Solarians," she says.

"Solarians! What do I care? The city is filled with people who read a lot of science fiction and never had this happen to them! Joseph Steele reads a lot of science fiction! K. M. Conrad, the editor of *Tremendous*, says that he reads four hundred science-fiction stories a *week* for his magazine! And they aren't even all good! What does it have to do with reading science fiction?"

"All right, Izzie," she says, "don't overreact." And Fox realizes that he has indeed done this. He is reaching, as a matter of fact, in exactly the same fashion that he had some months ago when his mother for the first and only time visited his furnished rooms (unannounced, of course) and had seen the piles and piles of science-fiction magazines. She had started by berating him and then had switched to a certain soothing tone of voice, a certain understatement of manner which infuriated Fox because he came to think that she thought him insane. The whole thing had ended very unpleasantly. They had had no contact since.

"I'm not overreacting," he says sullenly. "I mean, it's a pretty horrible thing to live through, don't you think? They aren't doing this to *you* or to your friend Teddy Wilkes. They're doing it to *me* and it's all I can do to stand it anymore. How would you like to know that at any moment a goddamned group of ugly aliens could seize your mind and put you in a goddamned spaceship and start to make threats and torture you about the fate of Earth? They say they're going to *torture* me next time, Susan! They say they won't *negotiate* anymore! It could be the whole fate of *Earth*! Do you think that that's a pleasant thing for me to go through? And you talk about overreaction!"

"Teddy Wilkes isn't my friend," Susan says, putting out the cigarette carefully after having not really smoked it at all. "He's just one of the people down there. I mean, I've *gone* with him a couple of times, and he took me to see *South Pacific* last month, but it wasn't what you would call a *date*. Certainly there was nothing between us. I don't think that Teddy Wilkes is too interested in girls anyway, to tell the truth. I think that he's interested in science fiction and Teddy Wilkes too much to ever get involved. You know, I thought the same thing about *you*, Izzie, for a while."

"All right," Fox says. "That's not the point."

"Well, what *is* the point?" Susan says. "I certainly don't think that it's fair of you to start blaming *me* for your problems. I didn't get you into this, you know. I mean, you don't think that *I* had anything to do with it, did you?"

"No," Fox says. Susan's unreasonableness stirs him. The fact is, he feels that for the very first time he is beginning to understand women. Unfortunately he is not sure that he wasn't better off looking at things in the previous way. It is something very difficult to figure out. He begins to understand that here, no less than as with the Rhelm people, he has been vaulted into another world of shuddering possibility, strange implication, multiplicity of motive far beyond his mild means to cope with it. It is really too much for him and he sinks back on the bed sighing, gasping, rubbing his eyes, truly overwhelmed by desperation and yet at the same time leaving just enough of a cautious crack in one exposed eyelid to be able to judge Susan's reaction to his seizure. There is no reason, after all, why he should have to go through this alone.

"Well, all right," she says after a time, leaning down to look at him. "All right, Izzie. I can see where it's been a terrible strain. I mean, *I* don't know whether it's really happening or not, but in any case it's something pretty terrible to live through, I suppose. The thing is that you shouldn't make remarks about people like Teddy Wilkes, who you don't even understand, without being sure that you really understand them if you follow what I mean."

Fox sighs, sinks back even further into the bed, tries to block out the whole thing. Possibly he could go to sleep and when he awakens it would be behind him: if not the Rhelm people (they seemed very determined and competent), then at least Susan—which would be something of a blessing.

"Anyway, I'll tell you what I think," she says. "If you want my best idea on the whole thing. You should come with me to the Solarians tonight and tell them the whole thing. Maybe they could help."

"I don't *want* to go to the Solarians," Fox mutters. "I'm a *collector*. There's nothing they can do to help me."

"How can you say that? They're all science-fiction people just like you and me and if *they* couldn't understand what's happening to you, who could? These aren't fools, you know, these are some of the brightest people in the city. If they can't give you a fair hearing and some ideas about what you might be able to do, then, Izzie, you're not really facing up to it. Maybe you're making the whole thing up and you just don't want other people to start tearing it apart."

This has been a cunning shot and Fox's awareness of the ploy does not, unfortunately, lessen his reaction. He sits bolt upright on the bed, eyes staring, hands curling and says, "It is *not* something I made up. How could I make *up* something like this? These people—I mean, these creatures—these aliens have seized my *mind!* They're out to destroy the whole planet! Why would I make something like that *up?* The whole fate of the universe could be at stake!"

"Oh, I didn't mean for you to get all upset. I mean, I didn't think that you were lying or *hallucinating* or anything. I just thought that if this thing were truly serious to you, and that you had the courage of your convictions, you would want to come down to the Solarians and talk to them about it. Isn't it at least that important? These aliens were important enough to you to take over your whole *mind* and to make you tell me all about it. So why don't you at least try to talk the whole thing over with a group of people who might be able to help you? I think they'd really like to learn about this, Izzinius." Her eyes now seem to be emitting a faint gleam, but whether it is for the sake of the

Solarians or only for a more intricate purpose, Fox does not know. "I mean, they could give you some really good ideas," she says.

"Listen, Susan," Fox says. "Do you really think that a group of science-fiction fans could save this planet? Could understand this situation and save it?"

"I most certainly do," she says. "Who else?"

Fox feels suddenly a wonderful kind of submissiveness, an absolute sense of relaxation spreading through him. It could be called apathy-on-the-cheap. He has never felt anything like this wonderful, soaring sense of disconnection which suddenly seems to place miles between himself and his motives; light years, between himself and causation, thrust him into a small shell of space where nothing at all matters. Too, it is time that he got out and socialized. He is undoubtedly leading a very narrow, enclosed life as Susan herself has pointed out; and part of the very problem might be ascribed to his isolation. If he had traveled in a crowd, if he had had a lot of friends, surely the Rhelm people would not have been so quick to disrupt his life, so contemptuous of his private affairs.

"All right," he says, "all right, then, I'll go."

"And you'll tell them everything?" she says.

"I'll tell them everything" Fox says, "if they want to listen."

"Oh, they'll listen," she says. "That's one thing you can say about the Solarians, they'll listen to *anything.*"

Overcome by his wonderful lassitude, bidding goodbye for no good reason to the shiftless, trapped Izzinius Fox of only a few hours in the past, Fox permits Susan to draw him against her. Then, for the longest time, he immerses himself in a certain kind of exploration, fear and palpitation tucked away neatly in one corner of his mind—that corner undoubtedly the one populated by the Rhelm people who, he hopes, will lay off long enough to get him educated.

They do and he is grateful but when everything is finished he is not able to quite convince himself that what has happened is more important than the fate of Terra although, he admits, one of the interesting aspects of it is that it makes it seem more important at the time. He puts it down to biology, one of the hard sciences he has never cared for, and drifts into a thick, dreamless sleep against Susan for an hour or two until Browning comes bumping up the stairs with another cabinet to be placed in the room, giving vacant disgusted glares at the magazines which, he has told Fox before, ought to be charged for double as extra tenants.

VII

A seizure, a discovery, a salvation.

Fox had not discovered science fiction so much as having fallen into it. He had bought and read a few books during his teens but had found the plots fairly dull and the writing for the most part at a level somewhat below what the city university's Department of English had told him to consider worthwhile. By the time he was sixteen he was entirely beyond it and never thought of it much again until one day, working on field time in the Department of Relief and Restoration, he found himself in the vicinity of that large clutter of used book and magazine shops which agglomerated near the Astor Place station of the Lexington Avenue IRT.

He didn't want to make the visit which was his assignment in that area (he was due to interview a dependent relative of a recipient to see whether or not the recipient would be able, out of his own grant, to lend the relative support, otherwise he would have to Expand the Case, one of the most depressing maneuvers available to someone in his position since it necessitated the filling out of thirty-seven separate forms in triplicate and with special addenda to the intermediary consultation section of the Central Office). And he didn't want the blank defiance of simply chucking it all and going home where undoubtedly his mother (at that time he still lived with his mother) would pump him almost hysterically for confidential information from the case records.

It was one of her chief pleasures now that most of his father's inheritances had run out along with his season's pass to all roller derby games *in perpetuo*. (His father, three months before his lamentable death, had been voted Roller Derby Fan of the Year and was presented at a magnificent ceremony with lifetime admission to all competition plus a pair of miniature skates and knives to commemorate his interest: unfortunately the Roller Derby had run into economic trouble in the large city and was now operating out of places like Bismarck, North Dakota, and Macon, Georgia—places where his mother in her poor health was unable to travel with the ease that she could get to Madison Square Garden.)

"My God," his mother would say. "You mean to say that that bitch has had three out-of-wedlock children and doesn't know how it happened to her? You mean to say that that man has been in Lexington, Kentucky, for three whole years and thinks that he only gets the shakes? You mean to say that people like this are riding the subways all the time, possibly sitting next to me or kneeing me right in the aisle? Thieves! Assassins! Murderers! What are we coming to if respectable people can be riding with things like this and never even know it! Tell me who else you know that has out-of-wedlock children. What's the all-time record? Who do you hear of that had the most out-of-wedlock children? Do they all think that it's spontaneous generation? Amazing! Terrible! What's the city coming to? Why don't you go out and get yourself a decent job?"

The whole thing was very depressing and somehow grim and terrible because more and more Fox found that he was comparing his mother unfavorably to the people the department serviced. She had the same drives and motives but far less energy and invention. But at that time he had not yet quite made the decision to leave home because his room was comfortable, food was always on the table, and the old lady charged him only forty dollars a week for all services which gave him fifteen dollars free and clear spending money which he did not know how to disburse.

He went into one of the bookstores, an odorous cave containing a few weeping old men, who were attempting to rip pages from medical textbooks and stuff them into their pockets, along with two exhausted clerks who were themselves totally absorbed in the Occult and Horoscope section and thus could not have cared less (no one quite knew who the owner was although it was suspected that he visited the store daily in the guise of one of the old men), and going eventually into the back room where he discovered Stuart Wiseman and Stuart Wiseman's Science-Fiction Book Service. From that moment he had, in a sense, discovered himself. He was not interested in the books. He was interested in the magazines.

Stuart had piles and piles of magazines. He had the three major ones: *Thrilling, Tremendous,* and *Thoughtful.* And all of the minor ones as well: *Terrific, Super Duper, Explosion, Marvelous Mystery Tales* and *Astonishment from the Frozen North.* Most of them were in mint condition; and Izzinius began to tremble as he reached his hands toward the stacks of magazines, ran his fingers through them, admired the colorful covers. It was as if he was holding the past in his hands. Not only his own past—which was certainly dull enough—but some kind of communal mystery which the magazines tapped into, a mystery which he could barely apprehend except in terms of the strange dates on the cover: April 1945, May 1946, March 1943. The covers themselves glinted with power, the contents pages with implication. And Fox had been overwhelmed with a sensation utterly foreign to his own nature and, apart from everything he had ever known, what he wanted to do was to *possess* those magazines; not only for their own sake but because in so doing he could possess the past itself. It was all too insubstantial, it all got away from you too quickly. February 1945 was a glimmer; May of 1946 an empty token. (What had he been doing in May of 1946? Oh yes, he had been a sophomore at the city university, trying to get into a house plan.) But with the help of the magazines it all came back to him. In a sense, then, he was being given a Second Chance by virtue of the magazines to go over his own past and do it right.

Of course all of these ideas and emotions did not go through him at the exact time of entrance into Stuart's store: that had only happened much later when he had been able to sort out, so to speak, the quality of his responses, the question of his destiny; a Sorting Out process which had begun that very day when he had walked out of Stuart's place with three issues of *Tremendous* locked away in his briefcase. One of them, at Stuart's advisement, was vol. 1, no. 1 itself—the very first issue of the magazine, which had then been called *Whizzing Planetoid Spheres in Orbit* but whose name and copyright had been changed when the publisher collapsed six issues later. The line from *Whizzing Planetoid* to *Tremendous,* however, had been very clear, as Stuart had pointed out to him: both had had the important "Tek Room" feature and K. M. Conrad, the first and only editor of *Tremendous,* had had a novelette in the first issue of *Whizzing Planetoid.*

It had cost him $30.00 net, an enormous amount of money—the most money which he had ever spent on a given object for his personal use in his life—and he had decided to build the collection around it since, as Stuart had pointed out to him at their first meeting, the principle of the collector was to *specialize* rather than scatter his shots and he, Stuart, could tell right off that Fox had the stuff of the real collector. Indeed he did.

Stuart had explained to him that there existed in science fiction basically three types of people: "professionals," who wrote for or edited the magazines, "fans," who were a social organization built up around the magazines and who often contributed to the letter columns and built up a whole web of social activities and rivalries based on their mutual interest, and the "collectors," who were mostly involved with trying to build up an accumulation of these magazines. The categories were not really mutually exclusive. Many professionals had been fans at one time or another and fans were often collectors. But as it turned out, collectors really had little to do with fans and rarely became professionals, and professionals tended to come more from the ranks of fans than collectors, who the professionals considered to be a little strange for being so interested in what they, the professionals, often considered so much crap. Stuart had been loquacious and quite sincere. He said that he personally saw it as a hierarchy where the collectors were probably on top. The professionals all spent the money the minute it came in and there wasn't a good deal of money in the field to begin with. The fans were merely killing time because they had neither the funds nor the discipline to service their obsession. But the collectors were the only ones possessing something with a true sense of purpose.

"Personally, in spite of the fact that I deal in this stuff and sell it, I'm more of a fan than a collector," Stuart had conceded. "I mean, I'm willing to sell any of this stuff if I can meet my price. The thing is that I don't think I have the simple *guts* to be a collector because then you really got to risk yourself, really got to take chances and risk getting hurt, which always happens if you can't get an issue you need to fill in. But right away, having a chance to get to know you and talk to you like this, Izzinius, I can see right away that you're a collector; you have the interest of the true collector. There's a certain kind of guy, who, when he comes into this shop, I can see right away, just by the way that he handles himself, just by a certain look he gets in his eyes, that he's the real thing. I know you got it. I've seen a lot of guys like you come in here wanting to be collectors, and I'm happy to say that I got a lot of them started the right way, built them up into big collectors, celebrities in the big time. Even dealers at conventions. The thing is that you start off slow and build up and you never know what's going to happen to you.

"Take Billy Wilberson Key … I knew Billy just four years ago when he came in with a quarter to pick up last month's issue of *Tremendous,* which he had missed on the newsstand due to a case of flu. Billy who was just buying *Tremendous* and throwing it out, no interest at all, Billy and I had a good talk and I showed him around this place and filled him in and now Billy's the biggest collector on the East Coast. There's going to be a *book* about Billy published by one of the fans soon and he's been on radio in all the Southern states, talking about his collection. So you see anything can happen once you get started right."

Fox had been fascinated and, in the weeks to come, he came to know Stuart very well. Far better, he was sure, than he had known any relative or dismal acquaintance in the city university let alone his coworkers in the department. Stuart had begun by coaching and guiding him into the proper channels and had then sat back, so to speak, while Fox took over the guidelines and started to tell Stuart what he needed and what rare issue he was seeking and what Stuart should try to get in stock for him next time. It had been, Stuart said, one of the most truly encouraging experiences of his life to see the way that Fox came along once he got involved; he had always known from the beginning that Izzinius had the stuff and to see him becoming a true collector was like watching a flower bloom in the desert.

"I'm proud of you, son," Stuart had told him confidentially, patting his back gently although Stuart was only three or four years older than Fox, maybe not even that. "I'm really proud of the way that you've come along. And if you don't mind I would like to say that I take some of the credit"

Then he had begun tentatively to urge Izzinius to come to meetings of the Solarians, go to vague conventions in the fall in distant cities, enter into some land of fan contests. There was no reason that he could not be a valuable addition to fandom now with his growing collection standing behind him.

"But you said that fans and collectors didn't mix," Fox pointed out.

Stuart said no, that wasn't quite the case at all, they mixed very well; it was just that in many cases the fans didn't have true respect for the collectors because the collectors, while they went around getting every issue in sight and naming the contents pages for years back, didn't seem to know what the magazines were quite *about*. They were very good on titles but not so good on remembering plots or meaning, which led the fans to feel contemptuous about the collectors who they regarded only as strange neurotics poking and prowling rather aimlessly around the outskirts of something which the fans themselves considered vital.

But Fox was hardly in that category, Stuart had pointed out. He was not only a collector but a *reading* collector: one who took home all the magazines to carefully study and absorb and whose knowledge of those magazines was in many cases as good as that of the professionals. This was the kind of person who was most valuable in fandom, Stuart had explained, because most of the fans, unfortunately, were so involved in their social lives and clubs and feuds that they had less and less time to actually *read* this stuff and thus were always in urgent need of someone competent like Fox, who had the files and kept up with the professionals, and who would be able to keep them abreast of the latest affairs in the external world of publishing.

Nevertheless, Fox had resisted, remembering Stuart's original distinction, and resolved that he would do nothing whatsoever to compromise his new and important sense of dedication. "I'm a *collector*." he found himself murmuring at odd intervals during the day, say, when he was making a phone call to a landlord or killing time in the stall in the lavatory, trying to pretend for the benefit of the supervisors that he had diarrhea and could not possibly discharge his duties that day no matter how he tried. "I'm a *collector; I collect* things; I have an important stock of *rare issues.*" And the feeling of pride and identity which had gone through him during these monologues was often so powerful, so truly consequential, that he was unable and unwilling to perform his job duties for the given day.

The thing was that his new passion trivialized everything, not only the job, even his mother. He moved away from her in the third month of his passion when she began to make comments about the strange magazines filling up her son's room; he simply put everything under cotton in a new valise and took off, went into Browning's rooms on a chance. And there, for the first time, was able to set up his collection properly, putting it all on the floor in narrow, carefully centered stacks so that the magazines would not have to be stored in the abnormal upright position (Stuart had warned him about this) and could get plenty of even pressure and air to sustain their pulp. Now the knowledge that he could come home at any hour and sit in isolation to consider his collection at leisure, without any pressure whatsoever, made the job itself almost unbearable: all that Fox found himself thinking of during this time was his selection of rare issues and the covers of magazines he felt particularly desirable. Sometimes the very aspect of the scenes he would occupy would seem to shimmer and dissolve in favor of a glowing cover, a contents page.

Looking at it objectively, Fox supposed that he was succumbing to a massive and somehow overriding obsession, but there was no question of objective. How *could* one possibly be detached when confronted by what was nothing less than a singular opportunity to encompass the whole of his life within a set of artifacts. He was not only possessing the magazines themselves; through them he had hold for the first time of a very dangerous and tricky past—a past which for once seemed to have acquired some kind of form and order.

"May 1949," he found himself mumbling, sometimes to his supervisors or clients at odd moments. "June 1950, October 1948, Oliver, Tyson, Steele and Conrad."

His hours at work began to dwindle as he used more and more of his field time (during which he was supposedly visiting various recipients of relief and restoration and thus building up the favorable public relations image of the agency) to go hunting for rare issues. Stuart remained his main source, of course, but he found a couple of other magazine stores in the neighborhood, one of which had a truly remarkable collection of *Thoughtfuls* in mint condition and all of which did not seem to know, as Stuart and Izzinius did, the sheer value of their goods. Whereas Stuart was charging him fifty cents for any issue of anything, no matter how recent or battered, these rival stores would often let their goods go for a dime or less; once, to astonished wonder, he was able to pick up a full year's run of *Saturn, Pluto, Mercury and Mars* (a magazine of fantasy) for fifty-five cents from a grim old bookshop keeper who helped Fox smuggle these copies into his briefcase with a series of strange glares, twitches and convulsions, mumbling in the meantime that he could not understand, simply could not understand, those goddamned magazine collectors.

But the trouble with the other magazine shops was that in not knowing the rare and precious value of their goods they paid little regard to them: stored them unevenly, sold them erratically, did not have anything approaching completion. And so, when Fox had used them to fill out the fringes of some minor collections, he found himself driven back to Stuart, who at least understood and who, at all times, could be counted upon to at least attempt a search for a rare issue for a modest deposit. There was no sense in exaggerating Stuart's worth. He was venal. He charged too much. He tended to lie about his stock and, most surprisingly, he did very little if any reading whatsoever of his magazines. But Stuart was still the most dependable dealer in the city, which, along with the fact that he had introduced Fox to the pursuit in the first place, meant that he was owed the most unusual loyalty. Fox gave it to him as the very least that he could do.

It was inevitable then that he would have to quit his job: his collection, his growing desires, and the need to put full time into cataloguing, indexing, arranging and purchases meant that he could no longer give to the department that which it so much needed. So he put in his notice, withdrew his balance from the pension fund, and moved full time into the collection business at about the same point in time that he became involved with both Susan and the Rhelm people. He did not choose to see any collaboration beyond coincidence in these two elements. In the first place the Rhelm people were malevolent while Susan was only mildly curious. And in the second place Susan could not possess the organizational ability, the sheer motivation and drive which seized the aliens. She explained to him often that she was merely going through a blank period in her life and intended to apply herself to something meaningful in just a little time, six months or so; but in the meantime science fiction provided her with a social outlet and she was having a genuine voyage of self-discovery in Browning's rooming house thanks to her growing sense of individuality and her growing realization that the world as a totality was insane—thanks to her close observations of Browning.

"He's just the same as you, Izzie, only in reverse," she had confided to him during one late-night discussion when, unable to sleep, she had come down to his room, taking him away from the August 1947 *Tremendous.* "You want to collect things and hold them all to yourself and Browning wants to put his possessions with everyone else; you want to dilate and he wants to expand."

Fox knew about dilation because doors and spaceships and people were always doing it in the magazines, but he was damned if he could see how this applied to him. He felt personally that he was expanding his horizons. For the first time that agonizing feeling of delimitation which had dogged him since his father's untimely death seemed to have left him. Then the Rhelm people got serious and things worked into a different stage.

Well, that was the way it was: win and lose. Life's a lottery; if you finally got involved in something that made you truly happy and fulfilled you were bound to find that new problems came up. It had been too good to be true after all. He bore the first visits of the Rhelm people (or his visits to them, he was never quite sure how to define this) almost cheerfully, a sense of humorous resignation controlling his responses. And for the first couple of times it hadn't been too bad at all, but then they had shown him that they weren't kidding around in the least. They were, in fact, damned serious, and things had taken a difficult turn.

Fox knew he was in a tight spot. He felt like one of the heroes in a Tech Jones serial now: hounded on all sides by malevolent, marauding aliens whose only motivation in destroying him seemed to be in keeping events going. But unlike Tech Jones's heroes he felt neither competent nor particularly desirable; in fact he felt that he was stumbling endlessly through a viscous agglomeration of matter, trying to find his way from the grayness into a corridor, in the corridor lurked marauders of a different hue, and in the control room more assassins yet, but he would win through. He would overcome; he would see the end of this.

Was it possible that Izzinius Fox could have lived so long, struggled so hard, sustained so much history merely to come to an abysmal end? It was not. And at the center of his despair lay a cheerful faith, a sense of abandoned commitment which he knew would sustain him as far as he had to go, incised into him with the same radiant sense of knowledge that was given him by the possession of a Rare Issue, an issue that he knew everyone else wanted but which only he had. And had it filed away. In mint condition. Neatly stacked on the floor of his rooms. Safe from everything but the prowls of Browning who, in addition to everything else, did not understand science fiction.

VIII

First stirrings of the knife; eternity weighed in a spaceship.

The Rhelm people get him on the way to the Solarians.

Once again there is no feeling of transition, not even a warning. One instant he is walking with Susan toward the subway stop (they will go up to One Hundred and Tenth Street, transfer to the West Side Broadway local and ride up two more stops to Teddy Wilkes's apartment which is the place of the meeting this week), talking quietly, feeling the absent brush of her hand in his, trying to stay on her left as a gentleman is supposed to although her weaving gait tends to put him more and more in the gutter, and the next he is wrenched inside, pulled outside, turned into pulp and transported mindless miles to the interior of the spaceship. He does not even have a chance to warn Susan what is happening to him; not that it would make any difference since all of this happens in no-time and she will not even know that he has been gone.

He finds himself seated, unbound, in the center of a circle. The circle is composed of aliens and they are talking cheerfully to one another, seemingly unaware of his presence. This goes on for quite a long time and Fox, with a discovered sense of delicacy, feels that he would be wrong to interrupt; they seem to be so *engaged* with one another. Animation is so rare that he is pleased to see it, even on this level.

The Arch-Leader strides in, carrying something which looks, to Fox's bedazzled eyes, vaguely like a movie projector. He waves at Fox cheerfully, enters into deep conference with two of the aliens, who get up and begin to do things with the projector-thing, seemingly trying to put it in working order. For some reason, this gives them difficulty and they begin to chatter at one another unhappily in their foreign tongue although, strangely, Fox can discern certain phrases which sound to him amazingly like "dirty bastards, sons of bitches, goddamned hell" and the like. Eventually, they do something to their satisfaction and withdraw.

The Arch-Leader comes to Fox's side and says, "I ask you again, have you changed your mind?"

"No," Fox says. "I have not changed my mind. I happen to be on very important business now—"

"We can't be concerned with that," the Arch-Leader says rather sharply. "Your personal life is of only personal importance; we are talking here of the fate of the universe. Come now, Fox, be reasonably sane about this. Won't you turn over the December '46 *Tremendous* to us?"

"No," he says. "I won't turn it over." The whole thing would be vaguely thrilling if he did not have the feeling that he had gone through this too many times already to sustain any sense of drama, let alone significance. "I won't betray my people. Earth triumphant! Ruling over the galaxy! Timeless search for destiny! Peoples of the world! Buy your own goddamned rare issue if you want; Stuart Wiseman could get it for you."

"Most unfortunate," the Arch-Leader says. "I thought that you might have reconsidered but, as with almost everything on this mission, I have been wrong. Do you realize, Fox, that due only to your egregious stubbornness I run the risk of being dropped from L-71 to L-68, for no reason other than the fact that you refuse to face simple reality? But of course the penalty is always paid by the innocent. Very well, then, are you ready for the torture to begin?"

"I'd rather not," Fox says, feeling a vague squeamishness in his joints. The fact is that he has always been something of a physical coward and reminding himself that nothing that the aliens can do can destroy him or go on for more than a few minutes is not, under the circumstances, particularly helpful. "Why don't you just respect my, uh, ideals, and I'll try to respect yours? There must be millions of people who would be *happy* to help you out."

"Ah, well," the Arch-Leader says. "We will begin on the psychological level, which, in any event, is usually the more effective with the so-called sentient races. You have no doubt noticed our machinery which happens to be a Lamning Vault Projector, catalogue number 4687B, and which has the ability to project scenes on a screen very much as one of your own products might. What we intend to do, Fox, is to try to show you some scenes of your past life. We find this to be strongly effective. All that you have to do is watch although, of course, if you feel a certain low necessity to scream I guess we can go along with that. It's all up to you, of course."

At the realization that his torture will be "emotional" rather than "physical", at the sound of the wonderful word "psychological" which in the alien's speech-organ seems to roll itself into a limp and delicate construction not entirely unlike the Oriental languages, Fox feels a sensation of relief and release so profound that he feels that he is about to sob. He has been offered the surest proof that the aliens cannot really touch him and, in the bargain, knowing that his mind is stronger than any of the minds which oppose him, he feels on the instant a sense of enormous release stirring through him with such power and constancy that it even diminishes that more trivial kind of relief which he felt, an hour or so before, with Susan. Surely there is nothing she can offer him ever, nothing that *any* girl can offer him, that would surpass the feeling of power he has now.

"All right," he says, leaning back on his palms and crossing his legs; a rather difficult bit of acrobatics on the slick and shiny floor, but something he accomplishes with ease. "If that's the way it's got to be, that's the way it's got to be, I guess."

He tries to put a little bit of trepidation in his tone. Obviously, it would stand him in better stead if the aliens thought that he was intimidated. There is no sense, truly, in pushing things.

"I don't like what you're doing to me, and I'm very afraid, but I'll never give in. Never," he adds, with what he feels to be a nice blend of terror and bravado.

"What we will do," the Arch-Leader says, "is run these scenes to completion, Fox. There is no way we will stop once we get started and the whole thing could be very unpleasant. Would you like to reconsider your decision?"

"Never," he says, and the Arch-Leader says "Excellent," with perhaps a little more pleasure than would be expected under the circumstances and the lights go out.

For a moment Fox feels an apprehensive twitch at the sound of the alien's voice, much as if something is in preparation beyond Fox's expectations—and the alien knows this. But then it goes away; he is too absorbed, after all, in looking at the events depicted on the white screen which appeared in ghastly illumination on the upper edges of the room in front of him. A series of yellow and green flickers around the edges and then the film is rolling. It is in black and white with the aspect of a 1930s horror film but the sound in particular is penetrating and bright and clear and Fox finds that he can not only apprehend everything without trouble but, indeed, cannot escape it.

He is looking at a movie of himself sitting with his father in Madison Square Garden, watching a roller derby. He appears to be eleven or twelve here but this is not absolutely sure; his father took him to the roller derby from his eighth birthday to his fourteenth and Fox was one of those men who undertook a delayed adolescence, emerging only into his slack-jawed maturity at eighteen. Thus he could be as young as nine here or perhaps as old as fourteen.

His old man is wearing a checkered vest and an emblem which says NEW YORK CHIEFS and is waving a pennant similarly inscribed. On his left sleeve is a large heart-shaped piece of cloth on which the name TUFFY BRESHEEN has been sewn. And it is this arm which he is using to wave the pennant, urging the New York Chiefs on to more success. Tuffy Bresheen, who had been the female star of the Chiefs during the late 1930s, had been one of his father's grand passions. He had once gotten her autograph in a delicatessen, written "To Milton, With Affection." Since then he and his image of Tuffy had been inseparable. He mentioned her several times a day, often interrupting otherwise dull family meals to tell his wife that if Tuffy Bresheen skated like Fox's mother cooked she would probably have broken her neck several years ago.

Fox sees that he is in the movie, sitting next to his father quietly: his usual stunned, detached aspect at these games; shaking his head and trying in this way to convince people in adjoining seats (it all comes back to him now) that he is seated next to this lunatic only by coincidence and has absolutely nothing to do with him, being a roller derby fan on his own hook. It is not very convincing and a feeling of woe spreads over the younger Fox's features, so deep and intense, so stricken and driven, that Fox, watching the movie, finds himself twitching in response; it has been a long time since he has remembered how truly painful his childhood was and, indeed, he has managed to convince himself that there was nothing wrong with his juvenescence at all. It was perfectly normal. A little yellowed and frozen at the edges, perhaps, but basically the same kind of existence which all of his contemporaries were being put through. But looking at this film, Fox comes to understand that it was not that simple at all and that he must have been suffering at the time even more than he would admit.

The soundtrack of the film snaps on violently and Fox hears crowd noises, screams, squeals, vague hoarse shouts in the background for blood.

"Kill those sonsofbitches!" a heavy man seated behind Fox and his father shouts.

His father half rises to his seat, waving the pennant and screams, "You yellow bastards, you ain't got no guts! Skate 'em down, Ray, skate 'em down! Knock them over!"

The younger Fox cringes in his seat, runs a thin adolescent hand over his forehead, sighs heavily, as his father nudges him in the ribs and says, "Listen, don't you *care*? Don't you even know what's going on here? Didja see that *foul?*"

"No," Fox says and tries to duck down in his seat But his father's hand falls on a shoulder, squeezing the boy into enormous pain, and he sits bolt upright, a look of shrieking pain in his eyes and says, "I saw it, I saw it!"

His father releases his grip and says, "You don't pay no goddamned attention. I never take you to this game again," which both the older and younger Fox knew perfectly well to be a lie because his father took him to every roller derby match held in New York for a period of several years, two or three times a week on the average, sometimes as many as four or five, and refused under any circumstances to let Fox seek his own devices.

"It's a wonderful sport; it'll make a man of you," his father had said. "You see a little mental toughness out there, a little physical mayhem, and you'll understand what life is really *like*. It isn't all a bowl of *soup*, you know."

Since Fox's father was a physical coward who spent the majority of his time either seeking or drawing unemployment insurance, there is a kind of ironic undertow to this advisement. But neither the present nor the past Foxes are able to take much comfort from this since the dreadful violence of the roller derby seems to virtually vibrate, one could say pulse, in the elder Fox's frame during his period of spectatorship and if he were to knock his son unconscious right here and now out of some vagrant streak of enthusiasm or response, it would certainly not be the first time and probably not the last.

The camera switches to a close-up of the roller derby itself: men and women skating frankly on a circular rink which, although made of wood, glistens with the coldness of ice; sticks swinging; faces dripping; mouths screaming. The object of the roller derby, of course, is for one member of a given team to skate ahead and completely lap every member of the other, thus scoring a single point (and a certain number of points becoming a "match"). These efforts are known as "sprints" and the participants are allowed to use any means to impede or assist the sprinter, which usually consists of members of his team attempting to act like blocking backs in football and shunt the opposition off the track while the opposition, in turn, tries to find a "hole" in the wall of fullbacks and, in getting to the sprinter, knock him completely off the track and into the seats where, for all they care, he should lie dead for a considerable length of time.

The women's teams, which wear the same emblems and alternate with the men, are particularly vicious. And since it is the women who are skating now, it is all that Fox can do to continue looking at the film. In close-up (although once he had thought they were sexually attractive) all the women look like dreadful avenging hags and are shouting oaths and imprecations at one another as they try to clear a path for one of their number: a broad-shouldered, mighty woman in her early thirties who is trying to engage in a sprint.

"Come on, Tuffy, you big bitch!" his father shrieks as the camera swings back to his face. "Knock them all dead, you animal you!"

The elder Fox swings his hand aimlessly, catching the younger Fox with a mighty cuff; the younger Fox seems to shudder and huddle in upon himself. Fox, himself, feels suddenly that he cannot look at this anymore. Seeing the movie at this time and in this way has suddenly made him realize something that he had never seen before and which insight he had sedulously avoided during that period of his life when he was capable of making it: he understands suddenly and with a kind of total clarity what his father had hoped to obtain from the roller derby (and what he never got) and he shouts "Stop it! Stop it!" staggering to his feet, looking hopelessly around the spaceship for, of all things, a light.

The Arch-Leader says behind him in a deadly monotone, "Of course we're not shutting this off, Izzinius. Do you think that it's as easy as that? Do you think that you can bury the past merely by escaping it? Sit and watch it!"

Shuddering, Fox feels himself slammed to his knees. His gaze is on the screen and Tuffy Bresheen is on a sprint; her skates coming down on the wood with clattering, stomping sounds that seem to shake the very projector, her mouth open and screaming, her stick held high above her head. "*Whoopee!*" she shrieks and knocks a small woman completely off the track and into the field. "*Take that!*" and clears the field fully.

The camera switches back to his father again, who has now risen to his feet and, leaning over, his hands cupped around his mouth is saying: "GET THEM, TUFFY. GET THOSE DIRTY BITCHES. YOU CAN DO IT!"

Tuffy screams "*Whoopee!*" again while people in surrounding seats look at his father in terror and awe.

And then the younger Fox is on his feet, screaming too, tugging his father by the elbow and saying, "Stop it. Stop this. It's got to stop, I can't stand it anymore," as the old man calmly, shatteringly, hits him on the head and the younger Fox falls back on his seat, gasping.

"*Stop it!*" Fox is screaming. "*Stop this, for the love of God. I can't take it anymore!*" And the lights go on, finally. Aliens, he is surrounded by aliens, all of them looking at him with wonder. The Arch-Leader, leaning over, is saying with infinite patience and warmth, "See, Izzinius, do you see it now? There are certain things about the way you people are constructed that permit you no surcease. You can never forget; you will never forget. It's always there, Izzinius."

And Fox says, "I can't stand this. I truly can't stand it."

"Well, of course you can't," the Arch-Leader says. "Who ever said that any one of you could? But our time is up, Izzinius, we'll have to let you return now. We expect to find you a lot more reasonable the next time, Izzinius. We'll be waiting for those transcripts." The scene goes away, everything goes away, and he is walking with Susan west on One Hundred and Nineteenth Street near Columbia University, gasping unevenly, sweat dripping down the panels of his face.

She turns and looks at him to say, "My God, did it happen again?" Speechless, he blinks his eyes and she says, not stopping (because they are late for the Solarians), "Was it bad?"

"Pretty bad; the worst yet. I don't think I can stand this anymore."

She says, squeezing his hand and lengthening her pace, "Well, then, Izzinius, we'll just have to *do* something about this."

For the moment, disoriented as he is, he has the horrid sensation that she is Tuffy Bresheen moving out on a sprint, but his shriek becomes a bubble in the haste and cold. In time he is able to remind himself that this is Susan, only Susan, and one way or the other she is taking him to some people who can help him. He believes. He wants to believe. On the other hand, there is always the possibility that all of these people whom he will see came out of circumstances exactly similar, in which case, he is in even deeper trouble than usual because he does not see how anybody who went through the particular set of experiences which he did is capable of making logical choices, let alone moving on them toward meaningful ends. It is all a bit too much for Fox.

And it occurs to him only then, after all of this, that his father never took him to a roller derby game in his life.

IX

Introduction to some Solarians, July 3, 1951.

The meeting of the Solarians is to occur in Teddy Wilkes's apartment on the fifth floor of an old apartment building near Columbia University. Getting into the elevator with Susan, two strange men, and a large dog, Fox closes his eyes, tries to cancel his usual apprehensions about self-service elevators (What if it stopped in mid-passage? Who would rescue them? Who would *care* to rescue them?) as it inches upward in a series of hideous creaks and whines, the cables seeming to barely sustain the car as it shoves its odorous weight upward.

"This is the first building on the block to have one of these automatic elevators. Isn't that wonderful?" Susan whispers, and Fox says that he supposes it is.

The men get off at the third floor although the dog, strangely reluctant, gives Fox a series of pleading, grievous looks as it is shoved out of the elevator with curses. The animal emits a high, piercing whine as the doors close, and Fox wonders pointlessly if it is somehow related to the Arch-Leader. He doubts the theory very much, but it is as sensible as most of the things which have been happening to him recently.

"Don't worry about a *thing*," Susan whispers as he feels the cable once again yank them upward. She strokes his elbow, puts a finger cheerfully in his side and pokes him. "They're nice people and everything's going to be *fine*. They'll be glad to meet you."

"I don't see the point," Fox mutters, "that's all. It's nothing at all personal but I just don't see the *point*," and would go on to expound on this theory except that the elevator, thankfully, groans into place at the fifth floor and releases them.

They stumble into the hall, Fox semi-tripping on the way out because the car does not come evenly to floor level, and find the door of the apartment on their left open. From it come sounds of classical music. Maybe it is Beethoven's *Eroica* symphony. But Fox has never liked music too much and does not care.

A large, sweating, bearded young man bounds out of the door and takes Susan by the arm. "Hello!" he says and runs his lips through her hair, then straightens her up and looks at her intently for a moment. "We're in the soup tonight, Sykes is flying again."

Then he takes note of Fox who has been looking at him with perhaps more astonishment than is truly explicable under the circumstances. The man, or perhaps he is a boy (it is very difficult to tell because of the beard and a certain confused look around the eyes which has more of an adolescent glint than manly glower), bends down to Susan and says, "Who is he? Is he friend? Is he fan? Is he foe?" And then, finding this apparently to be almost unbearably funny, moves off into a high-pitched giggle, which excludes Fox and Susan, as well as a series of chokes and sputters, well internalized; and things run their course which, as far as Fox can judge, takes several seconds.

"Oh stop it, Teddy," Susan says and slaps the man on the wrist "You know perfectly well that there are only friends here. This is Izzinius Fox, whom I've been telling you about. He's finally decided to come to one of our meetings. Izzy, this is Teddy Wilkes about whom you've heard so much."

"Oh, I haven't heard *that* much," Fox says. Which is probably not the right thing to say under the circumstances for Teddy Wilkes gives him a look of sheer loathing moderating only slightly toward the end to bemusement.

"Well, I haven't heard that much either about you, Fox. You're that collector, right?" He begins to prod them toward the door. "You're a little early," he says, "but then again these damned things never do start right on time. Why don't you just kind of get organized and watch Sykes for a little while? He's really carrying on. We're going to discuss *Thoughtful* tonight, Fox," he says, "I don't know if that would interest you very much though; you're a *Tremendous* man, I understand. This usually happens with people who can't adjust to new things, they hold onto the old stuff. Well, live and learn, why don't you just go right in."

Fox finds himself behind Susan in a long hallway. Wilkes slams the door behind them, gives Fox another glower and then disappears. The sounds of the *Eroica* are much louder now, of course, and Fox perceives that there is something wrong with the music; it seems to be higher pitched and at a much faster tempo than the performances he is accustomed to. And then, in a moment, he understands: this is probably one of the new microgroove records, the 33½, and Wilkes is playing it at a higher speed. It doesn't seem to make too much difference to Susan who smiles and nods and allows her hips to move a little more than is strictly necessary as she walks ahead of him into the living room, where she is instantly seized by two large and unbearded men who engage her in intense conversation, winding her toward the couch. Fox finds himself momentarily at loose ends.

There are seven or eight people in this large living room. In addition to Susan, the two men who have commandeered her, and Wilkes (who is now standing in a stiff posture by a bookcase, a pipe stuck between his jaws, reacting to the music with slow heaves and groans), three other men occupy positions of solitude at various ends of the room, standing immobile, a strange catatonic freeze seeming to come over them as they stare blindly at the lights.

In the center of the room a small desk and chair, probably for the purposes of formal meeting, have been placed. And this further restricts movement so that the combination of limited circles of space, along with the harsh overhead glinting of the lights, gives the room a rather surrealistic aspect. The interesting thing, to Fox, is that it looks in many ways strangely like the spaceship of the Rhelm people and he feels himself, pondering this, on the verge of a large insight, something having to do with the endless similarity of all sentient life, everywhere. (But perhaps again the spaceship *is* this room and his hallucinations have merely found extrinsic collaboration: what he must keep in mind at all times is the omnipresent realization that he *might* be insane; if he can hold onto that it may end up being the only small piece of sanity in the entire affair.)

He is interrupted by one of the three single males who comes over to him, taps him on the elbow, and without any introduction or prelude says, "What do you think of the Graffanatis faction? I mean, what's your position?"

"Graffanatis?" Fox said. "I don't think I know who or what you're talking about."

"Oh for Christ's *sake*," the man says. "Who is Wilkes bringing into these meetings? Is he really trying to pack them for ignorance? The Graffanatis faction, Miles Graffanatis, his position on the Plutonians. Don't you know what I'm *talking* about?" He is a small intense man in, perhaps, his early twenties; his face pockmarked by the remainders of an acne he has more or less successfully sabotaged with a clever, if too public, application of talcum. "You don't really want to talk about it do you?" he says. "You're going to play it cagy and innocent until the *vote* comes up and then you'll play it down the line. I wouldn't put anything past Wilkes, but why doesn't he let *us* pack the meetings?"

"I'm sorry," Fox says. "I really don't know what you're talking about."

At that moment, fortunately (for he is truly glad to see him), Wilkes comes over, clasps the small man by the hand and says, "Are you bothering my friend, Izzinius Fox? You really ought to watch that kind of stuff, Hollowaite; you just *leap* on people and before they know what's going on you've got them bound up. This is Harlow Hollowaite," he says to Fox. "He's not really a member, only an observer so to speak; don't listen to a thing that he says. Actually he's from the Graffanatis faction."

Hollowaite, for all of his small size, seems to expand with rage when he hears this, literally suspending himself from the floor, and says, "Wilkes, that's an evil and deadly thing to say and I won't stand for it. I don't have to *take* your abuse; I was in the Solarians before you were even a fan."

"Oh, all right," Wilkes says with a heavy chuckle and turns his back on both of them, motions to a corner and says, "Leave her alone, Sykes!" Blocked by the back of Wilkes, Fox can only guess what is going on but he assumes that the as-yet invisible Sykes has been making gestures toward Susan and he tries to move toward Wilkes's side and forward to protect her … but finds himself intercepted by Wilkes who says to him, "That Sykes, that Sykes, he is really *crazy.*"

"No he isn't," Harlow Hollowaite says. "He's the only sane man in the room except for me, now that you've gone and cracked up, Wilkes. You just don't understand his methods," and bursts into a thin, groaning cackle which much disconcerts Fox and for the moment dissuades him from moving toward Susan.

The Solarians are a very strange group, there is no question about it. He is quite sure that he has never been at anything quite like this before. But shaken as he is by the Rhelm people, their torture, Susan's anticipation, and his own dread, he is unable to make the kind of patient evaluation which he supposes he will get to later. The thing seems to be that they are all crazy.

The bell behind the open door rings and Wilkes, nodding vaguely, detaches himself to go there. Fox finds that he is looking straight on at Susan and the aforementioned Sykes; they seem to be in intense conversation on the couch. Sykes is a totally bald young man of thirty or so. As he approaches them Fox notes that Sykes has the ponderous gestures and delivery of a man much older and is so absorbed in whatever he is saying that he does not even notice Fox until Susan, looking up in the middle of a paragraph, smiles at him and says, "Steven, this is my friend, Izzinius Fox. He has the biggest file of *Tremendous* in the neighborhood and he's a wonderful collector of other things, too. You remember I was telling you about him?"

"No," Sykes says without looking up. "Susan, why are you interrupting me? Why are you diverting me from my course? Are you too my enemy, the enemy of free thought and expression lodged deep in the foul bosom of Teddy Wilkes's Solarians? Never a chance; never a chance. So when all of this was done, Graffanatis, he turns to me and do you know what he says? 'Screw the Solarians!' he says. 'I don't give a damn if the Solarians disintegrate! They are a dead issue, the hand of a dead past lying heavily upon the fair brow of science fiction!' I was amazed. I never heard of anything like it. The *gall*—"

"He's talking about Miles Graffanatis," Susan says. "The leader of the Plutonians."

"Yes," Fox says. "I already heard something about that."

"The Plutonians are a rival group. Miles was president of the Solarians until last month but then he took a splinter faction away and formed the Plutonians."

"Susan," Sykes says and puts a hand on her rib cage, draws it up toward her neck (which means that the bald man fondles her breasts intimately, but there is no sexuality in the gesture at all; he could be running his hand over a magazine cover and Susan shows no reaction, so Fox decides that he had better take no notice of this whatsoever; he is already in deep waters), "Susan, I wish you would outgrow this infantile pedanticism, this seeming need to explain the inexplicable to those who cannot understand."

"Sure he understands," Susan says. "He's an old friend. He lives in my rooming house."

"I don't care if he lives in your *bed*. There is no way that you can explain Miles Graffanatis to him. Unless," Sykes says, coming to a dead halt and looking up at Fox for the first time with strange, glittering eyes that seem to weave in his skull, "unless of course he *comes* from Miles Graffanatis and you've smuggled him into our meeting. That would explain everything, wouldn't it? This new stranger. The lack of true introduction. The inadequate cover story. The failure of this man to speak up and fully identify himself. That *would* explain everything, wouldn't it?" He fixes Fox with a dull stare, his lips working unevenly and says, "Explain yourself! Justify yourself! Describe your position, your ambitions, your mode!"

"I really can't," Fox says. "I'm only a collector."

"He's only a collector, Sykes," Susan says, patting the bald man's knees. "Really, he knows *nothing* about fandom."

"But not so sure about fanac, eh?" Sykes says. "You can have a little fanac outside of fandom, can't you? A ringer! Graffanatis sneaked into us a ringer!"

"Oh come on, Sykes," Susan says. "He's perfectly innocent. Besides the Plutonians have a policy of noninvolvement."

"I don't trust you," Sykes says, but his voice has diminished to a murmur. Sighing, he stands and says, "I should talk to Wilkes about my suspicions right now. Before this meeting slides into peril and disaster I should unburden myself of this difficult apogee or perhaps the word I am seeking is merely epiphany." He stumbles off shaking his head.

Fox slides down on the couch next to Susan and says, "I don't understand what's going on here. I mean to say that I never met any people quite like this in my life."

"Oh they're very nice," she says, nodding briskly. "The Solarians are a very nice bunch. What you've got to do, Izzinius, is come out of your shell and realize that it takes all kinds to make a world." Her eyes, however, are not on him but on the door. As she stares abstractedly there is another peal on the doorbell and then Stuart Wiseman comes into the room, wearing a green vest, Windsor knot, and red jacket, which gives him a more illustrious appearance than Fox would have believed possible.

"But listen," Fox says hurriedly, leaning over to whisper into her ear, "listen, Susan, you really can't expect me to just *tell* these people what's going on with me? How could they possibly understand?"

"You've got to get over these feelings of inferiority, Izzie," she says. "You're just as important and meaningful as anybody in this room and your trouble is that you have a low opinion of yourself. You'll just speak right up and they'll listen." Her voice, however, seems to contain very little conviction or energy.

Stuart has recognized him and plows through the room, stands in front of Fox, hands in pockets and says, "Well, I see that you came after all. Of course, you had better inducements than I could offer you, I'll admit that. What does bring you here, Fox?"

"Nothing much," Izzinius says.

"Hello, Stuart," says Susan. She seems to be staring at some point of space behind him.

"Hello, Susan. Are you and Izzinius here friends?"

"Yes," Fox says.

"I don't know what you'd call it," says Susan.

"Well, whatever," Stuart says and slides comfortably down on the couch between them, looks at Susan with some amusement and says, "you seem to be very tired tonight."

"I don't feel like talking too much, Stuart."

"You're not telling this man bad things about me, are you? You're not filling him full of tales of Stuart's venality and unction, could you be? After all, Susan, we're old friends."

"I don't feel like talking," Susan says. "Leave me alone, will you Stuart? Anyway, it looks like the meeting is going to be called to order now, we've got to be very quiet."

"She's a very self-involved person," Stuart says to Fox. "She tries to act as if other people's consequences meant something to her, but the fact is that she's too self-involved. You ought to be less self-involved, don't you think so, Susan? I met Miles Graffanatis in the shop this afternoon, he has some very nice things to say to you."

"I want to listen to the meeting," she says.

"What do you think of Miles Graffanatis?" Stuart says to Fox. "I suppose you've been filled in on the scandal."

"Not at all," Fox says. There seem to be peculiar cross-currents, undertows, winds of change sweeping through, and he feels more than slightly at sea. It is something like but practically worse than his conference with the Arch-Leader who at least has simulated frankness; what is going on inside Stuart and Susan at this moment strikes Fox as being of somewhat darker nature than anything which the aliens can foist on him. "I mean I just came because Susan wanted me to; I'm not a member of anything. I have no position. I'm not a fan, I'm a collector."

"Well, no time like the present, eh, Izzie?" Stuart says vaguely while Wilkes, who has come to stand behind the desk, begins to rap a large metal gavel rather aimlessly on its surfaces.

"Come to order!" Wilkes says, "The meeting is now in session!" Groaning, the Solarians take their places; most of them on the floor in front of Wilkes, Hollowaite, and another small man leaning from chairs somewhat to the rear of the desk. The *Eroica* is shut off. "This is the four hundred and seventeenth regular meeting of the Solarians," Wilkes says, "and we'll get right into it. First I want the old business and then we'll have the new business. But first the recording secretary should read the minutes of the last meeting."

Hollowaite stands and says, "I didn't take any minutes. I'm no longer recording secretary. I resign," and sits down as the room begins to fill with noise. "I don't have to take this kind of humiliation anymore!" he shouts.

Wilkes pounds the gavel and finally there is a kind of silence and Wilkes says, "We were aware of your resignation already, Harlow. All right. Does anyone want to give us a verbal summary of our previous meeting?"

Susan stands energetically and says, "Come off it, Teddy. This is no time for formal procedure or anything like that. I've brought along my friend, Izzinius Fox, who has some very important things to say and—"

"Point of order!" the man next to Hollowaite shouts, standing. "Point of order, we must proceed in a regular fashion; there is to be none of this!"

"Hear her out!" Sykes says against the wall. "Hear her out. She's probably detailed from the Plutonians anyway and Graffanatis will know everything that goes on—"

"I am *not* detailed from the Plutonians," Susan says, shaking with rage. "I have nothing to *do* with the Plutonians, Sykes, and I want to remind you that the night of the walkout *I* was the one who stayed here and defended the principles of the Solarians. *Where were you, Sykes?* I didn't see you after the meeting! You went out with Graffanatis, didn't you!"

"You lousy bitch!" Sykes shrieks and Wilkes slams the gavel while the room surges with noise.

Fox finds Stuart slamming him enthusiastically on the knee and saying, "Now, it will come out! *Now* will come out the truth!" and Fox stands to try to avoid the force of the blows which is really considerable under the circumstances.

"I don't have to take this!" Sykes screams. "If there's any disloyalty in this room, we know *exactly* from whence it comes and those parties will be dealt with most strongly!"

"Oh keep quiet," Susan says with enormous self-possession, her demeanor not only seemingly unaffected by Sykes's outburst but even improved. "We know exactly who you are, Sykes, all of the *true* Solarians in this room, and we aren't frightened any more. As I was saying, I brought along my friend, Izzinius Fox, who has some truly remarkable things to tell all of us and I think that this is so important that we ought to get to it right away. Now, Izzie—"

"Point of order!" Hollowaite shrieks. "We either proceed according to the constitution of this organization or we do not proceed at all. Anarchy may be for Graffanatis but we, I remind you, come from a better tradition and are more mature people."

"Then why did you resign as secretary?" Susan says, a remark which turns Hollowaite purple with rage. Then she turns to Wilkes and says, "Really, Teddy, I think that's the best way to do this. Izzinius came all the way up from the 70s to talk to us and this is very important. I know the whole story already."

"And so does Graffanatis!" Sykes bellows. "And everything going on here!"

"All right," Wilkes says, slamming the gavel abstractedly, "Enough of this. We can no longer sustain these feuds and petty anxieties and sustain our mission as Solarians. Susan is quite right, we have to proceed in an orderly way. But I really don't know if we should—" He comes to a stop and stares blindly around the room, seeming suddenly at sea. "I mean, I don't think we can just—"

"All right," Stuart says, slamming Fox on the knee again and standing. "I think that we can get a modicum of organization into this organization. I've been dealing with Fox for many months now and I can vouch for the fact that he's an honorable man, certainly has nothing to do with the Graffanatis faction, and will not compromise us in any way if we listen to what he has to say. Why don't we let Izzinius speak and then we can make some resolutions or something? The trouble with Susan is that she makes everything antagonistic, it has to be a battle, she doesn't understand that—"

"Listen here, Stuart," Susan says. But Wilkes slams the gavel with more power this time and, seeming to have been aided by Stuart's speech, says, "I think that the motion is on the floor. It is herewith resolved that the Solarians should hear, uh, Izzinius Fox tell us something. All those in favor—"

"Point of order!" Hollowaite says as the man next to him says, "Point of personal privilege!" Both go to their feet as they stare at one another with bemusement, then shake their heads and sit down.

"I hear a vote on the floor," Wilkes says. "Now, all those in favor say aye." There is silence and Susan, Stuart, Wilkes, a tall man in the corner, and Hollowaite say *aye*. "All those opposed say *nay*." Sykes shakes his head but says nothing. Izzinius rejects a mad impulse to say *nay* himself and run shrieking from the room. "Well, then," Wilkes says, "it appears that we have a unanimous—"

"You didn't call for abstentions," Sykes says. "Abstentions!" Hollowaite screams. "All right," Wilkes says, nodding. "Abstentions." Sykes, Hollowaite, and Hollowaite's companion say *abstain* in unison, sounding vaguely like frogs.

"Well, then," Wilkes says, "the motion has been carried by a vote of four to nothing with three abstentions. The chairman votes *present*. It is therewith, I mean, herefore resolved that Izzinius Fox will now—"

"Wait a minute," Sykes says, gesticulating violently toward Wilkes. "Just wait a minute. How can you vote present when we're forced to abstain? That's totally unfair."

"Chairman's prerogative on a vote in which he may have an interest is to vote present, the least level of commitment."

"Where'd you read that?" Hollowaite says, standing. "There's no such rule. You've either got to abstain or commit yourself to a position; you can't just vote present. What's to prevent *us* from voting present? What's to prevent the entire organization from crumbling with *present* votes? I demand that you vote and I want that to show up in the minutes."

"There are no minutes," Wilkes says. "We don't have a secretary. Do you remember?"

"None of your insults, Wilkes! I'll have you know that I received a very interesting phone call from Miles Graffanatis not three hours before I left to come to this meeting and Miles Graffanatis had a very interesting proposal to make about what my position might be in the Plutonians. Miles Graffanatis tends to think that I've been ignored in this organization, that I haven't received the position due my abilities and he'd like to change that. Of course I loyally said no and intend to have nothing more to do with him, but you are making things difficult for me, Wilkes, you are making things very, very difficult! The history of abuses in this organization is clearly documented and—"

But Hollowaite can be heard no more. His remark about Graffanatis has apparently created something of a sensation and now several people are trying to obtain the floor simultaneously, Sykes screaming loudest of all and finally obtaining silence by simple exercise of volume.

Izzinius finds himself shuddering with the sound, unconsciously putting his hands to his ear, and Susan leans over and whispers, "It doesn't matter. Don't worry about a thing. It's just procedural. You'll have the floor in just five or ten minutes; you have to let them get their energy out this way so that they'll be able to listen to you. You want to be listened to, don't you?"

Fox manages to nod, then shakes his head and says, "I don't think it's going to work. I just can't see how I could possibly talk to them. They don't really listen."

"Oh yes they do," Susan says. "The trouble with you, Izzinius, is that you come into something strange and right away you start to make value judgments. You'd be better off if you just respected people and their common sense and came to understand that there are certain ways of doing things. Now be patient." Fox shakes his head and tries to say something but the overwhelming bellow of Sykes's voice finally cancels the possibility of all conversation.

"I just want to know!" Sykes is screaming, "I just want to know how many other people in this room are agents of Miles Graffanatis! How many of you are not members of the Solarians at all but traitorous, treacherous invaders; South Bronx vermin come here to subvert our purposes, steal our confidences, and report everything to your infamous leader? How many! Who will tell the truth? *Where does Izzinius Fox come from?"*

Fox gets to his feet, waves frantically and shouts to the limit of his volume in an effort that leaves him weak and gasping. "I'M NOT A FAN, GODDAMNIT. I'M A COLLECTOR AND I NEVER HEARD OF MILES GRAFFANATIS IN MY LIFE!"

He sits down feeling that at last he has done something devastating, but, in the dead silence that follows his outburst, Sykes says quietly, "Someone will be able to explain why the young man is so defensive!"

And the meeting, at that point, becomes chaotic. What happens is that Fox quite loses control of his perception. His vision dances, hearing becomes erratic, concentration fails and he seems to be in a space surrounded only by vaguely gesturing forms, capering, screaming, dancing, parading. They are saying things to one another like "Neptunians!" and "Ugly traitors!" and "Infantile swine!" and "Graffanatis is the revolution!" And for the life of him it is all too much. It seems to all be slipping away. He is not only unable to deal with it (which would be the least of it), but a massive apathy which seems to sink leadenly through his limbs and joints makes him unwilling to. There is a certain failure of concern, in short, and Fox does not care anymore. He knows that this is dangerous symptomatology. A man in his condition, what with the fate of Earth at stake and the Rhelm people having to be fought off by the minute, a man in that kind of fix certainly should not abandon his sensibilities. But nevertheless he is tired, tired, and the slow dissolution of mood and scene which he contemplates seems to be not only the inevitable outcome of what has been happening to him but somehow the *deserved* one as well. He deserves it. He has worked too hard.

Somewhere in the distance he feels Susan pressing against him with increased urgency. Stuart is shouting something about fandom and fanac and gaffiation and neofans and bee enn effs. Wilkes is talking to him as well, soothingly and at length, but he hears nothing. If Graffanatis himself were to walk into the room at this point he knows that he would greet the villain only with a small bland smile.

He feels himself being separated from his seat and then escorted through a web of space. He has a feeling of transition, flight, but it is all narrow, detached, happening to someone of whom he has never heard and the giggles and moans he hears could, for all they matter to him, be his own. In fact they *are* his own, but only on the elevator, moving unevenly downward, does he become aware of this and then too it does not seem to matter. Susan and Stuart talk to him soothingly, carefully, at great length, trying to patiently sort out things for them and he listens with mild appreciation, considerate for their time and trouble. But if he was, at this moment, quite able to talk he would tell them that it is perfectly all right; he can manage without them, everything is fine. Like Graffanatis, he is in some space of his own, cemented to his own purpose, a fish in speckled water flicking brightly toward the canal as the ponderous and mindless sea scurries above him, befouling the surface with its own absent pollution.

X

Further notes on the Solarians; the restoration of purpose.

When he begins to feel like himself again he is sitting in a cafeteria—Stuart on his right, Susan across from him—and he is drinking a cup of coffee. Susan, meanwhile, is talking to him patiently, quietly, with gentle gestures: she has apparently been talking for some time and at the look of returning intelligence in his eyes she smiles but does not stop. She is telling him now—has been telling him for some time it appears—the history of the Graffanatis Imbroglio and he listens as carefully as he can while Stuart holds his wrist casually and looks down dully at his coffee cup.

"So Miles said when Sykes said that, he said, 'I can no longer exist in an organization which will not make the simplest commitment to basic realities!' And he stood up and said that everyone who agreed with him should join with him in walking out now. Well, it was a sensation of course, there was no question about that, but everybody was so stunned for a moment that no one moved. And Miles said, 'I can see that whatever courage remains in this blasted organization is limited only to me,' and went to the door. That was when they began to follow him. First Johnny Bernstein and then Hugh Bellows and Mark Julius and finally Gail Curtis went out with him; and Teddy didn't know what to *do*. I mean, it was a terrible thing to accuse a man of disloyalty and end by being ultimately disloyal to yourself, but Teddy put it to a vote and it was agreed that Miles had absolutely no right to do what he did and that the whole thing was terribly immature. It was really a solid vote of confidence in Teddy and the Solarians. But I guess," Susan finishes glumly, "I guess he's picked up, Miles I mean, I guess he's picked up a little support since then. I wouldn't be surprised if Sykes, Hollowaite, and that tall goon in the corner were all spies for Graffanatis. He's got the whole organization by the throat. So anyway, that kind of explains what happened tonight."

"They didn't listen to me, Susan," Fox says. "I was supposed to talk to them about what was happening to me; you said that this would be the solution to the whole situation and they wouldn't even listen."

"That's not quite the point," she says, rather sharply. "I mean, that's all well and good, Izzinius, and we're all sympathetic; but do you know what we've witnessed tonight? We've witnessed nothing less than the destruction and possible death of the Solarians."

"Which," Stuart says, "might be a damned good thing, all considered."

"Oh, you can't really say that, Stuart. Think of the *contribution* the Solarians have made over the past four years. The *dedication*. The *involvement*. And now it's all gone because Miles Graffanatis is a power-hungry lunatic. It's a sad, sad thing."

"I don't understand this," Fox finds himself saying. "I mean, I simply don't understand this. I never meant to know people like that. It's all so strange ..."

"What's also sad," Stuart says, ponderously, "is that Miles is not the only one to blame; Teddy Wilkes's own power drives have to be held to blame for a good deal of the difficulties we've seen. The trouble with Teddy is that he simply can't deal with people."

"Oh, sometimes," Susan says, "sometimes he can. But the thing is that the Plutonians have nothing to offer. They're just a splinter group in the first place and in the second they're just into sword-and-sorcery; they aren't science-fiction fans at all. They're *fantasists*. I don't quite know what's happened to us."

"Listen," Fox says, his feeling of disorientation gone but some disconnection setting in to take its place, "listen, maybe we should just forget the whole thing. I mean, I feel like going home and going to bed or something. Maybe in the morning things will look better."

"Oh nonsense, Izzinius," Susan says. "You're always so defensive about things and so careful about your health; you'd never be in this mess if you weren't so selfish in the first place. You know what I think we ought to do? I see only one solution."

"Don't tell me about Miles Graffanatis," Stuart says.

"That's exactly what I'm thinking about. I think that we all ought to go up to Miles. Izzie and you and me. We ought to talk to him. Maybe he can see the light of day. Maybe we can lead him to understand that the future of the Solarians is more important than the ambitions of any single person and that all of us have to make compromises. I agree that he should have been president. Teddy had been president for three months already—two whole terms; it was time for a change. He was greedy. But none of us understood how badly Miles wanted the presidency and he didn't understand that his time would have come anyway."

"Well, listen," Izzinius says, with a certain false briskness, draining his cup of coffee and pushing his chair back from the table. "Listen, that's all well and good. Why don't you just do that, Susan and Stuart, and I'll be getting along home. You can tell me—"

"Nonsense," Susan says and seizes his wrist. "That's nonsense, Izzy. You've got to go along with us. You've got to go up and tell Miles what you were going to tell the Solarians. It's the only way to shock him into an awareness of how serious things are. If he can understand that it was completely his fault that the Solarians were unable to listen to your story, if he is led to understand that it was his spies planted in there who broke up the meeting and deprived them of your revelation, he may come to his senses. It isn't that Miles isn't sensible when he wants to be, just that he doesn't like to *think*."

"Yeah," Stuart says. "What was that anyway that you wanted to talk about to them, Izzie? I was very interested; I'm sorry I didn't have a chance to hear."

"Nothing much," Fox says.

"He's being visited by some aliens," Susan says, "or more properly, the aliens are making *him* visit. They're in orbit outside the Earth and they keep on taking Izzie up to the spaceship to demand that he turn over evidence to them that will allow them to take over the Earth. They seem to want the Cupboard articles on the engineering of modern minds and they keep on seizing his consciousness and they won't let him go."

"You don't say?" Stuart says. 'That's very interesting. That's one I never heard of before. Must be very tough for you, hey, Izzie? Aliens!

Seizing your mind! Imagine that."

"It's pretty tough," Fox says. "There's no question about it."

"He's bearing up very well," Susan says. "But he needs help and I thought that the Solarians could give it to him. It's to our eternal discredit that we were unable to hear Izzie speak tonight. Now the thing to do is to go right up, to Miles Graffanatis and tell him what happened and make him listen to Izzie. That should bring him back to his senses, when he understands how important the issues are here and how the stakes are too high for this kind of immaturity. I think that he'll listen to reason."

"Sykes will probably be there already," Stuart says. "And that other one."

"Well, of course they'll be there, but they wouldn't tell Miles the *truth*. They'll just glamorize themselves. It isn't that Miles won't listen to reason if we give it to him."

"Look," Fox says, "look, I really don't feel very well; I'm quite tired and I think I have to go home. You can tell Graffanatis, I mean you can say to him what I would have said. Wouldn't it accomplish the same thing?"

Stuart shakes his head, and Susan says, "Never. He'd think that we were faking it or something because all that he'll hear from Sykes and Hollowaite will be lies. We have to confront him with the truth."

"Don't you want to help spread the truth, Izzie?" Stuart says. "Think of the consequences involved. Besides, I know I'd appreciate your cooperation. I just got a January 1947 *Tremendous* in and I think that I can sell it to you for half price. You need that one, right?"

"Stuart," Susan says, "must you always try to do business with people every second? Can't you sometimes just be friends with them? Besides, I've told Izzie already, I don't think that he should collect any more magazines; I think that that's one of the reasons he got into all this trouble in the first place. The collecting. If you had guided him the right way—"

"January 1947?" Fox says. "The January 1947 *Tremendous?*"

"In mint condition. Not even a bent flap. One of the most beautiful copies of this issue I've ever seen and right now I can tell you that it's going to be a rare one. The market is piling in on those. I can give it to you for two dollars or maybe a dollar seventy-five. How would that be?"

"That's the one with the Marlow cover, isn't it? The two fairies fighting inside the spaceship with the green ointment coming down from the ceiling and all those Druids watching? And the moon and rings of Saturn in the background?"

"That's the one," Stuart says with satisfaction. "It was Marlow's third and last cover for *Tremendous*, and most of us agree that it was the best. And it's got the new Vivaldi serial starting off in that one too."

"No it doesn't," Fox says. "The Vivaldi serial, *Killers of the Rulers* starts in the December 1946 issue and I know that because I have it. The *second* installment is in the January 1947 and then it finishes off in the February 1947. The December 1946 issue is the rare one, you know. That's the one that they're after."

"Well, I don't blame them," Stuart says. "It's a little beauty and the Oliver cover is striking. One of Oliver's best."

"No, I don't mean for that. That's the issue with Cupboard's articles in it."

"Oh yeah? Oh, of course, you're right. That's right. Well, in the last analysis, it's all a matter of taste. You like Cupboard, I like Oliver. And Steele. What a terrific magazine that late 1940 *Tremendous was.*"

"Stuart," Susan says, "you're not even *interested* in science fiction. You don't even *read* those magazines. All that you do is try to profiteer off people like Izzie who don't even know what's going on. I think it's disgusting."

"I *love* the magazines," Stuart says. "How could I be in this business if I didn't love them? You have no right to say that, Susan. The only thing is I can't be a collector because it takes guts to really give yourself over to something and admit that it's important to you. I don't have that kind of guts. That's why I admire Izzie so much; he comes right out and has conviction and that's something which very few of us have."

"No, that isn't true, Stuart," Susan says, "but we can't waste time talking about that now. I think it's just disgusting how you make people get involved with collections and all the time *laugh* at them. But we'll talk about that later. Right now, Izzie, I want to get up and go to Miles. I have a feeling that he's waiting for us. We'll tell him the whole story and Izzie will tell him what's going on and we'll settle this one right now, for once and for all. That's the whole thing."

She puts down her coffee cup with a clatter and stands, looking quite domineering. "Come on," she says, "let's go." Fox, feeling that he is somehow attached to her by a thin but cutting wire, stands up, and Stuart does as well. Fox puts on his coat mumbling something to the effect that he really does not care to go but he knows that the issue is settled. Susan's determination is really quite frightening and, in the bargain, he has two other motives. One is that he might as well talk to Graffanatis who, it seems, might be the only person who could truly understand and help him—at least he finds that he is now beginning to think in that way—and the other is that he really wants that January 1947 *Tremendous* and if going over to Graffanatis will be helpful in getting Stuart to lower his price, then it is well worth the undertaking.

It is time to bring things to a conclusion one way or the other; Fox can see that. "All right," he says, "all right, I'll go, I'll go." But they are already striding ahead of him briskly and he finds that instead of being greeted as the enormous concession which it surely is, to the contrary, his statement has become a desperate plea and, scuttling after them through the cafeteria after colliding with an old woman and a tray, Fox finds that he has to scream it, reiterate it, plead it through whistling lips as he strives to catch up with them before they go out the swinging doors. But before he can make it, guess who picks him up again? And drags him winging through unlimited stripes and banners of space. Scuttling in helpless submission, he permits the warp to take him where it will thinking: there must be a better way to do this, surely there must be an easier way to work out this scheme; but just as determined as ever that he will tell them nothing because the fate of the world remains at stake and in any event he has to talk first to Miles Graffanatis.

XI
The Arch-Leader also has internal troubles.

"Well," the Arch-Leader says, "how are you feeling?" This time they are alone again in the closeted humming whine of the main room. "You look very tired."

"I'm all right," Fox says. "I've had a difficult evening. I really couldn't bear to be tortured again just now, I might break down on you and then where would you be?" He feels almost flippant at the moment; there is one thing that can be said about the Solarians and that is this: when you have gone through one of their meetings you have, in a genuine sense, been prepared to see it all. There is very little that the aliens can do to him at this moment that he feels he has not already experienced, at least by proxy. "You still do want the articles, don't you?"

"Oh indeed," the Arch-Leader says. "Unfortunately, however, we've run into a little bit of a problem. Nothing serious but complicating. I wouldn't worry about it at all but it *does* make things difficult. Headquarters feels that we should release you."

"Really?"

"They feel that since our contacts have been unavailing it would be unwise to pursue this further; that what we obtain over resistance could be more dangerous than obtaining nothing at all. They want to dissolve the mission in fact and recall us; send out another expedition to take over. With someone else," the Arch-Leader says hastily. "I mean, they would try to deal with another human, you wouldn't be touched again."

"Well," Fox says, struggling to a sitting position and finding, by some happenstance, a steaming cup of coffee on his right which the alien motions him to drink. "Well, that's remarkable news. I mean, it solves everybody's problem, doesn't it? You can go home and I can live out my life in peace and nobody's unhappy because the decision has been made for us."

"Well, not quite," the creature says. "I have, of course, intergrammed back a reply of the utmost protest and I do believe that I have a good chance of winning my point since the commander on the spot has ultimate authority on the nature of the conditions, at least he can give the only informed opinion. I think that things are going along quite satisfactorily at this juncture and that it is only a matter of a little bit of time now until we reach a complete, er, meeting of the minds. On the other hand, Headquarters is participating in its usual obstructory course for the usual reasons. The point is that we cannot continue our treatment for the moment, all our activities are suspended by fiat until the debate is resolved. So you've just come along this time for the ride, so to speak, just to be reminded that we're very much in contact and still have our hand in. You note, of course, that the frequency of your visits is increasingly marked. That is all part of the procedure; eventually you would be visiting us ten to twelve times a day and at that time resistance seems to crumble entirely, usually by that tack alone. But I'm afraid that our procedure is such that we cannot continue treatment while a policy decision is being made. So there you are. Terribly sorry of course."

"Oh, of course," Fox says and drinks the coffee which is pleasantly bitter, even acrid—all in all far superior to what he has had in the cafeteria and far more revivifying. After all of the events of the evening, now superseded by this moment of peace he finds himself in a peculiar state which he imagines is very close to drunkenness (he has no way of being quite sure since he has never had a drink in his life). "But I guess you'll get through it. I've had quite an evening myself."

"Well, you see," the alien says in almost a friendly tone, "you're going through the same kind of thing that we're going through here; the interesting thing about sentient races is that they all conform to certain basic patterns of behavior and bureaucracy, which, for all the apparent diffusion of the races, tend to run remarkably parallel. In my case we have a Headquarters which is attempting to build up its appropriations from the government—oh yes, we run on governmental appropriations like everything else—and the best way that they can do this of course is to have increased missions, increased responsibilities, increased duplication for various tasks and so on and so forth. Now, you see, by calling our mission abandoned and sending a second expedition to do the same job they'll be able to double their appropriations for the effort and this will give them all kinds of sock in the central office. You do follow what I'm talking about, of course?"

"I think so," Fox says. "I used to work for the government myself. Our government, that is. The Department of Relief and Restoration."

"Well," the Arch-Leader says with an enormous sigh, "you know the way it is, bureaucracy is bureaucracy and so on and so forth and what they want to do is to send two for the price of two. But I don't mind saying that I'll fight until the last inch. My judgment will prevail and we'll finish the job."

"Well," Fox says, "I wish you luck. I mean, I can understand your position."

"That's very kind of you, inasmuch as after all you stand to pay the penalty if we're allowed to continue here. Very generous, if I may say so. You see, Izzinius, it's nothing personal here at all. We have only the kindliest feelings toward you. We just want to finish our job and get out. But I must say that your resistance has been admirable. I mean, one can respect a man who will defend his home species in the way that you have. Of course you understand that they're really not worth it and that the benefits will be incalculable after you submit. Otherwise, your race won't survive another fifty of your years. I don't see how you can do it."

"Well, you know," Fox says, uncrossing his legs and leaning back, feeling quite relaxed, the thing is that the Arch-Leader is the first fully reasonable creature with whom he seems to have dealt within the last few hours, "you know how it is. I mean there are no easy answers and so on. Actually, I don't think that things are that bad here but I can see where my opinion might be a little bit prejudiced. We're getting along. Of course life hasn't been all that it could have for me but I have hopes."

"Yes, I can understand that," the Arch-Leader says politely. "Would you like more coffee? No? Well, anyway, the thing is that there are forces already set in motion, which are not quite visible yet, and whose consequences will not be visible for twenty years, but which are already built deeply into the system on your planet. This can only have one outcome, a rather grim one, I must say. You people are really doing dreadful things to your environment you know, but, beyond that, this so-called technological explosion you're having down there has had the most disruptive effect on the lives of most people. More and more they find themselves totally disconnected from any sense of their acts, any sense of consequence and also any ability to influence their lives. They really can't get hold of their lives, you know, that's quite a major problem. Eventually that, along with overpopulation and the media that will allow you to see more and more of how the others live, will lead to the implantation of a dreadful rage in most of your people, a rage which seems to have no cause and no outlet but which must be channeled in some way. And the only way in which that rage will find direction, I am sorry to say, is in destruction. They'll try to strike out at the environment and at the technology which they dimly sense to be the root of the problem. But almost everything that they do will be intercepted, so to speak, by the others: other people that is, who get in the way. Oh, it will be dreadful, Fox! The riots, the famines, the pestilence, the murder, the strikes, the dislocation, the aimlessness, the slow topple and heave of civilization—and the question of atomic energy too, of course. And all of the loneliness and lost purposes and waste! Really, Fox, you ought to think twice about this whole thing! Do you really want to sentence your people to live in this fashion when a simple decision of yours could make a better life for all mankind? Of course not."

"In other words," Fox says, stricken by an interesting idea, "in other words, you're trying to say that all of life for everyone all the time will be like a Solarians' meeting. Is that right?"

"That's about right," the Arch-Leader says. "I mean, more or less. These 'Solarian' meetings—and I admit, I can hardly understand what is on you people's minds, I have never witnessed anything quite like that before and, as a matter of fact, had to tune it out from disgust after a time—these 'Solarian' meetings are quite restricted, the purposes are narrow; there is, if I might say so, only a single passion at the center whose resolution is the question at issue. There is also a consensus in that most of those there have agreed, it would seem, to disagree. But the situation which I am promising you is one of such magnitude and resources that it would be like a Solarians' meeting held in one of your oceans on a freezing dark night with everyone blindfolded and your 'moon' exerting a high tide, everyone struggling in viscosity, hating one another, trying to touch mostly for the purposes of destruction. Terrible stuff, Fox! Come now, why don't you simply turn over the transcripts?"

It is tempting and for only a moment Izzinius allows himself to consider this: for one thing, it would send the aliens away and, for another, it would stop the sudden visits and, for a third, it would help the Arch-Leader to protect his position and even win a promotion. Truly he wishes the creature no harm; he wishes that everyone was as reasonable as the Arch-Leader obviously wants to be. If he were to turn over the transcripts he would, in short, be helping a friend and getting himself out of a very difficult spot and this would unquestionably be a benefit. Also, if what the Arch-Leader contends is true, he would not only *not* be the betrayer of mankind but would indeed be responsible for its salvation since things as bad as what the creature predicts would certainly be unbearable for Izzinius Fox let alone the rest of humanity.

He tumbles all these thoughts through his mind for a moment and allows himself to consider the whole thing in all of its proportions, and finally shakes his head, biting his lips and says, "No. I can't do it. I'm sorry, you understand. There's nothing personal to this at all but I just can't."

"But listen," the Arch-Leader says, "if what I told you comes to pass, why then—"

"I know. I know what you're saying and I really understand and appreciate it. But you see, the thing is, I can't believe it. I can't believe that things are going to get that terrible and I'm afraid that you're just saying it to me to scare me into doing something which would be against the interests of the planet. Look, there's a lot of hope. We're not doing too badly in the war and it's the only war we've had for quite a few years and most people are living better than they ever did before and generally speaking people seem to be getting a bit brighter. I mean, I agree that there are probably some terrible things going on in Russia that we don't even *know* about, and Hitler was despicable and all that, but that was a kind of period the world had to live through and I think we've all learned from it. I mean, this war isn't as *big* as the last two in any way and it seems to be confined to a particular area with only a limited group of people fighting it and it isn't spreading. Isn't that something? And there's less poverty and need and people seem to be acting a little kinder to one another. No, I just don't think that it's going to turn out the way you say it is. It couldn't be quite that bad. We're not insane, after all, and we'd have to be insane to turn out the way you say we are."

"You'd be surprised," the Arch-Leader says with a sigh and then comes to his full height. "Oh well, I suppose that you can't have everything. It would have been nice if I had been able to coax you into reason and deliver the transcripts to Headquarters; very nice and reasonable. But life is very hard, very difficult and defeating; there is no reason to expect easy answers. I wish that you could be led to understand, Izzinius, that your heroism is irrelevant."

"*Everything* is relevant," Fox says. "For heaven's sake, you know that, don't you?"

"I'm truly sorry we had to torture you in the way we did but you understand that orders are orders. We are not unfeeling creatures, you realize; we *suffer*. Knowing that we caused you such anguish was very difficult for me and I want you to know that several of the crew protested on your behalf. You are not without your admirers here, Izzinius; I want you to know that."

"Oh that's all right. Looking back on it, I don't remember him ever taking me to the roller derby anyway, so the whole thing was made up and that's not too bad."

"Of *course* it's all made up!" the Arch-Leader says. "That's precisely the point, Izzinius. There is *nothing* worse than the imaginary past … unless, of course, it is the foreseeable future. I am afraid our time is about up. Would you like some more coffee?"

"No, thank you," Fox says courteously. "I've had quite a bit today already and I don't want to get caffeine nerves. And I'm smoking too much in the bargain."

"Just inquiring. We'll see you soon and I do hope that we'll be able to resolve this shortly. I'm sure that this little problem with Headquarters will work out for the best and then we'll simply be proceeding."

"Oh, I trust so," Fox says and feels the familiar pressure of unwinding, the imminence of passage. "Well, thank you very much for your time and trouble and frankness."

"Well, thank *you*, Izzinius," the Arch-Leader says. And through the clouds of his diffusion they wave at one another, a courtesy and cheerfulness of spirit quite enormous in this void. All the way back to Earth Izzinius finds himself tapping his foot and humming, not that it is a long trip of course or that his voice is very good or that he has ever had even an inadequate sense of rhythm.

XII

Graffanatis.

He catches up with Susan and Stuart on the sidewalk outside, virtually staggering into them. Stuart seizes him in an enormous grasping clutch and, looking at him, says, "You weren't trying to get away from us were you now, Izzy? That wouldn't be right, after we worked this whole thing out and like that."

"No he wasn't," Susan says sharply. "Really, Stuart, leave him go. Can't you see he's been on a trip?"

"A what?"

"He's been with his Rhelm people again. I've seen him come back twice already today. He gets a certain look on his face and his breathing gets labored. Look at him, he's gasping like a fish. That's the sign."

"Well," Stuart says, "well, Izzy, is that true? You were with those aliens of yours."

Fox nods and says, "I don't want to talk about it now. Could we just kind of leave it to the side?"

"He's very sensitive about this," Susan says. "It's kind of a sore point with him. You just kind of leave him alone after he comes back for a while and then he's okay."

"Is that so?" Stuart says. "You're right, his face looks exactly like a fish. So they really take you on a trip, eh, Izzie? That must be very interesting."

Feeling vaguely as if he were little more than an object being discussed at some random distance and to no effect, Fox says, "Listen, just forget the whole thing, will you? I think I'd like to go home now. We can discuss it tomorrow or something."

"Nonsense," Susan says and puts her hand on his sleeve, guides him into a subway kiosk; Stuart's weight nudges him gently from behind as they negotiate the stairs with some difficulty and go through the turnstiles. "That's nonsense, Izzinius, there's only one way that we can bring this thing to an end and give you the help you need and that's to see Miles Graffanatis." There are dim rumbles, tremors in the distance, filth on the platform seems to circulate in response. Stuart says with satisfaction, "Here's the train coming in right now. It's only a short ride."

"But why?" Fox says, still in Susan's hands, feeling her palm, as a matter of fact, begin to move up and down his sleeve with real enthusiasm. She leans against him and puts her face into his shoulder, a peculiar gesture under the circumstances since, whatever else there has been between him and Susan, it is nothing which he has equated with a physical bond. "Why is this so important? He can't help me. I'm sorry I mentioned this business in the first place," he adds pointlessly. "I should have kept it all to myself."

"Not at all," Stuart says and motions that they should stand back as, screaming hideously, the train staggers across their path of vision and halts with a groan. "What's the point of living if you don't have good friends you can confide in, people who can share your problems, people who can help you work out things?" Susan nods and they encircle him, push into the train.

He finds himself seated uncomfortably in an almost empty car between Susan and Stuart who thrust their knees into him, exchange glances over his head, seem to share a kind of feral knowledge as the train slips out of the station. Across from him, a young boy, no more than eight or nine, is sitting in silent intensity, gripping an issue of *Thoughtful* and reading it with such application that sweat seems to be coming out on his forehead. The magazine trembles in his hand, pages slip and clutter, and then the magazine falls to the floor. The boy scrambles to pick it up and then, crouching, looks up at them, sees Stuart, nods at him in a stricken way and then, folding the magazine under his armpit leaves the car rapidly, slamming the door up front as he passes into the next.

"I think I know him," Stuart says. "He's a fan from Brooklyn named Arthur Abbotson. I sold him that issue of *Thoughtful* just two days ago if I don't miss my guess."

"Then why did he run away from us?" Fox asks.

Stuart considers this for a moment, tilting his head back and closing his eyes, then leans forward shaking his head, opens his eyes to fullest width and says, "I don't know. A lot of people I meet in the store don't seem to want to have social contact on the outside. I can't really figure it. Maybe they're ashamed of what they're doing or some such."

"They aren't aware of fandom," Susan says. "If they knew there was such a thing as fandom they wouldn't feel so isolated or lonely or ashamed of themselves, and they'd find that they could enjoy it. That's been your tragedy, Izzinius, you stayed away from fandom too long. If you had listened to me weeks ago, none of this would ever have happened."

"None of what?"

"Well, you would have come to the Solarians while Miles was still there and you would have told everybody about this and Miles would have been so interested in what was going on and so taken with his responsibilities as a member to solve it that he never would have walked out to form the Plutonians. It would be a whole different situation. Frankly, Izzie, you've shown very little consideration for your friends here; you've been very selfish and in a way this whole thing is your fault."

"Yes," Stuart grunts vaguely, bobbing to his left, "yes, Izzie, she's got a point there. If you have trouble in science fiction you should go right away to your science-fiction friends to help you."

"But it wasn't science fiction," Fox points out.

There is silence for a moment, then Susan says, "Well, of course it's science fiction, Izzinius. Doesn't what's been happening to you sound exactly like science fiction? Anyway, it never would have happened to you at all if you hadn't gotten so absorbed in those silly magazines and lived to yourself and let them take over your mind. You know that's true, don't you?"

Whether or not it is true, this seems to be quite unanswerable. There is really very little to say. Fox begins to understand dimly that there is nothing he can say anymore that will make the slightest bit of difference and so, in the silence that follows Susan's remark, he succumbs again to a kind of disassociation, seeming to witness himself and his companions from a far, blank distance as the train agonizes its way through the tunnels, moaning faintly to itself on the turns. For a moment he feels that the disassociation may be the normal prelude to a seizure, but nothing happens and he comes to understand that the Arch-Leader is probably still waiting out his instructions; for the moment he has been left to his own devices.

As a matter of fact, he may be left *permanently* to his own devices; if the expedition is recalled to the home planet he assumes that this will be accomplished quickly and, all that sentiment to one side, he doubts very much if the Arch-Leader will find it necessary to summon him for a personal farewell. In the ultimate sense they have only been doing business together, nothing else, there is no reason why he should feel that he and the Arch-Leader have a *relationship*. One knows that this persistent desire of his to involve himself emotionally with people with whom he is merely contracting business should be carefully watched, and could, if left unchecked, lead to a very embarrassing kind of destruction. Nevertheless, he finds himself thinking the Arch-Leader is really not that bad a type: a little harassed, a little rigid, more than a little mechanical, but considering the branch of the civil service in which he is employed and the particular problems of alienation involved in any government work, the creature is not a bad sort at all, quite reasonable really; certainly far more reasonable than most of the civil service types with which Fox himself worked during his period of employment. Everything is relative after all, and if there is any malevolence in the air it seems to have come from the "Headquarters" rather than from the Arch-Leader himself, who, as has already been pointed out, simply wants to get a more stable level of position. Perhaps the creature is still awaiting official certification and needs to make the mission succeed in order to escape provisional status. This would certainly explain a lot.

He toys then, not entirely for the first time, with the idea of turning over, when all is said and done, the Cupboard Transcripts to the Arch-Leader. There would be very little to it and Stuart would almost certainly (for a price) be able to replace the rare issue for him. Certainly, if things are heading to as disastrous a pass here on Earth as the Arch-Leader had suggested, then it would be the better part of martyrdom to turn the damned planet over to the land of galactic union which might be able to run it sensibly. The fact that Fox himself does not think that things are that bad is not a conclusive judgment; he is not an expert after all and the aliens are far more experienced than him at cultural judgments. The fact is that they may be entirely right in what they are saying, in which case his discretion (turnover) would be the better part of valor (defiance). He has, in short, taken what he imagines to be a stand for humanity against the brutal and insensitive invaders, but almost everything that he has seen recently has been to reopen the question. Who is humane? Who is brutal? Certainly, the aliens seem to be far more rational than any of the humans with whom he has been dealing. The aliens at least know what they want and seem to have a clear and evident sense of purpose.

He is unable, in any event, to understand yet what there is precisely to this Cupboard article which would make it so desirable—indeed so pivotal—to the alien's sense of purpose. Izzinius is not quite sure of what Cupboard was suggesting. He was barely able to read the article; it was surrounded fore and aft by a long editorial, by K. M. Conrad, saying that it was the greatest blessing to humanity since the coming of segregation and the Christian era, which at times became so hysterical (an old tendency of Conrad's) as to be incomprehensible. And the article itself was terribly dull and seemed to lack Cupboard's usual stylistic precision, which he had shown to such advantage in his famous serials *Into the Altair Cluster* and *Clashing Rocket-ships Play Sterile War in the Glancing Void.*

Cupboard's theory was that the human brain could be schematized into four compartments named A, B, C and D, and that each of the compartments had a particular role to play in the development and activity of the person. A was the sexual part; B was the rational part; C was the punishment part; and D was the retribution part. The healthy adult was mostly controlled by C which kept his raging impulses in check and allowed B to make its modest contribution to his overall insight. But a person could, at any time in his prenatal or infant life, be "fired" by something which Cupboard called a "quadroon," which would tend to augment or reduce the power of any given area and thus force the individual to run "out of kilter." Quadroons resulted from "faulty input of emotional stimuli" and guaranteed in turn that there would be a "faulty output because of poor engineering."

What Cupboard had suggested was a method of engineering the human brain and development so that quadroons did not occur and the brain was thus able to stay in perfect balance. Specifically, Cupboard had recommended that the C area be built up by prenatal dialogues which the mother would hold with the unborn infant; she would advise the embryo to "always do the right thing" and "keep tight control" and so on and so forth while at the same time she would keep the A compartment in check, for instance, by saying that "sex is bad" or "sex is dreadful" or "sex is something you must be careful about"; the whole thing then was that humanity could be shaped into a perfect engineering model through the input of good quadroons instead of poor ones.

Ultimately, Cupboard predicted, there would be a quadroonless society in which human beings, raised out of the womb, would be brought up in laboratories where they could be measured electronically and the input could be carefully controlled at all levels. But the inefficiency of modern science being what it was, Cupboard had added that the quadroonless society would only be accomplished when there had come to maturity a group of individuals with good quadroons and, hence, the ability to act rationally. This, in his opinion, would take forty years or a little less depending upon the distribution of the hardcover book based upon his article and the series of Q-Institutes whose foundation he announced and which were to begin their work all over the United States within a very few months, with Cupboard himself as the sole proprietor.

It had struck Izzinius as being a shade simplistic or mechanical although, he could understand, looking into his own heart and mind (K. M. Conrad in his prologue to the article had advised readers to think or say NOTHING until they had examined the consequences of faulty quadroons in their own lives!), that he was suffering to some degree from faulty quadroons himself. In his case the C factor seemed to have entirely too much dominance over the others while the B was almost totally nonexistent. He would have paid a lot more attention to the article for that reason if Cupboard had not made a particular point of saying that *there was no such thing* as having too dominant a C component and that most human beings by nature were totally held in thrall by B; thoughts of sex, licentiousness, prurience, copulation, breeding, perversity and so on occupying them almost all the time and making it impossible for them to function as rational individuals.

Indeed, the article had ended with the ringing declaration: "Destroy the B compartment! Destroy these weak, pusillanimous desires that prevent us as men of freedom from achieving our own ends! Grant us, O Lord, perfect adjustment, perfect peace, and the end of this haunting specter of sex forever!" following which K. M. Conrad had appended the second part of his editorial along with a note that reprints of the article could be obtained from the Quadroon Foundation—whose mailing address was similar to that of *Tremendous* and whose vice president and chief recording secretary was K. M. Conrad himself.

For these reasons, along with a certain indifference to the nonfiction in the magazines—it really was often quite dull and hardly "scientific" at all—Fox had not paid much further attention to the efforts of the Quadroon Foundation, although he had been vaguely aware through letters in the THUMBNAILS sections of *Tremendous* and advertisements occasionally seen in most of the magazine that the Foundation was doing a tremendous job, expanding by leaps and bounds, so to speak, under the guidance and supervision of its founder/leader, whose aim was to put a Quadroon Testing and Curative Center in every American city containing a population of more than five hundred and whose aim was already well launched thanks to the efforts of many science-fiction writers who had stopped writing in order to devote their full efforts to the Foundation itself.

In this way, Fox came to understand, Conrad had lost two of his most valuable and persistent contributors: V. V. Vivaldi, author of "Killers of the Rulers" and "The Race of the Barbarians Against the Engineers to Destroy Civilization as We Know It", and Gertrude S. McMariantyre, who in several short stories published in the *Tremendous* of the late 1940s had secured her reputation as the leading woman writer in science fiction-apart from Margaret Tuttle, who, it was rumored, wrote all the stories of her more famous husband Roger Tuttle under his pen name of Maurice Tuttle. Fox had managed to put the whole thing out of mind as only a minor loss (he had never liked Vivaldi or McMariantyre that much anyway), and had forgotten it almost completely until the aliens had raised the whole subject again.

But if Cupboard had indeed discovered the secret of human

consciousness, the foundation of human worth, then certainly there had been something in the article and the foundation itself beyond his means of comprehension and perhaps he, Fox, had no idea to single-handedly make the decision to deny humanity these benefits. For a single awful moment the possibility occurs to him that the Arch-Leader might *himself* be a member of the foundation or at least working on retainer, but he then dismisses this out of hand; the foundation had made it very clear that it was a totally nonprofit institution devoted to Human Worth and he could hardly see Cupboard turning it over to a group of aliens, for whatever purposes. The whole thing is very confusing and dark. At this moment Fox is not sure that were the aliens to summon him he would not sigh and stretch and say, "Look, the hell with it. I'll give it to you." It would bring a lot of things to an end and possibly save a difficult situation. However, he is not granted that choice. Instead, he feels Stuart's elbow in his ribs, Susan's hand against his heart and then he is lifted, perhaps the word is propelled, out of his seat.

"Our stop," Susan says and they lead him through the doors, through the station and up the stairs. He is now in something approaching a numb, unblinking state; it is really much easier to simply walk along with them than try to exert any control of the situation. So he only nods when Susan says, "Miles lives right here, right above the subway station; he believes that the noise conjures thought."

They go into an odorous small building, whose mailboxes seem to have been literally hammered through into the stone, and up one flight of stairs, kicking papers and shreds of orange peel before them. ("Miles believes in trying to live as the masses live; he says that this is the only way you can cultivate a sense of reality," Susan confides.) Without knocking, they enter into an apartment, gloomily lit by a kerosene lamp, which contains in the living room only a table and a chair and behind which table and on which chair sits a huge man, perhaps four hundred pounds or more (it is difficult to tell in this light) who looks at them out of swollen eyes.

Tapping a cigarette gracefully on the table next to him, the fat man says, "So there you are. I knew you would come. I knew it would only be a matter of time. So this is our little doppelganger, eh?" he says, looking at Fox and Fox feels a thrill of loathing and terror go through him because in some trickery of this light Graffanatis looks exactly like the Arch-Leader only much larger and for all the aspect of the situation he could be back in the spaceship with the alien ready for his Final Interview. "Get out," he says to Susan and Stuart. Without a word they turn from Fox and are gone. He is left confronting Graffanatis in the empty room. It is one of the most difficult experiences of his life although, Fox suspects, it may have a good effect upon his C compartment.

XIII

The secret revealed.

"Sit down," Graffanatis says. Fox makes a gesture to indicate that he does not know where and Graffanatis barks. "On the floor, you idiot," while Fox scrambles for a place. "We have no time for amenities here," Graffanatis says. "The sooner we get our business finished, the better off we'll be."

"I suppose so," Fox says, just trying to make conversation. The fact is that he has been with Graffanatis for only thirty seconds or so and he is already convinced that he has never met anyone quite like this man in his life; waves of power seem to come off from the huge man in thick, uneven surges. Yet, for all his size, there is a curious delicacy in his gesture as he lifts a cigarette to his mouth, lights it and then inhales deeply, coughing.

"Sorry," Graffanatis says, "I'm a very heavy smoker as you see; I know that it's going to kill me along with the weight by the time I'm thirty or something like that but what the hell, you take your pleasure where you can and I wouldn't say I've had an excess of it. Well, Fox? Have you come to a decision?"

"Decision?" Fox says. "Decision about what? They brought me up here to talk to you and—"

"Nonsense," Graffanatis says. "I know exactly why they brought you up here and I know everything that's been going on. I tell you, Fox, we have no time for amenities here. I'm sorry to have thrown them out of the room so abruptly, but on the other hand they get exactly what they want and need. Types like Forsythe and Wiseman, alas, are to be manipulated. Sykes has given me a full report of your disgusting behavior at the Solarians."

"Disgusting behavior?" Fox says. "I didn't *do* anything. It all happened around me."

"Don't give me that nonsense," Graffanatis says, inhaling again and choking. "I told you, we have very little time for amenities here. You have to come to the point and stay at the point if you want to survive. Now you listen to me," he says, "Perhaps you'd better stand up, get to attention or something like that. I can see that you're one of those types who is thoroughly undisciplined, small passions and woes, odd obsessions circling in on you all the time, hence broken concentration. You're a sick man, Fox, do you now that? Your B compartment has run wild."

"B compartment?" Fox says, and is once again on the verge of a horrid insight. "Did you say B compartment?"

"Of course, what do you think, your C is in control? No, it's sad Fox, sad. You try to be reasonable with people, but they turn out time and again to be fundamentally insane. Quadroon therapy isn't fully applicable to the masses. Stand up you son of a bitch."

Shambling, rather stunned, Fox stands at a kind of loose attention before Graffanatis. Then, unwillingly under the fat man's glare, pulls himself into a posture of rigidity, his eyes flickering around the room. Unquestionably he is in a difficult situation; in fact, he has never experienced anything quite like this before. "I've never experienced anything quite like this before," he says.

"Well, of course you haven't; there's no reason why you should. You have been sequestered with your idiot magazines and your anal fixations too long, Fox; you can hardly be sensible. Look at me," Graffanatis says, putting out the cigarette and hacking phlegm through his nose with a practiced hand. "I said, *look at me*." Fox confronts the man's eyes, curiously white and rolling in his face, feels himself linked in, feels a sensation of falling, immersion. "Do you know who I am?" Graffanatis says. *"Do you know who I am now?"*

And Fox does. On the instant he knows who Graffanatis is, understands why he is in the room, begins to have some comprehension of what has happened to him now that it is far too late, of course, to change anything.

"I see you do," Graffanatis chuckles. "Well, Fox, it proves that even a collector can catch on. Do you know why you're here? *Do you?"*

"You want the article," Fox says weakly. "You want me to turn the article over to you."

"Oh, bullshit, Fox!" Graffanatis says with a somewhat effeminate gesture and then struggles, sneezing, for another cigarette. "If we wanted those, I mean if we need you for those you'd never even know that we were around. We've already got the article; we took it from your room while you were at the meeting. I would say that it's safely in Tom's hands by now and Tom's long gone."

"Tom?"

"The Arch-Leader. The one you think of as the Arch-Leader. Really a very nice fellow. A little bit weak on policies and has absolutely *no* understanding of science fiction, but really a sweet guy. No, that's all taken care of; we got that out."

"My December 1946 *Tremendous?*"

"No," Graffanatis says. "That was not necessary. We did not have to appropriate the whole issue; we merely ripped out the section containing the article. The cover is intact as is most of the rest of the table of contents."

"You mutilated it!"

"Well, that's the price you have to pay for involvement. It still has the cover, as I say."

"But that was a rare issue. I paid two dollars for that copy! You can't go in and steal property like that."

Graffanatis shakes his head despairingly and lights another cigarette, flicking the match against the wall. "You *collectors*," he says with loathing. "I mean, you people are really *impossible*. They *told* me about collectors when I got into fandom but I couldn't believe it. No, Fox, we don't need the transcripts from you; we've already got those. There *is* only one last thing to accomplish and then you can go on your way and we can go on ours. The article we no longer need, fortunately."

"Who's going to replace it? That's my property, you stole."

"I haven't the faintest idea," Graffanatis says. "It's none of my concern. Frankly, I think you'd be a lot better off, Fox, if you put away this whole question of collections and tried to get out into the world; tried to associate with people, lived a little bit. There's a whole lot more to science fiction than merely reading it you know. Speaking personally, I haven't read any science fiction for almost ten years. You keep up. You get filled in. It's not necessary to read these magazines much less have them. All you have to know is what's going on in them and it's always the same anyway." He tosses out the cigarette, grinds it into the rug and then reaches into his pack for another. Driblets of sweat run down his face and jowls; his eyes, shrouded by the fat, seem to look shrewdly through Fox, indeed, as if the interview has already been completed and there exists no purpose to him whatsoever.

"I really know I smoke too much," Graffanatis says. "I feel very guilty about it, to tell you the truth. It's an unpleasant habit and I find that I'm apologizing for it all the time. Nevertheless, it's just one of those few means of individual self-expression which I have within my ken. Tom and I have had numerous discussions about you, you know."

"Really?" Fox says. He would try to stand himself, but the room seems dense, enclosed by darkness. Also, to stand would lift the interview to a certain level he does not want to take yet. "That's quite interesting, I'm sure."

"Tom's a very nice fellow, you know. He's responsible for the whole fifth sector and he's done a bang-up job. Considering the kind of superiors he has, he's done simply remarkably."

"You know, Graffanatis," Fox says. "I really didn't think that you were a seditionist. You've betrayed the people of Earth, do you understand that? All the time that I was fighting in their defense you were acting toward their destruction. Don't you feel anything about that at all? Doesn't it mean a thing to you?"

"Oh my goodness," Graffanatis says and blows out a match, coughing, inserts the cigarette into his mouth with two hands and takes an enormous puff, exuding huge clouds of smoke behind which he can be seen only faintly for a while, shrouded by the density. "My goodness, Fox, you really have been reading science fiction too much; must you construe everything as this kind of megalomaniac engagement? I'm not a seditionist at all! I'm a savior!"

"Are you?"

"Well I should hope so," the huge man says. "I should certainly hope so. I mean in the first place are you really aware of the state that things have gotten into down here? There's no B compartment anywhere, everybody's dissipating like mad. That's the key to the whole thing, you know, people have lost any sense of effective self-control. And in the second place Cupboard has been a blessing. He's gotten a bad press and a lot of cruel misunderstanding, mostly because his ideas are actively dangerous to most of the people who run the world, but he's a great prophet, probably the only prophet since biblical times. Why, when I learned that he had finally reached his audience outside I felt such an enormous sense of relief that I knew I'd do everything within my power to advance the cause. Advance the cause, Fox! How many years do you think we have left on this planet?"

"I wanted to hold out. I thought it was important to stand in the breach. And all the time—"

"Well, that's a lot of nonsense, Fox. You don't even want to think about that. You're talking like all the rest of the Solarians; you have no sense of proportion or reality. When something truly important comes along you can't even understand it. Don't you know what's going on! Think about it, Fox! Licentiousness! Promiscuity! Breakdown! The destruction of society! The loss of all our values! Without control we have nothing and we've simply lost control." Graffanatis stubs out the cigarette choking and says, "Repression! Control! Discipline! We need a little bit of order in this world, Fox! Without order, we're all doomed! We've got to get away from the question of our base desires and discipline ourselves!"

Struggling to rise, Graffanatis seems to lose his balance, weaves, hangs onto the table desperately. Fox, out of some misguided sense of compassion, reaches across and helps the huge man to his feet, feeling the enormous dampness of the hands like paws clambering against his for grip. "Thank you," Graffanatis says, gasping. "Thank you. Cupboard was right! We must control ourselves! We must lock ourselves away from evil thoughts! We must develop agencies capable of ordering and suppressing all of the evil within us! That is what is necessary! And now it will be done! Fox, will you hand me one of those cigarettes on the table, I seem to have run out of reach. I really am embarrassed about my smoking habit but you know everybody dies sometime anyway, so you might as well die doing something that interests you rather than kowtowing to other men. Thank you. Would you light it please? The matches are right over there. Thank you. Ah. Thank you again. There has got to be an end to this dissipation! People must be put in their places and find their proper roles!"

"So," Fox says, putting the cigarettes back on the table, fondling the matches absently in his grasp as he leans away from the suffocating odor of Graffanatis's breath; the fumes from the cigarettes, the sweet and dense air seeming to circle tightly in the room. He decides that he will never smoke again. It is never a habit which has commanded his particular loyalty, but after this particular demonstration he will bring it to a rapid halt. "So, all the time that I thought I was the only one involved with them you were working behind the scenes to get the information. You were in league with them."

"Well," Graffanatis says, "you know how it is. I mean, you're likely to find a lot of intrigue in affairs as crucial as this and in any event I would have quit the Solarians anyway. They're really such a dismal bunch of cowards; all that they want to do is to sit and write resolutions or some such and they never get anything done. Activism! Movement! Change! That's what everything is about, Fox. But I was unable to make them see it. They're such inferior stock, really. They have no minds at all, not even the best of them. Pinheads, really. They never appreciated Cupboard. Do you know I wanted to send a resolution of thanks to *Tremendous* when the whole thing came out, just putting the Solarians on record as approving the Quadroon Theory and they wouldn't go along with that? They thought it would be too political. Well, there's really nothing you can do with a group of that nature, of course, other than to try to overcome them in the last analysis. It took me about three years to find the right way but I've always been very slow and thorough."

Graffanatis tosses the cigarette against the wall, letting a powder of sparks emit from it, and says, "Would you hand me that glass of water, please? The one on the table. My throat seems a bit raw." Fox passes over the glass and Graffanatis drinks hurriedly, coughing and choking only a little bit and then putting the glass down with a crash. "Well," he says, "in any event, I didn't summon you here merely to hold a dialogue on the background here, although, of course, you're entitled to know it. What I really want to ask you is this, Fox: can your confidence be trusted? Can what has gone on here be limited only to you? Or are you going to spread the news around? Because if you do the latter, I'm afraid that you'd make things very very difficult for us and we'd have to take stringent action. It's a few months until Tom can use the transcripts to get the plan into operation, and in the meantime we'd prefer very much not to be embarrassed. It would make things infinitely more difficult and they won't be easy anyway. It takes time to get any worthwhile plan into full operation, you know."

"He said that it would be immediate," Fox says. "That as soon as I yielded the article things would be settled."

"Well," Graffanatis says with a giggle, "well, in terms of *their* operation, it *is* immediate, I suppose; they live on an entirely different chronological scale than we do. What seems to be a long span of time for us really isn't that long for them. Also, you have to understand that in their land of complicated bureaucracy, there are a lot of forms to be filled out, a lot of things to be processed, a whole set of procedures to go through. Immediate for *them*, maybe. Actually, it will take about twenty years until things are at the point where they're really working and we can join the galactic union. Won't that be nice? To be part of a galaxy and everything? Just think of the opportunities we'll have. It's certainly superior to the way things are now. I've been promised a very important post, incidentally. I can't talk about it right now but I should have something to say about the membership requirements."

"I don't know," Fox says. "I guess I can be trusted. I mean, there's really nobody to tell, is there? Whoever might be in a position to do something would only think that we're all crazy anyway."

"Well," Graffanatis says, sitting. "You know, by some coincidence, that's exactly what I was telling Tom: that there really wasn't anything to worry about because people from our, uh, social circle really aren't in a position to get a serious hearing anywhere. Nevertheless, we can't take chances. What I must have is absolute assurance of your confidence. Tom said that you were a trustworthy individual in his opinion and he thought that your promise would be sufficient; I held out for more than that but I want to say that he thought that that would be enough. You seem to have impressed him very highly, I must note: I don't know why, but he said that you had 'remarkable ability and comprehension.' At least those were his words: 'remarkable ability and comprehension for someone of your race,' or something to that effect. He thought that your promise of confidence would then be sufficient and has more or less left things in my hands to resolve as I see fit.

"Would you mind if I had another cigarette? I promise that offer I have this one I'll lay off for forty minutes, at least that's the way that I try to pace myself. At least twice a day and sometimes three times I don't permit myself to smoke for a full forty minutes, so it evens out. Also, I don't smoke when I sleep so there's quite a period toward the end of the day when I get my lungs back in shape."

"I don't care," Fox says.

Graffanatis takes the pack, looks at it from all angles with an eagerness which seems to sift slowly toward disgust and says, "Goddamnit, I ran out again. I'm always telling myself to have an extra pack, for something like this and I never believe that it's really going to happen to me. One of these days I'm going to get caught short when the stores and bars are closed and I'll be in a real mess. Well," he says, rubbing his hands together unevenly, an expression of interest coming slowly over his face as his eyes seem to focus on other elements, "well, I'll just have to go down and get some. Unless you would like to; but of course that wouldn't be right, to release you for now, before the conclusion of the interview. So we'd just better sort of hurry things along and then go about our business. Tom wants me to exact a promise from you that you won't speak to anyone about this for a full year. Except for Susan of course, that's all right, and Stuart too: they've been in it from the first. And to me, if you want to drop up and maintain our relationship. But otherwise you are to advise no one, write no letters, make no hints and so on. Can I exact your word on that? I assure you, once things get truly organized, it will be a blessing. You won't regret any of this at all, not at all."

"Stuart's in on it?"

"And Susan as well," Graffanatis says, nodding. "They've both been very loyal and helpful here except, perhaps, a little bit too, uh, enthusiastic in playing out certain aspects of their roles. But of course they haven't been agents as long as I have."

"Ah," Fox says, with a feeling that at least he is getting to the bottom of it; for the first time since he has left the Solarians, he feels himself beginning to shift back into what he would call, for lack of a better word, Normal Focus, "Ah, then, you just tell me this: if Stuart is part of this, why didn't *he* turn over the issue? Why did they have to go to *me?* He must have had at least ten of them."

Graffanatis and looks at his hands. "Well," he says, "to tell the truth,

Stuart is very selfish about his rare issues and wanted to exact a price which the aliens wouldn't pay. They had to get approval from Headquarters, you know; all expenditures over a certain level must be counter-signed and what Stuart was requesting was a sum at the fifteenth level of approval—something which Tom simply couldn't get. Stuart can be quite selfish sometimes. He talks about the fate of Earth and so on, but what I really think is he's interested in is his magazines and making money and nothing else. It's something that had to be put up with; we couldn't force him to do anything."

"But you could force me."

"Well, of course we could," Graffanatis says with astonishment. "Of course we could; you were one of the *enemy*. Stuart was on *our* side. That was decided all at the beginning, before the whole thing got started. It wouldn't be fair to switch in the middle of a situation, you know that? Do you promise?"

"They're really going to take us over?"

"Uh huh," Graffanatis says. "First they have to break us down and then they'll take us over. It'll be better, you'll see. You and I, we'll be only about forty when we start to see the fruits of this and it'll make the whole thing worth it. Cupboard will be in his late sixties or so; it won't be so good for him. He's absolutely thrilled, of course. I was able to reach him finally by cable in Poinciana to tell him what role he had to play and he cabled back that he was most excited. Of course he's not been recognized in his own time over here, but he's never become bitter."

"All right," Fox says, a certain weariness descending over him, a desire to get out of it. It is not repudiation which has seized him so much as it is an enormous detachment: things are obviously too complex for him, have been from the start, and now he wants nothing other than to be on the other side of the situation. "All right, I promise. I won't tell anyone about this. Not that anyone would believe me, but I won't."

"And you won't write any letters and you'll stay away from the Solarian meetings as well?"

"Of course," Fox says. "I'm a *collector*. I have no interest in fandom at all." Already he is thinking that he must replace the December 1946 as soon as possible but he dreads what Stuart will ask for it. Possibly he will be able to make a package deal for that one and the promised January 1947, at least it is worth pursuing. "I'll keep it entirely to myself."

"That's excellent," Graffanatis says, nodding and coughing. "So we're really left now with only one last question. Tom has arranged a voluntary memory wipe for you: if you want to erase any memory of what's happened between us tonight, we can just go ahead and do that. If it will make you feel any better about the whole thing, that is. All that you will remember is a certain agreement of secrecy, nothing else. It might make things easier for you. Incidentally I intend to use it myself so you shouldn't think there's any element of danger in this at all. Actually, I think that the erasure of memory is one of the best gifts a fan can have and I'm looking forward to it."

"Well," Fox says, shaking his head, "well, no. I mean, if it's all the same to you, I'd just as soon keep my memory of all this. Not that I'd tell anyone or anything like that but it would be kind of a nice thing to *know*. So when the things start happening all around us I'll be able to recognize what's going on and have the prideful feeling that I had a little bit of a share in it."

"Well then," Graffanatis says, "well then, if that's the way you feel, your wishes will certainly be granted." A certain surliness seems to have come into his manner, replacing the kind of reasonableness which he has been showing now for several minutes. "Then there's no reason to talk any further about this, Fox. You've done what you have to do and so have I. And I see no reason to prolong our relationship. Under no circumstances whatsoever would I allow you to join the Plutonians, incidentally, so don't even ask. Stuart and Susan aren't even allowed to join. All this conspiracy stuff aside, I think that their positions on many issues are very weak and I do not want them corrupting the situation further, so don't even ask. All right, Fox, get out," Graffanatis says with enormous decision.

Fox staggers to his feet again, goes to the door, stops there, tries to turn to say something devastating. But the thing is that Graffanatis is already invisible, hidden in smoke and gloom, only the thin wheezing of his breath locating him in the darkness—and that but dimly. Looking at him from this aspect, Fox senses that he is looking at something else as well: perhaps it is his whole sense of the past, perhaps it is only an intimation of the future but it is profound, there is no doubt about it. For a moment he feels that he should say something—something signatory, something to put this into perspective—but he realizes on the heels of this that there is really nothing that can be said to Graffanatis because whatever has gone on between them has gone beyond simple epitaph or communion.

He leaves quickly, trudging the stairs in a fugue of such complexity that he is barely aware of the fact that Susan and Stuart have come from the darkness, have taken his arms, and with the gentleness of strangers, the absent grace of priests, are conveying him through the streets carefully, swaying his weight gently as they move him toward the subway and that piece of rest which he so surely deserves. They say nothing nor does Fox. There is nothing to say. He realizes that they are probably as astonished by consequence as he.

XIV

Brief epilogue

By 1962 the first tentative effects of the aliens' influence began to be felt. By 1963 there were further and more massive indications. By 1964 those indications had multiplied to the point where they seemed to control the public consciousness. By the late 1960s the consequences of Cupboard's theorem could be seen in almost every aspect of the nation's public and private lives. By the early 1970s the job was complete. The nation reeled slowly toward its period of ascension and then …

Fox didn't think about it too much. He had gone back to Relief and Restoration on a Special Reinstatement and had advanced to the level of assistant supervising technician, third class—an absorbing job which fully absorbed his capabilities. His wife Susan might have been helpful in certain discussions, but since she had elected the Memory Treatment she had little to say.

THE END

IN THE ENCLOSURE
By Barry N. Malzberg

Fredric Brown's *What Mad Universe* published in 1948 was the first true fan novel or, if you will have it, the first Truefen novel; its protagonist found himself entrapped in the imaginary world of a wild science fiction fan and battled his way toward recovery or escape in through a series of confrontations of the usual specters. Brown and Phil Klass (who was beginning to publish sardonic sf as "William Tenn") were sufficiently close for Brown to tell Klass "The fans are coming for us; the fans are going to overtake everything, *everything.*" And his novel, like an unsophisticated politician's campaign speech. gave a scattered and occasionally frightening set of speculations of what that brave new world might be, at least at science fiction conventions and fan publications. That was the first survey until my successor and then *Dwellers'* fraternal twin *Gather in the Hall of the Planets*, were the only such novels for the general market until Sharyn Crumb's *Bimbos of the Death Sun* came decades later.

There were the fanzines of course and the aforementioned conventions and all of the scuttlebutt surrounding the social construct but the general market had no real successor in the non-parochial floodlight until I took it upon myself to attempt this novel. The basis of that impulse remains as elusive to me now as it did at the time; I knew that there was some kind of audience (maybe unhappy parents of 14 year old fiendishly collecting sons) and more significantly I knew that Donald Wollheim, Ace Books' captain, science fiction writer and desperate cynic, would be a reasonable market. I wrote *Dwellers*, really more of a novella, intended as a half of a Wollheim Ace Double and patched it with astonishing speed and a cynicism well in accord with Wollheim's.

That cynicism was not spawned by vengeance and certainly not by contemplating grateful reception. The novel was not a celebration of fandom as I distantly perceived it at the time but it wasn't an attack either, it was a survey for the survey course my first half decade in science fiction was becoming. I felt that I was a ghost at the reception, a rookie trying to go from Class B to the majors through a welcomed resume. This was something of a register of naiveté of course, but beneath that something rather misguided and sadder; I thought that as the first true outsider to report on the kingdom I would win the gratitude of the hitherto unknown or abandoned.

That of course could only be a prescription for (at the very best) marginalization but an even more interesting souvenir of misapprehension. I was the stand-up comic or dramatic tragedian who simply misread the house. The novella was ignored by most and reviled by more than a few.

One fanzine reviewer, mercifully (for me) long departed from the Planet of Birth wrote in his column for THE WSFS JOURNAL "Malzberg should be killed for writing this novel"; he might have been reacting to what he perceived as an horrific accuracy. (Or then again he might not: Robert Silverberg read the novel and wrote me: "I was there. Where were you?") What remains powerfully interesting, more than half a century later, is the deadly, the frightening accuracy of the reportage. On the basis of the sketchiest research and a profound chutzpa I invented the characters, the milieu, the feuds and rivalries and the transcripts of fan society meetings with horrid accuracy. *I was making it up and it turned out to be true.*

Wholly dated now of course (just think of the Net, of Zoom, of worldcons, often international, with 5000-7000 attendees) the novel remains stunningly accurate for and prescriptive to its milieu. "First fandom will never die" was the battle cry of those first self-enlisted but its last surviving member died at 103 last year, the year of the worldcon in China. Two fates met and fused in the sprawling jungle science fiction had become.

This and the other fan novel adjoining (and characteriologically merged with) *Dwellers* might have made me a pariah in certain quarters (which, merged with its semi-semi sequel were even less pleased with *Beyond Apollo*) but they staked out the ground. That semi-semi sequel, *Gather in the Hall of the Planets*, sealed the deal.

April 2024: New Jersey

GATHER IN THE HALL OF THE PLANETS

BARRY N. MALZBERG

Writing as K. M. O'Donnell

Being a novelized version of the remarkable
interplanetary events that took place at the World
Science Fiction Convention of 1974

For
DONALD A. WOLLHEIM

PROLOGUE

In the August night, three aliens come to Kvass and sit to converse with him. He is not sure whether it is a dream or merely his drunkenness that makes the experience seem hallucinatory. "Listen, Kvass," the leader and apparent spokesman of the three aliens say, "the whole fate of your planet hangs in the balance now and you are charged with the task of saving it. Only you can rescue Earth from a fate more terrible than any of you could conceive. You'd better listen in."

"Come off it," Kvass says shakily, but with his customary ebullience. "I've been writing this stuff all my life. I don't believe a word of it when I'm writing it and I don't believe it when I'm away. It's just a question of making money. I could have gone to the sex novels but I have a certain integrity and besides the market there is too uncertain. And Westerns and mysteries are finished in paperback original. Pulp, it's all the same to me. I never even *liked* the stuff, I just read it when I was young and found that I could do it too."

"You'd better attend closely," the alien says with a certain grim intensity which rides over Kvass's protestations. Perhaps he is deaf. "What we are going to do is to infiltrate one of us, an alien, into the coming world science fiction convention at the Hotel Northport in New York City. This observer, this alien, this one of us will be present at all the goings-on of the convention and his path will cross yours many times. In fact, it will cross constantly. You will have to deduce who the alien is. If you cannot, we will conclude that your race is so stupid and without mental alertness that you are undeserving of an independent fate in the galaxy and we will move in on you. On the other hand, if you *are* able to deduce the identity of the alien, we will decide that you are a pretty tough and gritty little people after all and we will be afraid to mess around. So you see, the whole outcome rests with you. We have enough cosmic detonators to destroy your planet ten times over very quick so don't think that this is an empty threat."

"That's no test," Kvass says, deciding to play along with them for the time. If a group of aliens comes into your room in the strange hours of the night and talks to you about large issues seriously, it makes sense to deal with them on their own terms. It is this attitude which more than once has saved him from a writer's block even more deadly than the one which has seized him for the last several weeks. "You don't look like any human beings I've seen recently. In fact, you look pretty horrid. I'll just find the one that looks strange and turn him in to the authorities, right?"

"Oh, it won't be that easy, Kvass," the alien says with a rasp, shaking its tentacles so that small, bell-like protrusions squeal and ring in the spaces of his furnished apartment "You don't really think we're that naïve now, do you? I mean, you're dealing with a pretty shrewd, developed intelligence here. Masters of the galaxy, and so on. We have the ability to assume human size and shape and we will simply replace someone at the convention with one of our own who, having already sucked out his mind and history, will be able to, uh, pass for him. You'll have to deduce it by cleverness, Kvass old friend."

"You mean, you're going to abduct someone?"

"Someone you know very well, Kvass," the alien says with a chilling giggle, "someone as much a part of your life at the convention as the very hair on your head. This one we shall call the Other and when you think you have found him, you will simply say *unmask!* He will unmask, revealing his natural form and color and vanish with a shriek of exposure, thereby ending our plot. On the other hand," the alien says casually, "on the other hand, if you ask the *wrong* person to unmask, and that person turns out to be human we, who will be observing all of these events from afar, will chuckle at your stupidity and commence at once the destruction of your planet. Not that this should make you nervous."

"How can I believe you?" Kvass says, reaching to the corner table and his pipe. He puts it cautiously within his mouth which still seems to work. "How do I know this isn't all a practical joke or a horrid scheme? Maybe you'll destroy the Earth anyway. Maybe I'm imagining this. Maybe you're some people I know in disguise."

"This could be," the alien says judiciously, "but then again, you might as well take us seriously. After all, we'd be taking excessive means for a practical joke and then again we wouldn't go through this whole proposal simply to destroy you outright, would we? We'd just pull the trigger. No, a test is a test. It's perfectly fair. We try to be fair and reasonable about these matters."

"But why?" Kvass says, "why of all places would you take a world science fiction convention? Of all the unreasonable ideas—"

The alien produces a massive shrug. The two others shrug as well although with not nearly as much *élan*. "You know, Kvass," it says, "win a little, lose a little. It struck us as having a certain irony. Anyway, why not a world science fiction convention? It seems appropriate."

The three vanish. They leave Kvass quite alone except for his pipe, which seems to paint an unpleasant heat along his chin. Perhaps it is not tobacco but exit fire.

After a while, he stands and moves back to the bed, passing his typewriter on the way. The typewriter contains a sheet of paper with one paragraph. This paragraph has been there for several weeks and Kvass has been able to think of no particular way to improve it or to move beyond its simple substance. He shakes his head, collapses on the cold sheets, takes out his pipe and closes his eyes, telling himself that he will think of it no more.

No more. It is all part of the insane game he is playing with speculation and, in any event, the block has *got* to subside sooner or later; shortly after the convention (which is only a few weeks away) at the worst and after that things will be looking much better. He will put the whole thing out of his mind.

But of course, he does not quite. Not really. And not for a long time.

Kvass finds himself, in the month of August, thinking about the matter quite a bit and regarding the dim, polluted sunsets of the west side of New York with unnatural tears sometimes blocking the usual keenness of his vision.

Books by Sanford Kvass

NEBULA ROCKET ALERT (1963)
ROCKETS TO GANYMEDE (1963)
THE MISPELED MAGICIAN (1963) with *Marcus Stein*
THE BABES FROM BELTEGUESE (1964)
SCRBLZI (1964)
THE SORCERER OF SCRBLZ (1964)
THE SORCERESS OF SCRBLZ (1965)
THE BROTHERHOOD OF SCRBLZ (1965)
THE SIN OF SCRBLZ (1966)
THE RETURN OF SCRBLZ (1966)
THE WITCH WORLD OF PHARR (1967)
THE SORCERESS OF PHARR (1967)
THE MAGICIAN FROM PHARR (1968)
THE BROTHERHOOD OF PHARR (1968)
THE SCRBLZ FROM PHARR (1969)

THE HALLS OF DARKNESS (unpublished)
GROWING UP IN WHITE PLAINS (unpublished)
THE CORPORAL (unpublished)
THE SECRET OF SCRBLZ (unpublished)

Short-stories published in *Tremendous Science Fiction, Thrilling Science Fiction, Thoughtful Science Fiction, Planetoid Tales* and *The Magazine of Witchery*. Anthologized in *The Best from Tremendous: #14 and #16, Science Fiction You Love to Hate* edited by William Culp, *Best Short-Short Science Fiction 1963* and the *Annual Lupowitz Awards: #12*. Foreign editions in England, Spain and Brazil.

Winner Boilerplate Lupowitz Award 1964; most promising new writer.

Schedule of events
THE NEWYORICON
NEW YORK WORLD SCIENCE FICTION
CONVENTION
Hotel Northport

FRIDAY, September 2

5:00–(?)

Check-in, registration, assignment of rooms. Masquerade contestants
to the Great Hutch on the mezzanine. Participants on the panels will
please get their tags. THE BAR AND ROOM SERVICE WILL BE
OPEN ALL NIGHT FOR THE CONVENIENCE OF GUESTS.
Huckster rooms open 7 P.M. and are open all weekend.

SATURDAY, September 3

9:00

Wake-up and free time. Heralds and Messengers will knock on doors.
10:00-12:30
Panel: Is Science-Fiction Necessary? Harlow Houthwaite, Billy
Mitchum, Rose Foote
Panel: Science-Fiction in the Age of Technology: V. V. Vivaldi, William
Culp, Sanford Kvass, Michael Foote
Panel: The discovery of Hyper-space: John Steele, Katerina Elizabeth
Templeton
12:30-3:00
Lunch, free-time, nap-time, huckster's rooms. Masquerade contestants
rehearsal in the Great Hutch.
3:00
Grand and Glorious Auction: In which Harlow Houthwaite will be
auctioned off by Billy Mitchum to the lowest bidder. Also, Billy
Mitchum will be auctioned off by Harlow Houthwaite to anyone who
will have him. Also diverse other *celebrities* may auction themselves.

5:00
Cocktails, liqueurs, aperitifs and booze are served in the Grand
  Ballroom. Masquerade contestants final rehearsal in the Great Hutch.
7:45
Exceptional and never-to-be-forgotten grand *masquerade ball* in the
  Great Hutch … in which wondrously and before your very eyes,
  fannish friends and foes will attempt to impersonate the personna of
  your favorite *characters* of your favorite *science-fiction writers* under
  the tutelage and baton of Joseph Jacklin and his Merrie Old *Band*.
  Prizes, folly, foolishness, bedazzlement, and a wondrous *conclusion*
  with an assortment of *prizes*.

SUNDAY, September 4

12:00
Wake-up and free-time. Heralds and Messengers may be heard from.
1:00
Lupowitz Banquet #21. The Awards of the Associated Fans of America
5:00
SAYONARA

Registrants are reminded that they are guests of the Hotel Northport
  and the management of the hotel requests that they comport
  themselves at all times in accordance with that status.

Only those actually registered will be permitted in their hotel rooms.

No responsibility by the convention committee is assumed for the
  registrants.

No responsibility by the management of the Hotel Northport will be
  assumed for registrants.

You must be twenty-one or over to be served in the bar or to receive
  alcoholic beverages in room service.

Program and memory book edited and published by Billy Mitchum
  and through the courtesy of the *Explosive Magazine Newspaper* staff.

Participants in special Package Plan must check out at 3:30 P.M.
  Sunday; otherwise, higher rates must apply.

I

Sanford Kvass, winner of the 1963 Boilerplate Award from the fan clubs of America as the most promising new science fiction writer of the previous year (but that was a long time ago and besides there had been little competition; Kvass himself having had to publish only fifteen short stories and three novels to win it), hurls himself groaning over the naked body of Katie Elizabeth Templeton, preparing to make his long-delayed entrance as quickly as possible and find out, in her orgasm, if she is an alien … but as he does so, feeling his beard sink against her moistening shoulder with a rasp, there is a sound of banging on the door of his hotel room and from the corridor he hears shouts, peeps, high frantic squeals. "You dirty sons of bitches!" Kvass screams, quite losing control, hurling himself to a squat, "They won't let you live!" and, muttering, takes a shoe and throws it violently at the door, the smash inaudible in the larger goings-on. "I hate them," he says, "I hate them."

"Sanford," Katie Elizabeth Templeton, the dean of the computer rocketry adventure juvenile says, "Sanford, just quiet down and they'll go away, don't worry about it," and reaches her substantial arms toward him, but Kvass is beyond reason. An old neurosis makes him unable to copulate in public surroundings or to even avoid distraction and besides that, Katie Templeton is something of a problem on her own, not that Kvass would use the onslaught from the hall as an excuse to avoid his obligations.

"I can't stand it anymore," he says and goes to the foot of the bed, puts on his dressing gown and flicks on the overhead. "Besides, they'll be out there all night hammering unless I make them go away. You haven't been around conventions long enough to understand that, Katie." He shoves the covers over her, moving them way beyond neck level (she looks much better this way, really) and pats them into place. "Cover yourself," he says superfluously. "This should take just a second if I handle it right." He removes his pipe from the pocket of the gown and mouths it as he opens the door, trying to confront them in striking book-jacket profile. "Get out of here this minute," he screams to the hall. Three or four teen-agers are framed in the door. Behind them, he suspects an agglomeration of several more, perhaps a dozen or fifteen although it is difficult to tell in the murkily lit corridors of this large, ill-maintained hotel near the outskirts of the Wholesaling District, patrolled by malevolent personnel and occasionally dogs. Spiteful sounds fill the air; high, hard shrieks and the nearest teen-ager, a thin youth with a mad intensity around the forehead, thrusts a bottle in Sanford's face and says, "Entrance token! We've come to join the party."

"I'm afraid you've got the wrong room," Kvass says gently. "There's no party going on in here. I was sleeping, as a matter of fact."

"That's Sanford Kvass," someone says from the hallway. "I'd know him anywhere. Sanford Kvass is at the convention!"

"No," Kvass says, "I'm really afraid you have the wrong party this time. My name is Milton Oppenstein and I manage a small fur factory in the Midwest. I happen to be in town for liquidation proceedings and I don't know who you're talking about."

"Sanford Kvass," the voice says with the sureness of accusation, the ripeness of doom. "He's having a wonderful party in there and he won't let us come in. You'd better let us in, Kvass; your stuff stinks anyway. That novelette last month in *Thoughtful* was a disaster; you copped the whole idea from Vivaldi's *Raiders.*"

Kvass shudders and tries to close the door. He finds that a foot or feet, however, have been wedged within and decides to try a calmer, more reasonable tack. Fans are *important,* he reminds himself. They comprise an *audience* and indirectly pay him money which he needs. In addition, the alien might be among them (although this is doubtful) and possibilities should be investigated. He can hear Katie's faint whimpers and moans behind him on the bed; whether it is passion or fear (or even alienness) which drives her he does not know, but in any event Katie has never been at her best in uncontrolled situations and a certain sense of impending consequence overtakes him. He flings a hand to his heart as he steps into the hallway, pushes a body and closes the door behind him.

"I'm really sorry," he says. "You awakened me from a deep sleep, you see, and for a moment I hardly knew who I was. Yes, of course I'm Sanford Kvass. But I'm really sorry, children, you got a wrong tip. There's nothing going on in my room. I'm just trying to get a little sleep, I'm on a panel in the morning, as I'm sure you know, and I can't really burn the candle the way I used to." He tries a deflating giggle which comes out with an aspect of retching. "Getting older, you know."

"Nonsense, Kvass," the boy with the bottle says. Nevertheless he does give a step of ground, his eyes flicking from right to left in a hesitancy which Kvass *is* glad to see. "The word was definitely out that there was a big pro party in room four-fifty-nine. You can't put us off; we've taken over this entire hotel and we're on the trail."

"Ah," Kvass says, "I understand. This rumor was probably planted deliberately by certain enemies I have in a particular editorial faction who do not wish me well. The *truth* is, however, that no party for professionals is happening in my room because if there *were* a party for professionals, I would be drunk. Wouldn't I? You know my reputation for drinking. It isn't folklore at all, and surely if I were in the midst of a party of fellow professionals, I would hardly be as lucid as I am at this stage. In fact, I'd be drunk. I am, however, and as you can see, entirely sober and this is proof positive of the fact that nothing is going on. So if you'll simply permit me—"

"Let's just have a look," a thin girl near the mad-eyed boy says in a piercing voice. Kvass had not noticed her before; perhaps he was thinking of something else. "Let's just go in and have a look, Kvass. If there's no one there, well we were wrong and we apologize. On the other hand, if it turns out that you were lying—"

"I can't permit that," Kvass says. "My privacy is sacrosanct. Out of that, I generate my ideas."

"He's lying to us," the girl says flatly. "He's having a big party behind that soundproofed door and trying to exclude us. I say onward."

Perhaps the girl is the real leader. It usually works out that way. The fans begin to mumble dangerously, make shifting motions toward the door. Kvass wishes that he could talk to her in private, try to be reasonable, even deduce alienness but this is not the time. He will have to be very cautious.

"I said, onward," the girl repeats, rather hysterically, and moves toward him.

Kvass shrugs, removes the pipe from his mouth. From this moment on it can no longer be his responsibility. He has, after all, tried. Besides, there are larger issues on his mind than idiot fan crashers; a certain petulance overcomes him. He is, under these charged circumstances, certainly entitled to more consideration than he is getting.

"All right, then," he says, "I'll tell the truth. There is no party going on in my room. There is, however, one Katie Elizabeth Templeton with whose fiction you may be familiar although this is only her second convention. As you will see," Kvass says, using a heel to kick back on the door, forcing it open then with a crooked finger, letting a small murky sliver of light prowl its way through the corridor, "as you will see, she is now lying in my bed trustfully asleep. Katie has no room of her own and I thought it only generous of me to allow her to stay in mine. This hotel is booked solid. Katie is, of course, a professional but what is going on here, being limited to only the two of us, could hardly be allied a professional *party,* if you get the distinction."

Katie shrieks. That part is good; it is doubtful if an alien would succumb to embarrassment in that fashion. Under the shriek he hears a frantic rustle of bedclothes. "She's a bit nervous," he points out, "and not at her best in public situations. She began writing very late in life as science fiction writers go. But as you will see, that's all there is to it. Just she and me and the bed."

He stands to one side, motions with a flourish, allowing the fans to come over and look which, two by two and in straggles, they do, then turn away shaking their heads. Katie begins to curse in a whining mezzo. That part is perfectly all right as well, Katie retaining the ability to do the expected with more grace than he would be able to manage. In due course, the fans assemble once again in the hall, shaking their heads and looking at him with round, wistful eyes. They look much younger and somehow helpless. "Nothing," someone says, "absolutely nothing. He was telling the truth."

"Well, the hell with him then," someone else says, "if there's nothing going on *here,* I understand that there's an old-timers' meeting somewhere on the seventh floor and if not that then there are those all-night festival films in the basement. We don't have to stand here and look at Sanford Kvass anymore. Who needs Sanford Kvass?"

It is a good question. He bows his head in agreement, fingers his pipe, looks with guiltless and stricken eyes as the fans turn to shuffle their way down the corridor. "You could at least apologize," he says mildly but no one seems to be interested; an elevator door thuds open in the distance and they seem to be fixated in that direction. So after a time Kvass shrugs again—less eloquently but with more real feeling— and goes into his room where he finds Katie Elizabeth Templeton, fully dressed, in the act of smashing in one of the windows with a high-heeled shoe. It is characteristic and for that reason rather moving but it is also noisy and awkward and the shards of glass on the floor could cut a barefooted man dangerously.

"Come on, Katie," he says, aware of her general instability which shows up in a rather poorly-controlled sense of plotting and narrative pace. "There's no need to carry on like this. It's just a bunch of fans, cruising the hotel. They don't need sleep the way people do. They hear of parties, the rumors start and they begin to knock on doors. If I hadn't let them check us out they would have been here until sunrise. You've got to understand the convention situation; you don't have my experience. I've been at these things since I was thirteen years old and you learn a few things after a while."

"I'm through with you, Sanford," Katie says unresponsively, breaking the window finally in a thin rupturing spasm that causes a small shower of glass to momentarily circle her like a halo before collapsing to the floor. "I'm finished. You never had any manners, you never had any consideration and what it comes down to is that you're a lecherous idiot. You haven't done any work worth talking about for seven years, you failed to fulfill your promise, you're a silly drunk and furthermore you degrade everyone who becomes involved with you."

This seems to complete the case. "Katie," he says mildly, sitting on the bed, trying to keep the situation in gear, "I'm afraid that you're the one who doesn't understand. I can't talk about it but I have certain problems. I really do. Quite serious problems. And they weren't interested in looking at you, all they wanted to do was to check out the room. I wish I could talk to you about what's really on my mind but I just *can't*. You have to trust me."

"And furthermore," she says with a shriek, hobbling on one foot to put on her shoe, holding onto the walls with churning, well-manicured nails, "furthermore, you seduced *me;* all that this was supposed to be was just a drink, a friendly *drink*. I should have known—"

"Be reasonable, Katie," Kvass says. "Everyone went to sleep hours ago except the fans. You'll wake people up and bring the detectives in here."

"You're a *lousy* writer, Sanford! I won't hold it back anymore; it's time you were told. Your scenes have no weight, you never had an original idea in your life and all you've been doing for five years is rewriting the same basic plot. You never *had* that much promise. All you had were editorial contacts. It's people like you that made it so hard for people like *me* to get ahead!"

"You wanted to come up here, Katie," Kvass points out gently. His mood is restricted and benign; it does not seem to be an evening for gestures. "After the meeting. I said that I had a headache but you still wanted to come. It was your idea. Besides that, Katie, your stuff isn't so hot either. The whole computer adventure thing goes back to the nineteen-forties, and aside from the three editors who have bought your work, I can't think of any professional who's ever been around who thought you were any good at all. And, anyway, you were able to get those stories sold in ways that I couldn't."

"You bastard," she says, "you lousy bastard," and goes to the door. Well, that is a good thing, anyway. At the door, she flings open paneling, propels herself through the aperture like a spacecraft, though not without minor collision with the walls, and then faces around to confront him, the fine silvery blaze of her descending eyes nailing him dead-center. "You have no respect for any other single human being. All that you want to do is to use people for your own selfish ends and to have something to drink. I'll get you for this!" she cries. "I'll get you for this before I'm through! No one does this to Katie Elizabeth Templeton and just gets away with it!" She reaches out a long arm, seizes the doorknob, pulls the door closed with an awkward clatter that causes some filaments of wood to join the glass on the floor. Kvass hears a kick or two, a few random, muffled curses ... and then nothing at all. Apparently Katie Elizabeth Templeton has gone away, back to her own room. She will go to sleep in her own room tonight. Kvass has been caught in a lie again. The fans were misinformed. Katie Templeton has her own quarters and, despite the convention, the hotel is severely underbooked. World convention hotels usually are. Word has gotten around.

He sighs. He sighs enormously. Then he shakes his head with a glimmer of comprehension. It occurs to Kvass that Katie's threat is dangerous in that he has every reason to believe that the lady now takes herself seriously, but at the moment this is not the point. The point is that she definitely cannot be the alien. No alien would react to deprivation in precisely the fashion that she has. She is the old characteristic Katie, and God bless her, although preferably in absentia.

The threat he can deal with; he is in too much trouble to worry about that at the moment. Also, and he admits this, there is no way of disguising the pervasive sense of relief that has flooded him at her exit, a relief that, interestingly, extends even to the groin. The fans have done him a favor. He is obviously not the man that he would have been.

Kvass double-locks the door. He removes his dressing gown and lies upon the stiff hotel bed, only faintly damp now against him. He closes his eyes and tries to rest for a little while; rest is always important and he must take it where he can get it. There are a lot of people to sift and only one alien. *Why am I doing this?* Kvass mumbles and then, surprisingly, is asleep.

II

On his way to the panel in the morning Kvass passes through an enormous room off the lobby in which hundreds of teen-agers and adults are sitting or lying on chairs, staring at screens suspended from the ceiling and walls; it is the film festival, of course, and what has been scheduled is a multimedia experience coming from the simultaneous showing on different screens of twenty-five famous horror films of the past. It is a marathon event, planned to run through the three days of the convention but already, on the first morning, a certain debilitation has set in; people are staggering around the room with glazed expressions and many on the chairs appear to be somnolent or even in a drug-induced coma. A few couples toward the fringes of the room seem to be copulating with great difficulty, moving under great clumps of clothing and hair to make contact with one another and Kvass sighs, shudders, feels a twinge of nausea work through him and turns from the room in some haste. Conventions are not for him what they used to be and he has been around them for over twenty years.

While no one was watching, something seems to have been happening underneath the level of consciousness and now the products are all over the hotel, many of them in the multimedia room but quite a few around the lobby or coffeeshop and more than a scattering in the seller's room which Kvass also looks into briefly on his way toward the panel. As usual, the seller's room contains thirty or forty independent stands containing old magazines and books from behind which proprietors stand with uneasy expressions, wiping their eyes from the irritancy of pulp. But now there seem to be new elements in the room; there are large posters of nude people for one thing and for another an enormous autographed portrait of one of the Moon crews in full technological regalia is stretched across the ceiling. Kvass stares at the bloated faces, feeling a horrid familiarity in the aspect. No less than he they seem to be stranded in far fields, not quite trusting of the devices that are supposed to get them home; not precisely sure how they landed in the first place.

Noise runs through the place like fumes and assaults Kvass; he staggers, shakes his head and turns to flee toward the smaller room where the panel will be held. Science fiction, it seems, has changed a great deal since he came into the field; on the other hand there is always the possibility that the field has remained the same and it is only he, Kvass, who has somehow retrograded. Two fans intercept him at the door and ask for an autograph. He shudders and says that he never gives his autograph; it might be transcribed onto a check somehow and this would lead to difficulties.

"Come on," one of them says, taking him by the cuff of his jacket and holding him, so to speak, in gear. "It's only a second's worth. Everybody's cooperating."

"I don't want to," Kvass says. He tries to keep his head inclined away from the fans, always a good tactic at conventions, but then reminds himself of the peculiar nature of his quest and confronts them full-face. They appear to be sixteen or seventeen years old; rather indeterminate for sex, a strange, bland expression centered in their eyes and running down the panels of their faces. One of them appears to be male and the other female but, then again, perhaps it is the opposite way or no way at all. They look as alien as anyone else in the room but not more so. "I mean it," he says, "it's an old policy."

"He's drunk," the other fan says. "He's always drunk. Just let him out of here. No one cares about him anymore anyway."

"I gave up drinking many years ago," Kvass says and determinedly puts down a leading shoulder, inserts himself into a small exposed place and hurls himself past the fans, out of the room. "For your information, I have not been a serious drinker since nineteen sixty-four. I don't like the stuff and it never did anything for me anyway."

"Is that so, Kvass?" a voice says. Kvass reorients himself; finds that he is standing in a small hallway and that he has been addressing William Culp, the editor of *Thrilling* who, with a female companion, seems to be likewise on the way toward the panel room. "When did this begin?" The girl with Culp giggles but this appears to be serious business. "You look like hell," the editor says.

"Well, I *meant* to stop drinking," Kvass says. "I was always serious about that part of it and I've done some substantial cutting down in the last year. Listen, I'm really distracted, I don't feel like explaining myself now."

"I didn't want to be on this panel," Culp says pointlessly, taking the girl by the elbow and pushing ahead, down the hall, "just as soon as I learned that you were on it. Now I want you to cut out the side-remarks and stick to the point or I'll walk right off at ten in the morning, Kvass. I swear I will."

"I'm a changed man," Kvass says absently, looking at Culp's companion. "I'm entirely different. Something's happened, William; I can't enjoy a convention anymore. You see, I was visited by these three aliens who said that they were going to plant one of them in human disguise at this convention and if I couldn't detect his identity by the time it was over then they would destroy the planet. So of course I'm a little distracted."

"That's interesting," Culp says. "Of course the idea's been a little over-used. Anyway, we've got a little bit too much of an inventory now; I don't think that I'll be buying much for several months, but of course if you want to make a speculative submission—"

"You're Sanford Kvass," the girl says. She is a rather pretty girl, perhaps twenty-three or so, although it is harder and harder for Kvass to detect ages these days, and no one under the age of thirty, it would seem, would be able to deal properly with William Culp. "I've known you around for years but never had a chance to meet you."

"Oh, that's all right," Kvass says. He ducks his head under a piece of stray wood; they move into the panel room where rows and rows of chairs are lined up behind a long low desk with microphones. "I'm pleased to meet you now anyway."

"I'm Gloria Simpson."

"That's fine, Gloria," Kvass says. She is an attractive girl, but something else is on his mind. Culp has been too casual. He reaches forward quickly, seizes the disjointed editor by the lapels of his double-breasted suit jacket and turns him around into a posture of attention. Culp, grumbling, spins in his grasp, faces him, his face turning even greener in the poor lighting of the room, "Listen, Sanford—" he says.

"Hold on," says Kvass. He gives Culp a long level stare, trying to deduce the quality of his eyes, some twitch of his forehead, a bit of asymmetry in his posture which will disclose that he is not the William Culp who he has known for a decade but instead an alien cunningly infiltrated into the heart of the world science fiction convention. It is difficult to make a snap judgment of this sort; like most of the people he seems to know Culp has a bit of alienness in him from the start, and the strange, demented glaze that works through the editor's eyes and down through the sideburns is, perhaps, characteristic. "I don't know," he says and releases Culp. "It's hard to tell. They aren't being fair, they're too cunning."

"You're crazy," Culp says. "Sanford, I don't know what you're doing—"

Gloria begins to giggle, harshly, cups her mouth in her hands and then turns away. "I never saw anything like *this* convention," she says to no one, "Is *everybody* like this?"

"Let me explain," Kvass says and would indeed try to explain. He might as well lay the case in front of Culp in a detailed way; maybe Culp has some ideas and in any event things can hardly become more complicated.

"What it comes down to—"

But there is no time for explanation. All the time they have been moving; Culp and the girl caught in the currents of the room have been pushed slowly toward the front and now they are at the table itself where the other two celebrities are already sitting, casting stricken glances at the ashtrays. Culp pulls himself away fully and stalks to the far end of the table, sits, glaring. The girl seems to have been forgotten. Kvass takes a seat himself next to V. V. Vivaldi, the eminent first-generation writer of alien fiction, and puts his head in his hands, tries to put the scene at a far distance. Clearly, nothing is working out. The girl leans over the table and touches Kvass gently on the wrist, gives him a knowing smile. "I've always enjoyed your work," she says.

"I'm pleased to hear it."

"You're really a very good writer. You can't imagine how exciting it is to me to finally be able to meet all these science fiction people. Until I met William, I had no idea that I would actually be seeing and talking to all of you."

"William has been in science fiction for twenty-five years," Kvass says pointlessly. "He hasn't really been *writing* much of it recently but he's editing and maybe that's more important. He used to be good, you know,"

"If you want to meet me later on, maybe for a drink this evening, I wish you would," the girl says and tosses her head back, does something with her posture which demonstrates her breasts, moves her head back and fixes Kvass with a gesture of unusual concentration. "I mean, there are so many things I'd like to talk to you about and I've read a lot of your stories—"

"Hell," V. V. Vivaldi says, shaking his head. "The air in this room is absolutely foul." His shoulders twitch, he seems on the verge of making a vigorous physical gesture and then slides back on his chair, "Hasn't been any good since nineteen fifty-one. That was the last good convention. Cleveland, I think, or maybe it was Pittsburgh. They all jumble together. They had a nice sensible group of people running the show in nineteen fifty-one. The awards made sense too."

"Could we meet?" the girl says, trying to ignore V. V. Vivaldi, which is somewhat easier than it might have been ten years ago but still something of a challenge as his attention now seems to be caught by her and he gives her a long, sullen look. "That would be really nice."

"You're with William."

"Oh, William is just my *escort;* he *took* me here. I'm not tied to him or anything." She puts a hand atop his; Kvass wonders if he feels a rasp of alienness, decides that it is only his own reaction. "Of course, if you don't want to—"

"Followers," Vivaldi says. "The whole scene has been taken over by followers. Now there was a time when you had a nice hard core; you had the editors and the writers and a few readers. But now you can't get together anymore; it's just full of parasites."

"Listen," Kvass says intensely, turning his back on Vivaldi. "I don't think you understand. Well, Gloria—how can I best put this without hurting your feelings?—I'm not the man I used to be. I've aged a good deal and I've had a lot of trouble recently with a writing block and some other things and, all in all, I just think it would be better if you found some other writers. I mean, it's not at all personal, you're very attractive and five years ago I would have been delighted but—"

"Well," the girl says and looks at him bleakly, "if that's what you think I am."

"I don't think anything—"

"If that's what you think I am, you're in for a surprise, Mr. Vass. I don't like your attitude at all."

"Kvass. Sanford Kvass."

"Just stay away from me," she says. "Just you don't try talking to me, because if you do I'll make things very unpleasant. You're a *lousy* writer. I *never* liked your stuff. I was just saying what I was saying to be polite. You better not get near me, Vass, or I'll make things bad for you. I go way back, I know a lot of stuff."

"You can meet me," Vivaldi says, looking up again, fixing the girl with a glittering gaze, his steel-frame spectacles catching the muddled light of the room. "I'm V. V. Vivaldi."

"I'm with Mr. Culp," she says and turns, walks down the length of the table, whispers something to a distracted Culp and then leaves. Kvass watches her walk down the aisle and out the door, hoping for a backward glance, a tilt of the hand, anything to indicate that there is no permanency of bad relations. Nothing develops, however. He sighs, twists down into his seat and slumps over, as enervated as if he had been drinking all night, which is hardly the case. It would not surprise him in the least if Katie Elizabeth Templeton were to now come to the table and whisper a few threats at him, were even to declare his incompetency as the subject of the panel. This does not appear to be a period during which he is having much success with women. On the other hand, he cannot recall precisely when his luck ever *was* much different; for Kvass there have always been a series of perilous involvements leading to difficult scenes, most of them in public. "I must change my life," he mutters. He wonders if he should give up the alien hunt as a gesture of sincerity and decides that he had better not, just quite yet.

"Snip," V. V. Vivaldi says to him, staring ahead, his lips not quite moving. "Miserable arrogant little tart I tell you, it's a whole changed generation. They didn't used to carry on like that in nineteen fifty-one. They would have called the sergeant at arms over and thrown her out. Of course they had sergeants at arms in those days; now they don't even have any common respect left. Youth running wild, that's what it is. Milt, isn't that who you are? Milton Dunning?"

"No," Kvass says, recalling that Milton Dunning, author of the *Rocket to Rocket* series in the old *Marvelous Tales,* has not been seen at a convention for some twenty-five years. "I'm not he. I'm Kvass. Sanford Kvass. We've met a few times. I got your autograph in nineteen forty-eight."

"Oh," Vivaldi says, "of course. I like your stuff, Kvass. Generally I don't read mysteries, but now and then I make an exception and you write a very tight line. That miserable little tart has no respect left."

"Yes," Kvass says and turns away, hoping to end the discussion. V. V. Vivaldi is a giant of the field, still turning out an adventure series at the rate of four titles a year, but he is also five feet three inches and slightly out of touch due to his involvement in a programming therapy institute which absorbed his total energies from the end of 1953 until only two years ago. For these reasons and due to certain financial difficulties of the programming therapy institute, Vivaldi is even more disconnected than he was during his heyday, although this in itself is not necessarily a drawback; most science fiction writers are somewhat disconnected. It is impossible to deduce whether he is an alien or not but Kvass decides that he will have to take a chance on the latter, Vivaldi not being a good candidate for abduction in any case.

He sees Katie Elizabeth Templeton seated in a center row, surrounded by young people who are taking her autograph, and shudders, retracts even more deeply into himself. To his immense gratitude, the panel is called to order by the convention chairman, who is acting as moderator. The chairman, whose name Kvass is sure he knows but which he cannot quite catch, says that he is particularly grateful to the four eminent personalities who have volunteered to come this morning to put their knowledge in the hands of the audience, and then introduces them one by one. The fourth member of the panel, Kvass finds to his discomfiture, is Michael Foote, an ex-writer and publishing house editor with whom he had a disastrous experience in 1965 and who has, subsequently, rejected every one of Kvass's submissions to his house as not being at the proper standards. As Foote realizes that Kvass is on the panel they exchange a look of sheer loathing, a kind of high agitation mingling with the revulsion in Foote's eyes so that his very goatee seems to twitch. Vivaldi stands when he is introduced and says that he has prepared some notes from which he would like to make his introductory statement, and the chairman says that he appreciates the dean of science fiction doing this very thing but the panel has not yet properly begun. Vivaldi subsides, muttering, and two adolescents detach themselves from their seating, run to the front of the room and seize Vivaldi's hands, one to each.

"Your autograph," one of them says. "Could we have your autograph?" and Vivaldi turns gray. Despite his background in programming therapy he seems unable to handle the situation and it remains for Kvass to stand, detach the adolescents and wave them back to their seats.

"Mr. Vivaldi really isn't feeling very well right now," Kvass confides and the smaller adolescent looks at him brightly and says, "How do you know?" Kvass is on the verge of answering the question seriously when the chairman says that it is now time for the introductory comments, and the panel is in progress.

The subject of the panel, Kvass finds out, is science fiction in the Moon age. Now that technology has advanced to the point where much of science fiction is reality, does the field still have a unique contribution to make in aiding the sense of wonder, and will the word-rates increase or will people become less interested in science fiction because it will become only another kind of adventure story and eventually will be phased out? The moderator puts the question in a high, harsh voice, his tone moving between an adolescent quaver and a baritone insolence and Kvass, totally unprepared, shakes his head.

V. V. Vivaldi says that he would like to make the first statement if he might and stands to read a long passage on the question of magical adventure. He pays his respect to Morton Tolliver Williams, the famous originator of the school of magical adventure on whom he is writing a full-length biography as well as a sequel to some of his works, and then reminds everyone in the audience that programming therapy still works and the fact that it has been discredited by the institutions and bureaucracy of organized science is an ornament to its strength. This last declaration leaves the audience with slightly glazed expressions, but then it is relatively early in the morning on the first full day of the convention—and there is only so much for which V. V. Vivaldi can be held accountable.

"I won't talk about programming therapy," Mike Foote says, standing in place and looking balefully at the room. "In fact, I won't even talk about science fiction and technology this morning. I think that we've had to face up to the fact—the more advanced people in the field, that is—that science fiction is a dying institution and the only way we'll be able to keep it alive is by going outside it and writing what's closest to our hearts and minds. We've got to get a better grade of writer and a better grade of story that has nothing to do with the weak old pulp tradition of our field, and at least in my publishing house I've tried to do just that. We've published six or seven books in the last three months alone that I think could be defined as the new literature—"

"Now come on, Mike," Culp says, sitting in place. "Don't start with literary lectures again." He giggles rather hysterically; Culp and Foote were at some time in the past married to the same woman, although at different times. There is an uneasy undercurrent of knowledge to all of their banter, as if what they desperately want to do is to sit down and exchange dirty stories and anatomical reminiscences but cannot possibly do so because their mutual wife is married yet a third time, to

Murray K. Bloom, possibly the most influential writer of their generation, and Bloom has a nasty temper. "No one wants to hear about literature. The fact is, Mike, that science fiction is *science* fiction; it is a genre with certain rules and certain goals and once you stop obeying those rules and goals you're no longer writing it. You may be writing very well and it may even be rather *outstanding* in the literary sense but it has nothing to do with the field. You're discussing something else entirely."

"Your trouble, Culp," Foote says with rather fine timing, "is that you're doing superb work, you're writing the best science fiction of the nineteen-thirties." There are mingled gasps in the audience, one-half of which or more is probably not aware that Culp and Foote have been carrying on this dispute in public for over a decade with no clear winner and that for all their seeming ill will, they are bound together by a series of mysteries so horrid that they can only evade them. "Your magazines show it and are a retrograde influence upon our field."

"The magazines are very important," Vivaldi says, "Without magazines we wouldn't have books and without books, where would we be, I ask you. Think about that. That's an important point."

"You either play by the rules or get out of the game," Culp says rather smugly and folds his hands across his chest, bows his head so that the fine series of indentations furrowing his scalp can be seen. "Of course if you can't be civilized—"

"I'm sure that I'll listen to your statement, William," Foote says, "when it's time for you to make it. In the meantime, you can do me the courtesy of listening to mine."

"You never listen, Mike, that's your trouble. You listen to nothing except what you hear in your head. That's why you probably quit writing; you got sick of your own voice."

"Now listen," the moderator says uncomfortably. "We're trying to have a calm, reasoned discussion here, and these distinguished gentlemen surely understand that. Now I hope—"

"Excuse me," Kvass says, standing. He feels unsteady on his feet; perhaps it is a fatal stroke or heart attack coming upon him, although it is probably only the usual, a touch of disorientation overlaying his very serious problems. "I don't feel very well. Perhaps I may be excused; these gentlemen are doing very well and I have nothing to say."

"No you don't, Kvass," Culp calls to him from his edge of the table. "You're going to stay here and explain yourself."

"That's right," Foote says, waving his arms rather stiffly. "You're going to stay and take it like the rest of us. Do you think that we have any desire to be here?" He sits unsteadily, leans past Vivaldi so that he can fix Kvass with a menacing stare. "Frankly, I don't like your attitude," Foote says, but he says this in a rather plaintive fashion. The truth is that Culp and Foote do not get along very well and need an interposition in order to function at their best level. "Come on," Foote says. "Make your statement."

"I have no statement," Kvass says. Standing now, his disorientation settling down to a high murmur in his chest and heels, beginning to feel more confident, he strides from behind the table and moves toward the door. "I have nothing to say. I cannot add to the discussion here. In my opinion, science fiction has no real relevance to the machine age because the word-rates are too low; but then it can be a steady market for a certain kind of person and I wish them well. I used to want to write mysteries, you know; that was what I wanted to do, but I found that it was almost a closed corporation and anyway I had no taste for murder. I am a changed man," he says, standing by the door, confronting the room, noting with some detachment that he seems, at last, to be the focus of attention. "I am not the Sanford Kvass whom many of you think you know. There have been enormous realignments, great changes. The fact is that I have no position on almost anything. I have an announcement to make."

"Stop that man," Vivaldi says, bouncing on his chair. "That man is a thorough disgrace to the field of science fiction. That man has no manners."

"An announcement!" Kvass screams. This seems to bring the audience to a kind of respectful attention. He clears his throat. "I am resigning from the field of science fiction. From now on, from this moment that is to say, I will no longer read it, I will not write it and I certainly will not discuss it. I want nothing further to do with the field," he says and tries to draw in slow, even breaths, a certain shortness of respiration taking some of the drama out of his declaration. "Although, of course, I like all of you or some of you very much," Kvass whispers and leaves the room hurriedly.

He keeps his head down. He moves his feet rapidly. He passes a room in which a fan celebrity is being auctioned off to the highest bidder for his services. He passes a smaller room where several people holding beer cans seem to be involved in a murderous but punch-less fistfight. He passes an open elevator in which the operator, a sullen expression on his face, is leaning against the cage of the car, looking at the proceedings in front of him with a certain revulsion. He is determined to see none of it. Behind him he hears footsteps, murmurs, shouts. Perhaps a delegation has been appointed from the panel to pursue him and change his mind, but he is an old hand at evasion; he knows every stairwell in every hotel in New York.

Rapidly coalescing within him now he feels the Decision; the Decision has been at the rim for hours and hours but at last it has burst forth in its naked fury, much like Katie Elizabeth Templeton, and he can only follow it, although not to a Templeton conclusion. He is going to leave the convention. He is going to leave the convention at the earliest instant and sever his connections with science fiction. His leaving the convention will mean that the alien presence there will be undetected and the aliens will move in due course to the destruction of his planet, but that is simply one of the prices he will have to pay for leaving his chosen occupation and his friends. In any event, the pain of loss will not be prolonged and his exit from science fiction will be the most dramatic and far-reaching since V. V. Vivaldi's of almost two decades ago.

It is simply too much. It is too much for Kvass. He cannot interview everyone at the convention and deduce from these interviews whether they are aliens or not. He cannot go around seizing people by the lapels and looking for a hint of difference in their eyes. It is simply beyond him.

For the fact of the matter is that they are *all* aliens and that is all there is to it. Science fiction has been founded upon deviation for too long; now it is impossible to sort out the extraterrestials from *homo bizarrus. I hope they take us out fast,* the stricken Kvass mumbles and in lieu of elevator finds a stairwell and bolts the four flights to his room.

In there, looking as stolid as ever, his literary agent greets him. He has been waiting for Kvass for a long time very patiently and now it is time to have a discussion. Kvass owes an outstanding advance of eight hundred dollars. "Would you care to pay me now?" Morton Millman, tall, distressed, fiftyish, ex-welder and mystery writer asks, "Or do I have to take severe action? You can't avoid me forever, Sanford."

III

Gullibility has always been one of Sanford's weaknesses although he feels that he has gone a long way in his later years toward correcting that tendency. Perhaps it is the reason he turned to writing science fiction originally; having been too long manipulated by people who preyed upon his ignorance and good will, he figured that he could turn the tables by learning how to tell a few whoppers himself. Of course science fiction has matured a great deal in recent years and now concentrates upon "modern realism," but the originating impulse seems clear.

In Sanford's freshman year at the State University, his roommate, a round, demented young man who had some family money behind him and who was taking wrestling lessons on the side had convinced Sanford that he, the roommate, was an emissary from the planet Mars who had been assigned to live with Sanford for a year so that "we can keep a close eye on you. We've been watching you for a long time, Kvass, but now we have to move in and really keep things in order." Kvass had dismissed these whimsicalities with a shrug and nervous tic; later on, however, when his roommate had made a fraternity and Kvass had not, Kvass had had second thoughts and as events turned out he wound up pleading for his life one November night in his room, the sound of upstate crickets and snow-machines coming through all the spaces of the dormitory and giving a rather wild rural overcast to Kvass's memories of the event. "All right," he had told his roommate, who had listened to all this cross-legged on the bed, expressionlessly holding an unlit cigarette. "All right, here's the deal then; I'll watch my step and I'll stay out of people's way and I'll never, never tell them the truth of the Martian invasion if you'll only release me from this."

"I don't know," his roommate had said, twirling the cigarette. "Understand, on my own I'd give you a full release, but it isn't just me. I'm only a sort of agent; there's a whole bureaucracy up there that I have to protect. I'd have to clear it with them."

"Well, can't you tell them that I promise not to make any difficulties and I'll never bother Martians again as long as I live?" Kvass asked. Well, he had been seventeen years old and from a rather sheltered background; perhaps there was some kind of a defense for this although even now he would be hard-pressed to find out exactly what grounds he could cite. He had done some reading in the pulp magazines and had been a bit short on sexual experience at that age, also the very environment of the State University, being constricted to two dormitories and five buildings, most of them under demolition or repair, had done strange things to many a psyche. There were all kinds of factors to take into account, the point was that Kvass is still not sure that he is able to put them on a balance sheet. His roommate, at least, he has not seen for twelve years, although on the publication of his third novel he received a fan letter from him on the letterhead of a hotel in Omaha, Nebraska congratulating Kvass upon being one of the few from the State University to "come out of the darkness."

"I'll think about it," his roommate said. "I'll take it up with the board. That's the most I can promise at this time," and three days later after ominous silence had announced that the board had allowed to let

Kvass go, conditional upon his being hypnotized so that the entire events having to do with the secret of the Martians would be wiped from his consciousness. In a panic Kvass had said that he would never sacrifice his *mind,* his mind being the only thing that he felt he had left. The roommate had said that in that case he could only go back to the board, but he doubted that they would feel inclined to be merciful since Kvass knew too much already. Kvass had gone through four days of torment at the end of which he had gone to the Dean of Men and placed the whole story in his hands, telling the Dean that he had better take some radical action before the Martians took over the entire State University complex. Possibly he had been a little incoherent; in any event, the Dean, a round man in his late twenties who sat under portraits of the ten first Presidents of the United States, had apparently taken the matter to heart and called a full-scale conference in his office between his roommate, himself, the Dean of Faculty and a few other members of the dormitory.

As a result of this intense conference Kvass's rooming had been shifted to a private cubicle on the second floor and his roommate had been placed under disciplinary probation for a period of three months and warned not to be caught in the act of speaking to or threatening Kvass. Shortly after that, his ex-roommate had slipped a note under his door informing him that the great Martian invasion operation had been temporarily suspended because of certain difficulties, but he better watch his step *anyway.* However, by that time Kvass had already found and become deeply emotionally involved with Wilma Politz, who took away the focus of his concentration from Martians and placed it on her breasts.

After Wilma—who had really been, all things considered, a great help—there was Carol Schulmann, whose father owned a fur factory but who really wanted to be a mathematician; and after Carol Schulmann it had been Martha K. Smith, Ph.D. (assistant professor of English at the State University) who had been in her way probably the greatest help of all, initiating Kvass into certain complexities and ironies of the flesh which even now, some fifteen years later, he is still unable to fully explain. After Martha K. Smith his terrain, so to speak, had really widened. In one sense then everything since Wilma Politz had been in a straight line—a complexity of experience which he was still sorting out. But in another fashion Wilma Politz had been a diversion, an important diversion but nevertheless merely an interruption which had diverted him from the basic task for a decade and a half and which left him, at the age of thirty-three, still not quite able to solve the question of the Martians. Possibly it was the Martian invasion which had been on his mind all the time and now it was merely catching up with him.

Kvass has gone a long way; he has voyaged here and retracted there, he has become successively a college graduate, a science fiction writer, a computer systems operator, a published science fiction writer, an applicant for public assistance, a husband, an adulterer, a divorcee; a winner of a major award at a world science fiction convention and the author of some eight published novels of speculation. He has every right at this stage of his life to consider himself in the category of veteran, but he cannot get over the feeling that at the center, underneath the compensatory bearded façade which he has worked up so carefully, a pure streak of gullible insanity remains and it is this streak which has been at issue all the time.

There *can't* be any aliens, they wouldn't *do* something like this, Kvass has been mumbling to himself through the month of August, and if there *were* any aliens, they wouldn't be coming *to me,* they'd go to someone who could be *useful* to them. Although the rational part of his consciousness has been accepting this gratefully, another part of him has not been listening at all and now, seized by grimness, Kvass is willing to bet that he knows what that part is. He has been sitting on it for fifteen years, but the truth will out sooner or later—to say nothing of the forgotten parts of oneself. That is why he has come to the world science fiction convention determined to look colleagues, cohorts, strangers and enemies in the eyes and ferret the alien among them.

But there are natural limits to anything. Kvass believes that he has found his and not a moment too soon. The aliens may take over the planet or destroy it or leave it alone, that is distinctly their problem and their choice, not his anymore, because he is getting out. *Not me, Jack,* Kvass has been singing atonally to himself in the instants in the corridor before he opened his door to find his literary agent. *Find yourself another rabbit; I'm out of the State University.*

It is the block. That must be his real problem; he has never had a writing block as insistent and humiliating as what has seized him in the last few months and it has left him, like a paralyzed patient, full of energy with no easy outlet. But the block will go away as all of them somehow have managed in the past and he will be able to write again and the editors will welcome his fulfilled contracts with glad cries and he will make thousands upon thousands of dollars to replenish his accounts and pay off his debtors and get even with his literary agent and somewhere in the future lies the best novel he will ever write; it is only a question of getting to it. It will be a novel of neurasthenia and will describe how the protagonist, by projecting his blight into the universe, managed to convince himself that the world was ending and that it was all his own fault. The novel will be good enough to sell to hardcover—for one thing it will not be science fiction—and the paperback resale will be for several thousand dollars at a heightened royalty rate. He will sell a million paperback copies of his novel, Kvass decides, and on the fifty thousand dollars, wisely invested, will put himself into a position where he will never have to write another line, except for bank correspondence, as long as he lives.

That is the ticket. It is all laid out before him. Thinking this, Kvass unlocks the door of his room and finds his literary agent therein and from this confrontation, the more dramatic and truly serious events of the weekend begin.

IV

"I've been looking all over for you, Sanford," Millman says. "I knew you would be here, but there wasn't even any indication that you had checked into the hotel and I had just about given up. Fortunately I ran into Katie Templeton, who told me where your room was. She seems to be mad at you, Sanford."

Kvass walks to the window, observes the fine gray view of the street and thinks about jumping but decides against it because he is only on the fourth floor and a fall would seriously damage him while undoubtedly still leaving him alive and unreconciled to his fate. "I checked in under a pen name," he said. "It's about the only way you can get any peace at all at these things; you know that, Morton."

"I don't know anything," Millman says, and swallows while holding his head inclined toward the ceiling, a devastating habit of his which causes Kvass's own Adam's apple to quiver in sympathy and almost become dislodged. "I've been going to world science fiction conventions for nineteen years and I don't know a thing, Sanford. Do you know that this is my twentieth? Where's the money? I want it."

This is another familiar trait of Millman's, an ability to be seemingly distracted from issues only to get maddeningly back to the point with sickening insistence. "Listen," Kvass says, knowing that the only tack he can take at this time with his agent is one of reasonableness. "I've had a little trouble. I really have. You know that."

"Of course I know that. You were supposed to deliver the Crescent novel six months ago; that's the only reason I advanced you the money. One thousand dollars on delivery, less commission and outstanding charges. Eight hundred dollars. I want that money."

"I got hung up," Kvass says. "I'm really having a lot of trouble writing these days, Morty. The thing doesn't seem to flow as it used to. Really, I tore up three completed drafts of the novel already because I didn't think it was up to standard. I wanted it to be right." He feels a dread smile convulsing the corners of his mouth, a molasses kind of sweetness seizing the angles of his face and turning them in unbidden directions. "I'm at a stage now where I feel I have to present my best work," Kvass murmurs and tries to leave the room.

"Don't give me any of that, you wretched hack," Millman says, shifting imperceptibly into a screaming tone. "You never did a second draft in your entire life; you've never been on time for a contract since I knew you and you have no intention of doing that book. Well, you don't have to worry about that because you're four months late and they just fired you. They called me the day before yesterday and told me to forget about the delivery; they're breaking the contract."

"I won't refund the money," Kvass says.

"You don't have to refund the money, you idiot, *they're* canceling. They're dropping the whole science fiction line effective immediately and converting to sex books. If you had delivered the book when you were supposed to deliver it you would have had two thousand dollars and all the rights back too because they would have released it, but now you've only got a thousand and you can't even write the book. I want my money, Sanford, I mean that. I can't go on advancing people and being screwed this way. Give me the money."

"I don't have the money," Kvass says. He wheels, passes the bathroom, finds the chair and sits on it, his hands folded earnestly, looking at Millman face to face. Reasonableness perhaps will work; Millman, a bachelor, has the largest collection of science fiction magazines on the East Coast and in his more youthful days was a member of the First Federation of Associated Fans. To this day he retains the capacity to be cajoled by science fiction writers who are, whatever else they may be, the olympian heroes of his youth. "Really, Morty, I've had a lot of trouble recently, I'm not kidding. That's why I dropped out of touch because you know that basically I like to talk with you at least once a week; I don't think of you as merely an agent but a friend. A lot of things have been closing in on me, but recently they seem to be straightening out and I'm sure that if you only show some patience, everything will work out. I've decided to write straight novels."

"I want my money."

"Of course you want your money, Morty. Everybody wants the money, it's a universal constant; I'm not denying that but money isn't the *only* thing. Do you think I'd steal eight hundred dollars from you?"

"Yes, I think you would."

"Well, there's nothing to say about that," Kvass says. He stands, goes to the closet, takes out his trunk and opens it on the bed. "I don't even know why I checked into the hotel," he says. "I live within commuting distance; I have no business being here at all. Of course being in the hotel meant that I could check out people more closely, but I don't want to do any checking out anymore so that's that. I'm going home."

"What's wrong with you, Sanford?" Millman says. His voice is infused with concern; Kvass would be moved if he did not observe Millman simultaneously removing a pipe from his suit pocket and placing it between his lips in some kind of mirror of Kvass's own habit. Millman, abandoning demands for the moment, has decided to become the Sympathetic Agent. "You haven't been yourself for a long time. Your stuff wasn't up to standard and now you aren't working at all. How are you supporting yourself? Is there some way I can help you?"

"You can advance me another eight hundred."

"Go to hell," Millman says and stands. "I can see that you don't want to be reasonable. You don't want to deal with people anymore, Sanford, you just want to exploit them. That's your problem. That's exactly what Katie Templeton said to me this afternoon and she's right. I don't think there's a shred of altruism left in you, it's all self-interest. I'm dropping you from the list."

"Listen," Kvass says. "I've got trouble."

"I know you got trouble."

"No, you don't understand," Kvass says. "I *really* have trouble." He goes over to Millman, takes him by the coat lapels (this seems to be the gesture he has selected for alien-detection, for all the good that it does him; perhaps he has convinced himself that the alien would reveal himself through an uneven press) and inspects him carefully. The agent's sallow face bends, flutters, leans away from him; his shoulders heave with what seems to be concealed retching, a certain weakness through the span of chest gives an insubstantiality to the contact. Morton seems to be the same as previous; there is no indication, in other words, that he is a doppelganger. "I guess I can tell you," Kvass says.

"What are you talking about? You *assaulted* me."

"I had to check something out. No, really, I'm going to tell you. You see, about three weeks ago—"

There is a hideous pounding on the door, the sound of panels imploding, shuffling of feet in the hallway, the rap of metal against cheap wood. "Open up," voices shout "Open up the goddamned door!"

Kvass says, "You see, I told you, that's the way it's been ever since I came here," and with a despairing shrug goes over and unbolts. "There's no party here, you see," he says to the hall. "I'm just having a discussion with my literary agent and in a little while—"

"None of that, buddy," a short man says. He is holding a large dog on a leash and the dog, apparently poorly trained, snuffles at Kvass familiarly, looks for an open cuff. "Where's the disturbance?"

"There's no disturbance in here."

"We got reports that there was a disturbance in one of the rooms on this floor. You better watch your step. We're keeping an eye on you. Off, Princess! Off, goddamnit! Who's that guy on the bed?"

"He's my literary agent"

"What's a literary agent?"

"Listen, officer," Kvass says, in his mildest, most pleading tone. "I don't know what kind of report you got but as you see, there's no problem here at all. The two of us are having a discussion." Princess leaps up again, totters on her rear legs, falls heavily and clumsily against Kvass, almost upsetting him and then collapses moaning to the floor, licking at her front paws. "Goddamnit," the hotel detective says. "You hurt my dog."

"I didn't hurt her. She attacked me."

"I can't stand you rocketry nuts," the detective says, giving a fierce yank to Princess's leash, producing a throttling noise from the animal. "All those damned kids and you're more trouble than it's worth. Where do these kids come from?"

"It's not rocketry," Kvass says, "it's science fiction."

"I don't care what it is. We're keeping an eye on you, just remember that. We don't have to put up with any of your nonsense, we got these dogs and a very close liaison with the police department. We can put fifty cops in here in half a minute if I say the word. I used to be a lieutenant in the department."

"Sanford," Millman says, licking his lips, leaning back on the bed with an expression of panic vaulting all the angles of his face. "Sanford, get that man out of here. Get that *dog* out of here. I can't stand it anymore."

"He doesn't like dogs," Kvass says, recollecting some aspect of Millman's youth which has become part of the major history of fandom. "He had trouble with one once."

"Oh yeah? Well, I don't like him, what do you think of that? We had a disturbance report, that's what we had. On the fourth floor."

"Please," Millman says, hunching his knees toward his face, a pitiful expression of torment forcing his mouth into a pucker. "Please get out of here. I'll pay you anything, just get out. I can't stand it anymore."

"I think I'll search the premises," the detective says, as if stricken by an idea. "I think I'll subject this room to a thorough search. Maybe you're hiding heroin. All of you people are on drugs; I know what's cooking here."

"No," Kvass says, assaulted by a horrid sense of cunning which overtakes him. "No, I don't think you'll find *heroin* anywhere around. No one's on hard drugs in the field that I know of. On the other hand—"

"On the other hand—what?"

"On the other hand," Kvass says casually, leaning over to lay a tentative pat on Princess's nose, then moving his hand down to feel the folds of flesh around her collar. She feels no worse than Katie Elizabeth Templeton and is a hell of a lot more dignified, snuffling in sudden gratitude as Kvass hits a concealed pleasure-nerve. "On the other hand, this man who I really do not know but who forced his way into my premises without my knowledge or consent, this very literary agent on the bed—"

"Yes?" the detective says, coming to attention, his nostrils flaring, his eyes taking on a canine fire. His name might well be Prince. "What about him?"

"This very literary agent," Kvass says, sidestepping neatly so that Princess and Prince will have a clear run to the bed on which Millman now sits, reduced six inches and fifty pounds by fear, his birdlike chest heaving in sudden comprehension because he has known Kvass for a long time, "whose name is Morton Millman is known affectionately throughout our field as 'the pot' not because of his postural characteristics which *do* verge in that direction but because he is the freest, frankest purveyor of freakout cheer that you have ever seen, carrying on his persons at all times—"

"Do you mean?" Prince asks. Princess says *woof* and similarly gives him an imploring expression.

"I mean—" Kvass says and dodges toward the door, moves over the threshold in a lurch while Prince and Princess, emitting glad cries, spring toward the bed. Over these cries he hears Millman's shriek and a babble of sound not quite connected into words, hears certain bumps and shudders as bodies make readjustments in the area of the windows … but that is no longer his concern. He is halfway down the hall, three-quarters of the way in fact and, seeing a staircase dodges into it and makes his way downward as quickly as possible, leaving the three to their own devices, which he is sure will be manifold and complex, although not striving toward any resolution for a good long time to come.

He will take a different tack. He must interpret the entrance of the

Prince and the Princess as fortunate, perhaps even planned. The game need not necessarily be over yet; never despair, where there's a will there's a way. A chicken in every pot, a silver lining to every cloud, a gleaming stairway to paradise and in any event, Millman, the cheap bastard, will not even trust an old client for eight hundred dollars which he does not even *need* anyway, so the hell with him. He can always mail back the money in small amounts from a concealed address, far from New York's great literary hot center.

V

There was 1958 at Chicago during which John Steele, the editor of *Tremendous,* had became publicly drunk and performed an unspeakable act in the Grand Foyer of the Hotel Loop during the day of the banquet, thereby rendering his relationship with contributors somewhat tenuous for years to come. There had been 1961 (or maybe it was 1964) at Cleveland when Harlow Houthwaite, chairman of the ex-fans of America and now a leading ornament of the television situation comedy guild, had been auctioned off for miscellaneous services to Katie Elizabeth Templeton for three dollars and sixty-five cents top bid, thereby unpleasantly affecting his reputation for months to come. There had been 1967 at New York when Karl Kable Feldman, author of a best-selling sex novel, had been awarded a fan prize in absentia for his contributions to the field as an ex-science fiction writer and had appeared in the rooms of the convention at midnight insanely drunk and ready to destroy much valuable property because he felt that his reputation had been ruined. There had been 1954 at Las Vegas, Nevada (that had been a good one during which Kvass had managed, at his first convention, to pick up a Volume I Number I of *Tremendous* from an ignorant fan for fifteen cents) but none of these conventions, in recollection or the real, seem likely to equal this one in New York during the Year of Our Lord.

Exclusive of Kvass's own private difficulties with the aliens (which in any event are not part of the convention program), the New York Convention has already yielded the following events: two fans, unwittingly it is assumed, have set fire to a small area in the screening room and the ensuing blaze has destroyed three chairs, four panels of wood on the floor, six multimedia projectors and the skirt of Diana Pope, Queen Poetess of science fiction, who had been trying to make herself heard in a call not to panic.

Harlow Houthwaite, threatened with physical violence by William

Culp for calling him the eunuch of the science fiction editors, has announced his third total resignation from the publishing of science fiction and has offered to turn over any reprint royalties on his short stories to the newly founded Campaign to Change Over the Editors.

Fifteen hundred fans and professionals, assembled in the grand hall for a rehearsal of the masquerade some hours hence have been terrorized by the invasion of some five hundred rats released by person or persons unknown who not only caused chaos but destroyed several hundred costumes, now unusable for the peak event of the convention.

Four editors have been assaulted in hotel corridors and at the snack bar and one of them, Billy Mitchum, the editor of *Vanquished Stories,* the least influential and worst paying market in science fiction, has been sent to the first aid room with assorted injuries, delaying his appearance at the cocktail party for seventeen minutes.

Marcus Stein, no longer writing science fiction but famous in the nineteen-fifties as the author of the Weird Magician series, has once again appeared in full medieval pastoral costume, complete with sword and slingshot, and has ranged through the rooms of the convention calling for a wench to amuse him. "Goddamnit!" Marcus has shrieked. "This is the only goddamned field I know where the professionals can't get laid by the amateurs. I can't stand it anymore! My backlog, my royalties for a screw!" and has used his blunt but still menacing sword to make threatening gestures at the buttocks of various young girls who have reacted to him with horror or condescension, much unlike the good old days at Seattle or Abilene in the early nineteen-sixties when Marcus Stein, then youthful and at the top of his form, had been able to carry on virtually public seductions through his method. That was before he gained almost a hundred pounds and was unable to find a tailor to make satisfactory alterations for his once-in-a-lifetime costume.

Also, it has been the convention during which Katie Elizabeth Templeton has passed among many groups of fans, professionals and editors muttering the name of Sanford Kvass and stating that in some way he would be "richly rewarded" for characteriological defects which Katie Elizabeth Templeton could clearly now see were incurable.

Also, it has been the convention at which a youthful reporter for one of the daily newspapers, dispatched there to get some minor color for the weekend section on the convention has moved from person to person within the walls of the convention asking what "the real truth of all you nuts is; do you still write about monsters or *is* the Moon voyage making you more realistic?" Surprisingly he has not yet been assaulted, although Michael Foote and a group of his friends from the

Old New Paltz Faction of the nineteen-forties have bribed the kitchen staff to insert somnolents in the reporter's place-set salad should he stay for the banquet as promised. They also intend, via bribery of the waiter, to put regurgitatives in the wine bottle which the young reporter will use.

In addition to that, it has been the convention at which Stanley X. Lupowitz, the oldest living member at fifty-one of the Fans In Revolt group of the nineteen-thirties, has created a flaring scandal at the annual meeting of the survivors of that group by telling an interminably long dirty story containing expletives and scatological terms, all of which were, unknown to him, broadcast to the convention at large by secret microphones and amplifiers which a clever group of young fans had planted in the meeting room prior to assembly. Lupowitz has denied responsibility for the speech but his voice-tones are unmistakable and the dirty story, in any event, is one which has long been associated with him although he has never told it so richly.

In addition to that, it is the convention at which V. V. Vivaldi, remitting to liquor for the first time in ten years, has come out four-square for programming therapy and has been attempting to psychically rewrite large random numbers of people who he is able to contact through a station he has taken up in the middle cubicle of the hotel lounge men's room.

It is the convention at which Billy Mitchum, after being attacked in the hall, has announced that he is leaving his position and will sue his publisher for aggravated damages as being the real figure behind his assault; if his publisher had allowed Billy Mitchum to pay the half-cent-a-word rate which Billy Mitchum had been fighting for, there would have been hardly so much hostility toward him.

It is also the fifteenth straight world convention in a row during which Dr. William Peebles—the noted nuclear physicist and, by virtue of his two published stories in the nineteen-forties, "science fiction's golden emissary to the outside world"—has gotten sick on liquor and passed out, this time at the entrance to the ladies' room serving the Grand Hall and other functions.

It is also the tenth straight world convention during which Mae Silvers, ex-science fiction writer and now part-owner of the Regal Rock Lounge Circus in the East Village of Manhattan, has been able to find someone in the field to have intercourse with her, this time Barney Middleton, fifty-year-old "fan of the year" in 1968.

Sanford Kvass has been relatively inconspicuous at this convention, unlike the old days.

Michael Foote has circulated among certain professionals in

attendance soliciting contributions for a Ban The War bookmark which he intends to have printed up cheaply by the million from a garage in New Smithtown and distribute to all retail outlets as "science fiction's blow against the horror."

Stuart Wiseman, running a seller's table, has misrepresented merchandise and cheated two young fans out of their life's-savings for damaged (and hence worthless) copies of the old *Space Station*.

The hotel has hired two extra detectives.

The hotel manager has asked the convention chairman if he can wrap things up a day or two early.

A couch before the elevator door on the seventeenth floor has been stolen.

The hotel bar has been closed for the duration.

Benny Martin, endeavoring to amuse fellow-fans with his familiar fiddle playing during the auctions, has been unable to continue because of a broken E-string. The string was sabotaged cleverly by enemies of the violinist who overtightened the peg before the concert.

The weather outside has been exceedingly foul, the air coming in thick damp waves of pollution, causing all of the activities to remain confined within the hotel.

Morton Millman, the long-time friend and leading agent of science fiction, has been arrested by local police (on referral of the hotel detective) for suspected possession of large quantities of narcotics and now languishes in the city jail under moderate bail. Although it would be quite easy for any one of a number of people to post bond in time for Millman to return to the convention a certain indifference to his condition has sprung up spontaneously among all sources and the general feeling seems to be that Morton Millman, the literary agent, is exactly where he should be at the present time, although possibly for the wrong reasons.

VI

All of this information, as well as more than that, Kvass has picked up at the gigantic talk-to-the-professionals cocktail party conducted in the dine and dance room of the hotel on the first night of the convention. Huddled shoulder to shoulder, buttock to buttock, with the giants of the field, to say nothing of several thousand fans, Kvass has succumbed to an airy feeling of disconnection, a sense of release from past sins and obligations, immersion in a delightful present which seems eternal. Probably it has to do with the fact that he is drinking again; it has been a long time since he has systematically applied himself to alcohol as he has for the first hour of this gathering. Seven or eight double Scotches gone, a glassy spin to his amble, Kvass now finds himself in a group of several fellow professionals who were being alternately baited and petitioned for autographs by a large, moving flock of youngsters who circulate throughout the room. In between the interruption of the fans Kvass is conducting an earnest conversation with Stanley Lupowitz, senior member of the Fans In Revolt, who is filling him in on all the details of the convention. V. V. Vivaldi is also in this circle; Billy Mitchum is on the outskirts and John Steele himself is drinking from a small tumbler an unnamed substance and giving crazed jocular looks to the room. But it is largely Lupowitz with whom Kvass now finds himself engaged. "You don't say," he says to Lupowitz every thirty seconds or so, not out of any need to keep talking (Lupowitz will never stop talking) but only to maintain a sense of connection.

In the back of his mind, now and then, a vagrant thought or two about aliens will extrude but Kvass ignores them. The aliens will have to take care of themselves; Kvass is going to enjoy the world science fiction convention and be damned. It only happens once a year or so, once a decade or less in New York City, and he is entitled to join with his colleagues in a Labor Day weekend of fun and professional discussions.

"And then," Stanley Lupowitz is saying, "right there before the whole group I said to him, 'Michael Foote, you are betraying the causes of the Solar Ring and are a destructive influence to greater fandom in Brooklyn! Michael Foote, you are found out! I am exiling you from the League!'"

"You don't say," Kvass murmurs. Lupowitz is referring to a famous incident of thirty-five years ago, catalogued in his five-volume memoir of fan history, during which he engineered the expulsion of Michael Foote, then twelve years old, from the League of Wonder Readers of Brooklyn because of Foote's attempts to set up a closet-revolution in the heart of the group. The story is familiar and has, indeed, been a plot element in at least sixteen novels written in their older years by ex-members of the League, but Lupowitz never wearies of retelling it, probably from a feeling (Kvass can understand this) that he has never yet quite got it right. "And do you know the funny thing?" Lupowitz says. "Do you know the kicker to the whole affair? Michael wasn't even a Communist. It was a false implication. I found some literature in his locker at school about the party and I thought that he was a member but actually he was holding it for Bill Peebles, who *was* a member. Would you believe it?"

"You don't say," Kvass says. He twirls his glass, watches the Scotch catch the glint of the ceiling fluorescence—this is part of the magic of drinking—and then takes down three somewhat watered ounces in a gulp, feeling them shimmer their way directly into his small intestine from which they will shortly emerge, he is sure, at approximately the same rate as he has taken them. "You really don't say?"

"I do say," Stanley Lupowitz says. There is a momentary lull in the conversation—Lupowitz functions in terms of stories and set-pieces but has a certain difficulty in the transitions with which Kvass, the blocked writer, can only sympathize. "You can't imagine how Mike Foote was in those days. Of course he hasn't changed."

"Fuck you, Stanley," Michael Foote says, turning around from an intense conversation with his wife, Rose Salmonson Foote, with whom he always seems to find new topics of conversation. "All I know is that you're three months late on that goddamned biography."

"That's right," Lupowitz says, his face turning a mottled green as Kvass regards him through the empty glass. "I wanted to get it right. It's got to be a good clean draft, Michael. This one has got to sell a hundred thousand copies; everyone's waiting for it."

"Oh yes," Foote says. "Everybody's waiting for an eight-hundred page biography of V. V. Vivaldi and the Nebraska Group, there's no question about it. What's this about clean drafts, Stan? We know perfectly well you can't tell the difference between a period and a comma."

"Hah!" Stanley Lupowitz says, his voice booming out unevenly over the thousands of bodies, the hundreds of sounds in the room. "Hah, hah, Michael! You haven't changed at all. You're the same arrogant little bastard you always were."

As usual, the Lupowitz boom attracts a good deal of attention and Kvass, not wishing to be associated with it at this instant—the most important thing about a satisfactory drunk is maintaining a relative inconspicuousness—decides to dislodge himself in search of another drink. The bar however, is at the far side of the room and in order to get there Kvass must transverse thousands of bodies, tens of thousands of limbs, appendages, projections, etc. The mere contemplation of the walk fills him with a shuddering sense of dependency; he is really in no condition to take on this kind of responsibility. What he needs is an escort.

"I need a drink," Kvass murmurs to himself in the tiniest of free-lancer's voices and then begins, with difficulty, to move through the area of the room.

"You never even *met* V. V. Vivaldi," Foote is now advising Lupowitz. "Can I at least get you an introduction?"

Kvass, from the throes of inebriation, finds himself thinking what a genuinely vicious person his old friend Michael Foote is. He used to be a good writer, of course, and a good deal of his troubles may be traced back (no less than Kvass's) to a writer's block. Nevertheless, there must be better things to do on a Saturday night in New York City than to abuse Stanley Lupowitz.

"Whoops!" Kvass says as he jars against a figure, rights himself, finds his feet kicked precipitately away from him by someone else and lands in a kneeling posture on the floor, two silvery ice cubes whisking like fish down the open dress of Katie Elizabeth Templeton who, it seems, has been in intense conversation with a group of editors.

"You lousy bastard!" Katie shrieks, abandoning her difficult public femininity and turning Kvass-ward; when she recognizes him her face suffuses as if many clots had gathered in her cheeks and she says, *"You,* it's you again! I'm going to get you for this now. I really am."

Kvass turns his palms upward (balancing the glass with an index finger) in a gesture of *nolo contendre* and smiles desperately. "I didn't know," he says. "I'm sorry, Katie," and then he sees the left hook coming.

Katie Elizabeth Templeton is gathering strength and force; Katie Elizabeth Templeton is reaching deep into her history to emerge with a stinging left hook that is somehow intrinsic to her quest for human relationships and Kvass, succumbing once again to his feeling of detachment (but with a good overlay of panic as well; he recognizes at least three of the editors to whom Katie has been talking; he needs these markets), floats like a butterfly, stings like a bee, slips the hook and a following jab and, discovering a small space between bodies to his left, runs to daylight.

"There he goes!" Katie shouts behind him. "Stop that man!" but the atmosphere of the party is such that her voice lacks carrying power and in any event she could be making jocular reference to someone's wardrobe.

Kvass does not look back; he does not balance alternatives. He merely pushes himself through mobs of people, mumbling alternate apologies and threats, thrusting himself through layers of damp to a kind of ascension which he finds at the exit, and past the exit he begins to move with increasing speed, thinking of a secure place. His room is obviously out of the question at this time and he does not know other locations well enough to take a chance. The hotel facilities have been closed off for the duration of the convention and the streets themselves are not worth the risk at this hour. Kvass finds himself leaning against the wall in an abandoned corridor, still somehow holding onto his empty glass, breathing hard and searching the ceiling for electronic devices. It seems as good a place as any to take a momentary break. There is no one in this corridor and in addition he does not feel strictly as well as he thought he did; alcohol has cut a thin bright ribbon through his sensibility. The ribbon now seems to be tightening and certain important parts of the brain appear to be constricting.

"Woof!" moans Kvass in a tone which sounds very much like Princess's and leans heavily against the wall watching the ceiling move. He thinks briefly about passing out but decides against it; it is too demanding and would only lead to problems of disposal later on. In any event, he has to impress editors who will shortly be coming out of the room in a flood.

A familiar voice in the corridor says, "Kvass, you're a disgrace," and from the depths of his sunken eyes, he looks upward. The alien spokesman—just one of them this time, perhaps the others are on a more important detail—is sitting cross-legged in the hallway, looking at him with an expression which mingles concern and distaste, although his form is so grotesque to contemplate that it is difficult to get into niceties of implication. "A disgrace," the alien says again. "I really thought that you would turn out better than this."

"Leave me alone," Kvass burbles. "I'm drunk; can't you see that? Besides, I quit. I quit this morning. I don't care anymore."

"I knew you would say that," the alien says. There is a brilliant, flaring pain within Kvass's skull and a series of ominous wrenches in the vicinity of his belt-line. He feels as if all the liquids of his body are trapped by gravity and moving violently toward the nearest exit and then, suddenly, he feels entirely different. Cold sober, he looks at the alien who appears now even more horrible. "That takes care of one part of it," the alien says. "Liquor is no escape."

"I can't stand it," Kvass says. "It took me hours to get drunk. You can't do this to me."

"Sit down, Kvass," the alien says, and pats the floor ominously with a tentacle. "I want to have a discussion with you. We're very disappointed in you, Sanford."

"They'll see us," Kvass says. "There are ten thousand people down the corridor and about a hundred hotel detectives. Someone's going to find us."

The alien waves his tentacles. "That's my problem. I can take the risk. Besides, *I* should be the one worried about interruptions. They're likely to turn on me."

"You don't understand," Kvass points out "All of science fiction is in there. Writers. Critics. Editors. Even a couple of publishers. If they come out and find me talking to a ten-foot long, green tentacled alien, my markets will be destroyed. I'll lose my reputation. I'll never be able to establish myself again."

"I'd say you'd done a pretty good job already of destroying yourself, Kvass," the alien says. "We've been keeping a close watch on you and we're increasingly disturbed by your behavior. You're not even trying."

"I want to get drunk."

"You've been drunk and you know perfectly well that that's no solution. Do you realize that you're holding up entire galaxies by your stupid unwillingness to carry out your assignment? There are millions of people standing by on triple-time and all because you aren't reasonable. The wealth that you've misappropriated."

"I can't find any alien," Kvass says. "Don't you understand? It's impossible. The alien could be any single one of them and they're all crazy. I'm in no condition to take your test."

"Then you know exactly what the consequences will be."

"Of course I know what the consequences will be. You've made that clear. It's just a chance I've got to take. I'll tell you the truth—things haven't been working out the way I hoped they would for a very long time now. It's been up and down for many years, but when you get right to the end of it the fact is that I'm just a pulp writer and right now not even a producing one. And as far as the emotional part of it is concerned, I just can't seem to get into stable relationships. More or less I blame other people for that but it may be my fault. Anyway, I can't see spending another thirty years or whatever writing paperback and getting stuck with people like Katie Elizabeth Templeton," Kvass says and shrugs. "So to tell you how I honestly feel at this moment, I'd just as soon see the whole thing go. What the hell? Maybe it's for the best. It's not going anywhere in particular and maybe we can put it together in some better way at some time in the future. You know," Kvass says and giggles, "it's pretty hard to take the long view when you're a commercial writer. You stick with the front end; there's no long-range income. I just can't see the percentage."

"You're being very selfish," the alien says. "You're looking at this thing from a very personal point of view. There are a lot of consequences, you know."

"Well then," Kvass says, "you probably judged what sort of person you were dealing with from the start. You said you've been keeping an eye on me, right? So you know the background; you could have done better. Why don't you give the assignment to someone else? Give it to V. V. Vivaldi. I'm sure that he'd give you a real run for your money. He'd take you seriously. There are lots of people like that. Give it to Stanley Lupowitz. I'm sure he'll figure out something."

The alien sighs and crunches against the wall uncomfortably, causing pieces of plaster to sift precariously and fall in a small rain in his vicinity. He flexes his tentacles, looks at the skylight. "Oh, Kvass," he says, "you're impossible. Listen, give me a cigarette, will you?"

"A cigarette?"

"I said, a cigarette."

"All right," Kvass says. "Why the hell not?" He removes one from his pack, hands it over to the creature, who takes it very deftly indeed and waits politely for a light, then palms it deftly and puts it into an orifice somewhere in the vicinity of the lower back.

"Ah," it says, "that's good. Well, why shouldn't we smoke, Kvass? Do you see any reason at all against it?"

"Oh no. Not in the least. It struck me as quite natural."

"And we're not as vulnerable to it as you people. Listen, Kvass," the alien says, a certain beneficence creeping into its tone and posture, clouds of smoke spilling from its anal area, a small halo of smoke around its grotesque head. "I want to talk very frankly to you. You put us in a hell of a spot."

"Well, it's mutual."

"No, you listen to me. Maybe we shouldn't have selected you for the test; maybe you weren't the right candidate after all, but then our researchers indicated that you were adequate and when the researchers say go, we go. It's too late to make a switch now. We need your cooperation and you've got to give it to us. We're committed now; we can't switch to someone else. For what it's worth, we may have made a mistake in the selection and I'm sure that I would be authorized to issue you an apology."

"So destroy the place."

"No," the alien says with a twitch of the head area; it puts the cigarette now into what appears to be an ear and takes in enormous quantities of smoke which spill from the tips of the tentacles. "We can't do that. We have a set policy and procedure in cases of this sort and it holds that there's got to be a fair test. It's got to be done under the code."

"I don't want to do it."

"But you've *got* to do it, Sanford; don't you understand," the alien says with a strange pleading tone. "We can't just move in and wipe out the place. We have to have authorization. We're a very small unit; we operate on a limited jurisdiction and Headquarters, although they give us a lot of latitude, is very strict with methodology and results. We can't just peremptorily knock out a culture; we have to have the test."

"So we're saved," Kvass says. "That's what it is, we're *saved*. If I don't cooperate in your rigged test, then you can't blow us up. The hell with you."

"No," the alien says mournfully, streaming smoke now from three-quarters of its body or more. Perhaps it is on fire. "I told you, Sanford, I'm on your side. I'm basically sympathetic and I must warn you. It isn't that way at all, because we've had hundreds of thousands standing by on triple-time for the destruction and we've got to go ahead and do it or it'll be a dead loss. The agency will be bankrupted. Regardless of the consequences, your planet must be destroyed on Monday; we've got too much invested in the project to pull people off at this time. We'll just have to face the consequences at Headquarters when they find that we've gone ahead and done it without administering a fair test. We'll probably lose our certification and spheres of influence; this isn't going to do our reputation any good at all. But business is business."

"Unless I deduce the alien."

"Oh yes, of course. Unless you deduce the alien. If you deduce the alien, we, uh, won't be able to do anything at all."

"But you didn't really expect that," Kvass says.

"No," the alien says frankly, "we really didn't expect that at all."

"But business is business."

"Yes, business is business."

"You're asking me, in other words, to save *your* ass. To participate in the conditions of the assignment so that you'll look good at Headquarters."

"That's right, Sanford," the alien says, and uses a tentacle to put the cigarette out delicately in the rug. There is a flutter of ash and a foul stench which seems to disconcert it little if at all. "We're asking you to be altruistic."

"You want to destroy *my* world but I should be sympathetic."

"Why not?" the alien says. "We selected you because you were farsighted and were capable of generous impulse. Besides, you always have a chance. You might win after all."

"Has anyone?"

The alien looks at Kvass, then turns away and seems to peer in the direction of the cocktail party. It is strangely quiet, Kvass realizes; sounds from the room seem to have ceased and the panting sounds of the hotel cooling unit likewise do not seem to be present.

"Well," the alien says, "someone almost got it once. They guessed right after the deadline, two or three seconds as a matter of fact. Of course it was too late then and destruction was already in process, but it was a near thing."

"You've run this a lot of times before, I gather."

"Oh yes," the alien concedes with a rather dapper flick of tentacle. "I must admit that we have. It turns out that we're rather of an imperialistic kind of culture if you follow what I'm saying. We need a good deal of real estate on which to organize."

"So I should get you off the hook by cooperating."

"You might as well, Sanford," the alien says. "No matter how small the chance is, you can still strive for success. You wouldn't feel right, otherwise. Besides, you must know that we're very important to you. Our culture and means and methods, you understand. You don't understand the facts of the case at all."

"No I don't," Kvass says. He looks somewhat nervously in the direction of the banquet hall and says, "Aren't we taking a little bit too much time here? We're going to be found. As sure as Stanley Lupowitz is in that room, we're going to be found and there's going to be a lot of explanation which I don't want to make."

"Don't worry," the alien says. "We can stop time. Briefly of course; it's a small trick but a very taxing one and you can reach diminishing returns. Sanford, haven't you ever heard of the Book of Apocalypse?"

"I read it a long time ago. I'm not really too interested in the subject."

"Well," the alien says, "think about it." Its limbs begin to tremble and a certain sense of dilation seems to spread over its repulsive but honest features. "I can see that I'm a bit overextended, so we're going to have to cancel this right now, Sanford. I ask you to think about everything. I ask you to take it under advisement."

"I can't stand it," Kvass says. "I simply can't stand it."

"Well, that's *your* problem, not ours. Do you want to condemn two billion of your fellow creatures to an abrupt and terrible death just because you did not have the willingness to stand and fight for them?"

"Three and a half billion. We've had a bit of a population problem recently."

"Three and a half billion then. We can't keep up with everything. You'd be the one to know about that. The guilt would be just that more onerous, Sanford,"

"Not if we're destroyed,"

"Remember the Book of Apocalypse, Sanford," the alien says solemnly, looking at Kvass with a fine intentness, bringing its several eyes past an oblong shape into circles, then it vanishes—there is one thing about these aliens, they are good on their exits and entrances—and leaves him sitting; in a rather disjointed posture in the hallway. At the same time, he hears renewed noises beginning from the banquet hall and three adolescents race by him, holding their bellies, shouting.

"Out of the way, man!" one of them says to the stumbling Kvass, narrowly missing the administration of a strong kick. "Don't you understand that there's action down the hall! Away, away!" he cries and joins the others. Behind them, moving solemnly but in a determined shuffle, is a horse or rather two men in a horse costume; the costume is painted in pink polka dots and has reins and a halter imprinted thereupon. The horse is groaning and wheezing but making pretty fair time for all of that (about seven minutes and fourteen seconds for the three-furlong baby sprint distance, Kvass judges) and it follows the three adolescents into the distance, its unevenly worn rear legs moving in an unpleasantly sexual scuttle as it merges with the fluorescence and is gone.

That must be that idiot Homer Helmut Schwartz in his goddamned horse costume, Kvass thinks as he staggers to his feet and moves down the backstretch. Schwartz is a fixture of the world science fiction conventions, has been since 1941 when he came in third in class in the masquerade ball dressed as the vulture-thing in V. V. Vivaldi's *Monstrous Planet.*

He has done much better than that since—first in class for twelve years running as a matter of fact—but Kvass can be goddamned if he can think of a single piece of science fiction, his own included, in which a horse has been a major character. Of course, the field is changing quickly; it is moving nearer and nearer conventional literature in its stylization and pursuit of the characteriological. And one never knows, one can fall behind hopelessly in a matter of only a few months, perhaps there *is* a horse figuring prominently in some of the inner-personality fiction and he has simply missed it. He has fallen behind upon a lot of his reading nowadays.

Mumbling, Kvass follows Homer Helmut Schwartz, His mind is not on the fate of the universe yet; it is concerned with horsemanship in modern science fiction, but as things have been going recently this can only be taken as a generalized improvement. From horses to destruction is such a very small step, Kvass understands; the chasm could now be bridged at any time at all.

VII

The thing is that you fall into it. For a long time the idea of writing has been appealing, maybe it is a question of self-expression, maybe only a sedentary way of pointing out to girls that you too have existence. Perhaps it has to do with the fact that something is bothering you and the only way that you can take it to terms is to get it down on paper, usually in a lying kind of way that may have to do, in the long run, with truth. For a long time you are incapable of doing much at all; the stories come out too abrupt or too stupid or too much like something you have read, or fail to make much sense of what was in your head when you started. This is when most people quit, but the serious ones— the ones that find their options slowly closing off as they fall into it— do not. Eventually, maybe at the age of twenty-two or so, sometimes earlier than that, never much later, you find yourself capable of putting down something on paper that is a passable approximation of what you wanted to say when the whole thing started. If you are lucky, if you have some vague idea of the places that publish the kind of story you have been writing and if you try to write that story so it seems it could fit into one of those places, you may even be able to sell it. For money. For one cent or two cents or very possibly three cents a word, whatever it is. It isn't much, but in terms of the original act (putting words on paper, that is) it always seems to be more than you really deserve. The thing about writing stories and getting money for them is that no matter how hard you work and how little the money is, somehow, it seems like *stealing*. The money gets between you and what the business of putting things down on paper is really all about; and what that is about, of course, is *suffering*. There is no point in getting into writing, none whatsoever, unless it is painful, but at the same time it hurts good because at long last you have the opportunity to tell people what you think of them. In a disguised kind of way, of course.

After a while, if the money begins to come in regularly you become dependent on it, at least to the extent where you need it to live on. Meanwhile you've written a novel or two, possibly more like nine or ten if you're interested in writing for a living right at the start and you go to paperback. The money is never enough, but then on the other hand you aren't *entitled to* it. At the root of it you're still stealing, so although you're unhappy about the quality of income you have—which seems to be somewhat less than a certified civil service worker—you aren't unhappy enough to go out and look for a way to make a living. Besides, the hours are tenable and the more difficult editors can be avoided or lied to for months on end.

Eventually you find yourself a "professional writer"; that is, writing is your only source of income and you have been doing it for so long that you are fundamentally unemployable anywhere else. That is to say that if you decided to quit writing and walked into an employment agency for some kind of help they would want to know what you had been doing with a certain amount of time. If you tell them that you have spent that time writing books they feel that you have been on heroin or perhaps have been under the weather for a long time, serving a certain amount of years as atonement for a sex violation.

(By this time you *have* been writing books for quite a while; short stories don't pay enough to be worth the effort of generating new ideas all the time. Anyway, although the wordage rates are about the same it is easier to sell fifty thousand words and make fifteen hundred dollars than five thousand words for a hundred and fifty. Most of the fifty thousand words can be repetitious or go into the same material in a variety of ways; one simply doesn't have to *think*.)

At around the time that you become a "professional writer" a startling realization hits you. It may come during the course of writing a book or more likely in the periods (longer and longer and more agonizing) in between books, and that realization is that what you are doing has absolutely no connection with what you thought you were going to do when you fell into it in the first place. You are not getting down anything on paper which is of particular point or purpose to you nor is writing a means of letting the world Know Where You Stand; to the contrary it is a matter of raising fifteen hundred dollars for fifty thousand words and come fair weather or foul, come good times or bad the fifty thousand words have got to be produced often enough to keep up the lifestyle which is mostly concerned with the avoidance of writing except during periods of desperation. You are no longer interested in what you are doing; it seems inconceivable that a sane human being could have any interest in what you are doing; it seems impossible that what you are doing has any relation to anything, but still you keep on because the money is absolutely necessary and in any event, one must keep busy.

Besides, there is an audience out there. At some point along the way, people have gotten around to "reading" your "books"; they have certain "responses" toward your "books," and every now and then they give indication, through postcards or strange notes to one another in the subculture called "fanzines" that what you have been doing has some connection to them after all. And this is the most insane thing of all, because although it is impossible to imagine that anyone could take this seriously, there are people who find it consequential. They form "opinions." They purchase copies in enough quantities sometimes to guarantee "royalty rates." Many of them turn out to want to be "writers" themselves and ask for advice. They want to know if it is best to go for the specialized sale at the beginning or whether they should go right out and try to sell a big commercial novel so that they can make "big money" and spend the rest of their lives "doing the kind of work that we really want to be doing."

Sometimes, although it is rare enough to be a Special Event, it is even possible to get laid as the indirect result of your writing, although ten will get you a hundred that the woman who begins to gasp out her inner urgings underneath you has never read a word of yours in her entire life and could not care less. She is interested only in your "reputation" and is apt to become extremely difficult if you try to find out what her "opinions" are on your "work." (Of course, a "professional writer" has long since gone past the point where he is interested in anyone's opinion on his work, since he has none of his own; but every now and then there is a novitiate who finds himself published before deflowered and it is from this type of individual that the troubles may come.) Later on, once the affair has cooled, if it has gotten to the stage of being an affair, the woman may pick up on your work and begin to read everything in a high state of querulousness. But this is reasonably abstract, all other things being equal, and by that time you could hardly have much concern. Only a lunatic would expect to induce seduction through the written word nowadays.

So, you are a "professional writer." You grow a beard. Perhaps you grow a sideburn-and-mustache kit as well; perhaps you simply cultivate very long hair and a taste for obscenity mingled with pipe smoking. This hardly matters; what matters is that the increasing conviction that you do not know what the hell you are doing has begun to soak out to the outside life and corrections are in order. One cannot exist in a state of amorphousness and doubts, not that and stand any chance of copping second serial rights at any rate. The point is that you "cultivate" an "image." The "image," unlike the work you do, arises out of specific attitudes and has clear definition. If you are fortunate, the "image" is so clearly delineated and so publicly effective that it is possible to get behind it not only in the personal affairs bit (which is routine) but in the writing itself; that is, you begin to write what you are expected to write and what you know you can get through with the least amount of struggle. At the point that you have reached then, say a point of thirty-three years occupying a couple of furnished rooms in an apartment-hotel on the upper west side of Manhattan, with a well-stocked liquor cabinet, a good selection of pipes from the four corners of the world and a ten-foot long shelf containing your editions in English, Spanish, British, Norwegian, Japanese, French, Hungarian and Slovak. (The Japanese are particularly slow-paying and infuriating in their refusal to send authors' copies, not that you could read a word of them anyway.)

Well, at that point, Kvass decides, there is only one thing you can do to demonstrate to the universe, not to say yourself, that you remain a sane, balanced, realistic man. What you do is to go down to the World

Science Fiction Convention (which is happily being held in your home city for once) and go around this world science fiction convention hunting for aliens. To save the world from destruction.

Of course. Why not? What is so unreasonable about that? What is so unreasonable about "professional writing"?

Kvass decides that he will rededicate himself. He will try. The fate of the world is at stake. Furthermore, the peremptory lurch into sobriety has left him edged with bitterness; he cannot permit the Earth to be tampered with by creatures who hold within their technology such means and such total incomprehension of what the point of liquor is.

VIII

Much later, not exactly sure of how he got there, Kvass finds himself at the afternoon rock festival sponsored by the United Fans of America. It was obviously the intention of the UFA to have a quiet gathering, limited to certified participants in fandom, at which certain examples of the Music of the Space Age could be played by a small combo and then discussed in a controlled way by expert fans. But there has never been a convention quite like this one before; there are ten thousand registrants, most without credentials or qualifying background of any sort, and it seems that almost half of them have crowded into the Cotillion Room of the Hotel Northport to share in the festival of astronautics. The music is being provided by a four man combo known as the Maddened Hound (perhaps Kvass has not got the name quite right; in any case he has been assured that they are all dedicated science fiction fans). The Hound, stimulated by narcotics and the atmosphere of the room, has long since broken away from the more conventional space music that it has been playing and is now, massed guitars and drums thumping, beginning to break some entirely new ground. A nauseating whine breaks through the amplifiers always threatening to but not quite making it into a diminished seventh or so and Kvass is certain that behind the more rhythmic sounds he can hear obscenities, sexual invitations and speculation. Science fiction is not quite what it was when he broke into it nor, for that matter, are fans.

He is jammed against a wall, held in place by a good clump of bodies, working on a glass of club soda which he seems to have been holding for the last hour or so. Exactly what he is doing at the festival of space music he is not sure; certainly this is not the kind of thing that appeals to him and, in any event, Kvass knows that he should be fraternizing with his friends and fellow professionals, keeping his markets and options open and not wasting his time with a group of fans who, beyond everything else, do not even seem to know who he is. Possibly he had the idea that the search would be better conducted here than otherwise. It is more likely that the alien would be planted in the persona of a fan rather than a professional because fans come in more quantity and are less easily recognizable. But now, all good intentions blunted, Kvass rubs his back against the wall quieting an itch in a kind of despair. The whole thing is unreasonable. There simply seems no good way to begin.

Marcus Stein, in full medieval costume, thrusts himself through the crowd and taps Kvass on the shoulder. No one seems to pay him any attention whatsoever. It has been a good long time since Marcus Stein was able to make any sensation at conventions whatsoever.

"Sanford," he says in a penetrating tenor, apparently somewhat drunk, not that this makes any difference to the full range of Stein's behavior. "What are you doing here?"

"I'm listening to the music," Kvass says. He does not like Marcus Stein, although he should have expected sooner or later to have to deal with him. Several years ago Stein and Kvass collaborated on a series of short stories for *Tremendous* about an engineer detective who solved problems through a wondrous machine, and this kind of association, not to say the checks they have shared, cannot be put away, although Kvass rather wishes that it could. Somehow the checks always wound up being split unevenly by Stein's agent who was doing the marketing, but Stein insisted that this was only fair because he had had the idea and, anyway, John Steele was a friend of his and not of Kvass's. "Contacts, remember, are the most important thing," Stein had reminded Kvass over and over again, usually just before he left the hotel room they had been sharing for a night's exploration, leaving Kvass with a few incoherent pages of outline and plot ideas which were supposed to be his full half of the collaboration.

"Contacts are nothing," Kvass says five years later. "They only give you the illusion of accomplishment."

"What's that, Sanford? Hey, look at that cunt over there. You ever seen an ass like that? You know, it's a whole new generation out there, Sanford, growing up under our noses while we've been trying to back out on contracts and stay away from Katie Elizabeth Templeton. We wasted the best years of our lives. God, would I like to suck that out."

"So go ahead and try it," Kvass says somewhat petulantly. It is one thing for Stein the ex-collaborator to remind him of fraud and misuse but when he cannot even get the man to pay *attention*. "Go on," Kvass says. "I don't care. Go ahead and make her. Take her right on the floor if you can find a spot on the floor. Stop talking so much."

"Oh I don't know, Sanford," Stein says heavily and with a sigh puts his sword to rest on the floor beside him, unclenches his hand. "It's a feeling of consuming age coming over one, that's what it is. It's hard to take these children seriously; they lack our background, Sanford, they lack our minds, our struggles. What could we possibly say to them? Oh baby," Stein says to a young, abstracted girl pushing her way by him in peasant costume, her skirt somewhere barely below her waist. "Oh baby, I could go down on you. Could I *ever* go down on you, sweetheart."

The girl stops, turns, gives Stein a careful look and says, "Well, why don't you?"

"Why *don't* I?"

"Why not?" she says. "My room is number six-fifty-four and I should be up there in ten minutes or so to change my clothes for the masquerade ball. If you want to come up, you're perfectly willing to. Take your chances." She examines Kvass, shrugs. "Bring your friend along if you want to." She moves away from them, twitching her hips abstractedly. Kvass thinks of following her, decides that he has other things on his mind. "Well?" he says.

"Well, what? It's a whole new generation out there, just like I told you, Sanford. It isn't the same at all. Oh God," Stein says, bending over and picking up the sword, hefting it with a grunt. "They just make me feel very old."

"Why don't you go up and screw her? She sounded direct enough."

"Why don't *you,* Sanford?"

"I don't go around conventions asking to go down on people, Marcus. *You* do. Here's your chance."

Stein shakes his head with a pitying, weary expression and says, "It's like I always knew it to be, Sanford. It's always the same. You haven't changed at all, really, have you? You don't understand."

"I don't understand anything. They didn't call your bluff five or six years ago; is that what I don't understand?"

"I married well, Sanford," Stein says. Three years ago, through a series of manipulations incomprehensible to all of his old friends in science fiction, Stein had married the lead actress on an important daytime television serial; since then he has been living, although not always companionably, in a townhouse on the east side of Manhattan and his appearances with his old circles are limited to world science fiction conventions and occasional drinking sessions with the editors' club. "I'm a settled, happily married man—until my wife decides to leave me, that is, and then I'll collect alimony. I don't chase around anymore. I just like to keep a hand in, or on I should more properly say. Now your situation on the other hand is absolutely critical."

"Hey, Marcus, would you notice if there seem to be any aliens around the convention? People who don't seem quite human, that is to say; people a little bit out of the ordinary."

"Hundreds," says Stein, putting the sword back into place. "God, it's impossible in this costume. I've never been so hot. I think I'll have to go upstairs and take off the boots anyway. Maybe the jerkin, now that I come to think of it."

"Because if you see anybody who might be an alien and could spot them for me, you'd be doing me an enormous favor."

"I'll keep an eye out," Stein says. "You haven't been doing much writing lately, have you?"

"I have so. I sold a novel only a few months ago."

"Because I've heard that you've been having a little trouble. That it isn't coming as easily as it used to."

"It's coming very easily."

"Oh, I'm sure it is, I'm sure it is. I always felt that production picked up as you grew older. You're in the most productive sphere, Sanford; I was a *whirlwind* when I was thirty-five. But just in case you're having a little bit of trouble—"

"I'm thirty-three."

"Okay," Stein says, "okay, you're thirty-three. I thought that you were thirty-five, but if you say you're thirty-three then that's fine too. Anyway, I have a really great idea for a time-travel series which I think could work out to three or four books without any trouble at all. It would just be an adventure series based on the single gimmick and that way you wouldn't have to *think;* you'd just be writing three books instead of one but it would all be from the same idea. It would be effortless, Sanford, because the gimmick is really unusual and would hold the whole thing together. If you wanted to hear it from me I'm sure that we could work out something very advantageous. Now, I wouldn't stop with just giving you the *gimmick,* even though that in itself is worth everything, because all you would have to do is just to write them. Even so I would be happy to do some touchup on the final drafts and I even have a couple of scenes and characters that I would throw in at no further charge as well. I think you'd be very likely to get serial rights on this one as well. I still know that John is looking for something by me and even though you'd be doing most of the writing, I'd offer you my name as a full half-credit. You can even put my name *first* and that way—"

"In other words you'd give me an idea and make the submission of the final draft and for that you want fifty percent."

"Oh no," Stein says with a bedazzled expression, the imitation jewelry on his jerkin glinting under the lights which illuminate the Maddened Hound. "Oh no. I would have to have at least seventy-five percent. Well, possibly seventy but *never* less than two-thirds. I'm giving you the idea, I'm giving you the worksheets, I'm giving you editorial services and I know that this is a two thousand a book series; maybe even more. *Writing* it is no problem at all, it would just be like typing the alphabet for two hundred pages, that's how simple it is."

"No," says Kvass. "No, Marcus, I was wrong. You're not an alien. There's no question about it."

Stein seems the slightest bit disconcerted. "What's that?" he says. "Alien? What are you talking about?"

"I thought that you might be, that they would now be taunting me by infiltrating the *doppelganger* right into my presence and daring me," Kvass says, struggling now to make himself quite heard above the Maddened Hound, which seems to have managed critical repairs to its amplifiers during the progress of the concert and is now using huge knives of sound to carve the crowd into astonished sections which huddle in amusement as the group really lets free. "*Daring* me to take a chance that they knew I wouldn't, but I was quite wrong. I didn't understand their methods at all; I still have no comprehension of the cunning. You're not an alien at all; you're the same goddamned Marcus Stein and to hell with you."

"Sanford—"

"To *hell* with you, you're nothing but a lecherous aging hack who isn't even able to follow up on his fantasies. Besides that, you were always cheating on your sections; I was supposed to write five thousand words and then you were supposed to write five thousand words— remember, alternate shifts when we were turning out that crap?—but you always had a way of getting into scenes with short lines of dialogue and lots of extra paragraphs to show that this was a tough-talking novel. I stood for it all the time because I thought that that was the only way I was going to be able to make the sales and I needed the money. But you're a son of a bitch, Marcus; you still are and you always were and I bet I know now why your wife cries so beautifully and why they kicked her off that series with lung disease. To hell with you, Marcus," Kvass says. "To hell with the whole thing," and strides away.

It is a truly magnificent moment, a moment that he intimates he has been rehearsing subvocally for many years and well worth waiting for. But as do most of his long-awaited moments it does not work out quite as he had hoped; he catches a foot in mid-stride, finds another knee at the beginning of a totter and has to hang on desperately to a miscellaneous body to avoid going to the floor in the crowd. When he recovers his balance he finds that he has been holding desperately onto the large, harnessed breasts of a fifty-year-old rock fan who looks at him with enormous and rising interest.

"Excuse me," Kvass says and bolts, hearing behind him cries which might be either passionate or deprived depending upon location and point of view. He finds an exit and by sheer force of will propels his body through several others into an empty space and then toward the door. "I'll fix them," he mutters, not sure exactly who he will fix or how, but this gives him the illusion of progress, orderly movement toward an orderly outcome. "I'll fix them now, I know the answer, I certainly know the answer."

William Culp and Michael Foote are in the alcove, seemingly in intense conversation about some shared memory or another but Kvass's rather spectacular approach has interrupted them and they look at him with attention.

"Fix who, Sanford?" Foote asks.

"What *is* the answer?" Culp says.

Kvass says nothing, mumbles, grunts, pushes his way by the two popular and influential editorial figures and into the wastes of the corridors. Behind him, Culp and Foote begin again an intense disagreement on the subject of sexuality in science fiction, but by this time Kvass is almost out of earshot and even if he was not, he could not care less. He solved the sexuality in science fiction convention a long time ago and has never seen it necessary to change his approach. Keep sex out of the fiction and in the social life and from this basic tension let the themes of megalomania flourish.

"Yes indeed, yes indeed," Kvass murmurs, looking for the moment only for a small place to put himself for a little while but, remembering that his room is sealed off and under constant surveillance, decides that his options are somewhat limited. He decides to take up the girl fan on her offer. The whole thing is to stay resourceful.

IX

The first world science fiction convention was held in New York City in 1939. A group of New York fans who had, by corresponding with one another through the nineteen-thirties, set up a loose network or organizations called "fan clubs" decided that they would like to meet the professional writers who had been tenanting the magazines through which the fans had originally gotten in touch with one another. The convention was moderately successful and had an attendance of some two hundred. It was decided at that time that the convention would become an annual institution to be moved among the cities of the United States.

By the mid-forties the convention had doubled in attendance in an alcoholic content and had become internationalized through plans to hold it in London at some time in the near future and in a foreign country once every five or six years thereafter.

In the early nineteen-fifties the fan awards were instituted. Now the convention included a formal banquet during which the Generation of Fandom awarded plaques in several categories: best writer, best short story writer, best old writer, best newcoming writer, best fan writer, best fan publisher, best artist, most renowned public figure, best politician and so on. The plaques, nicknamed "Lupowitzes" after the last name of the originator of the idea, soon became highly coveted in the field of science fiction. Sanford Kvass, in collaboration with Marcus Stein, won a Lupowitz in 1963: the Boilermaker award for the best new writer of the year. The "boilermaker" is a bar term for a drink composed of whiskey with a beer chaser and the reason why this particular subdivision of the Lupowitz was so named has not been determined.

By the early nineteen-sixties average attendance at world science fiction conventions had moved over the one thousand mark and the activities of the conventions had become ritualized. The panels, masquerade ball, magazine tables and so on were listed in a full program with specific locations and/or times, and a commission was demanded by the convention committee in order to participate in the regularized activities of the convention. Also, at around this time, Sanford Kvass discovered that a world science fiction convention was a place in which one could get laid; it was nothing exceptional—in terms of the opportunities and possibilities offered it was somewhere midway between a whorehouse and a rather energetic church picnic— but it opened up an entirely new chain of circumstance through which to clamber through three days of one's life. Even if most of the contacts were hurried and with people who you could just as easily have been doing it with years before, it still offered a certain baroque reassurance that one's alternatives were not totally closed off with the selection of profession.

By 1970, the world science fiction convention had celebrated the twenty-fifth anniversary of the bombing of Dresden by taking place in Heidelberg and a wondrous modern chain of communications was utilized for the first time to speed the news of the winners of the Lupowitzes and minor awards to the mainland of the United States.

Shortly thereafter, the world science fiction convention broke the five thousand mark in attendance for the first time—there were six thousand and thirty-one in attendance at the New England convention in 1971—and it soon became apparent that the original two hundred (all of whom were still alive) had given birth to something whose time at last had come.

There are seventeen thousand people in attendance at the world science fiction convention at the Hotel Northport. Slightly over half of them are actual registrants, paying a fee of twenty dollars to be entered in the convention rollbook with their names inscribed against a number for eternity. Slightly over half of this half have contrived, somehow, to find residence in the twenty-three story hotel during the period of the convention. Exactly how this has been managed—and particularly in the face of a room on the fourth floor (capable of sleeping fourteen) having been closed up by police security for the duration—is hard to determine. It is a triumph in geometry, spatial relations and the intricate science of physics which would have been appreciated by any of the pulp magazine editors in the nineteen-thirties who started the whole thing by giving letter space in their magazines … and permitting correspondents to insert their addresses at the end of the letters so that they would be able, somehow, to get in touch with one another.

Perhaps, Kvass thinks as he lays the girl in room six-fifty-four (she is really a hell of a good lay although somewhere she has managed to pick up a number of tics, nervous responses and sub-vocalizations which he finds quite alarming as he moves toward centrality), perhaps the whole thing would never have come about if the editors' publishers had not been greedy and decided to capitalize on the monomania of science fiction readers by using their letters to fill up a lot of free space. Perhaps if the publishers had had a spirit of adventure, and had decided to spring another twenty-five dollars on publication for a ten thousand word novelette, these seventeen thousand would, all ignorant of one another, be scattered through the bedrooms, the lecture halls and the cocktail lounges of a nation, only a strange wandering expression around the eyes in odd moments indicative of a certain sense of loss.

No, Kvass thinks, plunging all the way into the girl in room six-fifty-four, feeling her relax at last into a compromising rhythm, *no, it wouldn't have worked out anyway*. It is only a false hope suspended on the discredited alternate-universe theory. Somehow they would have gotten together. Somehow they would have found one another. Somehow, the whole thing would have been reconstructed in exactly this way toward this end so that Sanford Kvass, at the end of any cycle of time, would be in this room with this girl in this posture, shouting his bemusement into the night, wondering if there had been another way to look at it, ever. He doubts it. This he doubts extremely.

He wonders if the aliens had anything to do, in the first place, with the publishers, the editors, and the letter columns.

X

The girl is named Laurette Coombs, but would rather be called Laurie. She was born in 1945 which was the year that her mother had seen *The Glass Menagerie* and had been very impressed by the lead actress, Laurette Taylor. Though this puts her age as somewhat over twenty-five, she does not want to be identified with the older generation in any way whatsoever. Actually, she was born again six years ago, when she was nineteen, and worked into an entirely different lifestyle. By any reckoning whatsoever then she is six years old and has nothing to do with conventional people of her age who are, by this time, already half-dead.

"Tell me," she says to Kvass who, not really concerned with the matter, is working mournfully on his pipe again on the easy chair, trying to put the experience into perspective. "Tell me the truth. I can take it. Am I good? Am I a good lay? I mean, I don't care what you say; I have the confidence within myself and you can't hurt me no matter how it comes out. But am I good in bed? Have you ever enjoyed sex as much? Be honest. If you have, tell me. Oh, I guess I'm being a little uncool but you've got to let the whole thing out, that's all there is to it, until you can come to terms—"

"You were okay," Kvass says and puts the pipe between his leaden jaws, tries to look stolid and judicial. "You were fine."

"Well, that's good. It's very important for me to hear you say that although I don't want you to lie."

"That's okay," Kvass says. "Really, you were fine." He readjusts his garments which have been rather hastily reapplied since Laurette has advised him that her "friend" who is also "rooming with her for these days" has a way of showing up at odd times in her room on any pretext and since he is "very unsure really of his masculine image" she doesn't want to "upset him." "Fine," Kvass says. "You were fine." He tries to move from the chair, but finds an easy, oozing reluctance of limbs, the contours of the chair fit him perfectly and it is surprising how much at this moment he merely wants to sit. "Don't worry about it," he adds.

"Are you at the convention too?" she says after an uneasy pause, examining herself rather abstractedly in the mirror while she does something with her peasant dress. "I could swear that I saw you down the stairs just a while ago. Didn't I?"

"You invited me up here."

"Oh yeah," she says. "That's right. I asked you to come up here. You or your friend. Well, that was just kind of kidding around if you know what I mean. Not that I mind you being up here. That's fine. Have you, uh, like read science fiction for a long time? It's my thing. Really, I never knew a freakier bunch of people."

"I write it."

"Oh, then you're an editor?"

"Listen, Laurie," Kvass says. "I have a problem. You see, I was visited by some aliens about four weeks ago; they said that they were going to infiltrate one of their number in disguise into this world science fiction convention and that the one in disguise would be assuming the role of almost anyone and I had to detect him. If I didn't, if I couldn't establish where the alien was, who was the one only pretending to be human and actually an alien, they were going to destroy the planet. I was just a testee, you see. The whole thing was an examination, although of course there were these big consequences."

"What a *groove*."

"So I figured that I might as well go along with it because, who knows, the aliens might be telling the truth and then that would be the end of the world which is the only world we know. But I've been running into some real problems since the convention began. I don't know *who* the hell the alien is. It could be anyone and as you say it's a weird crowd. Do you have any ideas how we might be able to find out?"

"Jesus," the girl says and leans back in the chair, folds her arms at the line of her forehead, permits her breasts to thrust forward as her eyes retract. "Jesus, that's really a tough one, isn't it? Having an alien in the convention and all. I wouldn't know what to tell you."

"It's probably a practical joke or a hallucination, you see, but just in case it isn't, I think that something should be done. Anyway, I don't know if I can afford to take the chance of seeing the planet destroyed or not. You understand the dilemma?"

"Oh sure," Laurette Coombs says. "Of course I do. Boy, you're really in the middle, aren't you? This is my second convention, but actually I think of it only as the first because when I went seven years ago I wasn't born yet. It's quite something."

"What do you suggest, Laurette?"

"Well, you could like go around to people checking them out. I guess an alien wouldn't look like the rest of us, right? Listen, there's no point in you looking at me like that; there's no way we can make love again. Bobby's due to walk in any second and I'll have to explain how you got here, let alone everything else. So you can just put that thought out of your head even though I can see in your eyes that that's the only thing you're thinking of."

"That's perfectly all right, Laurette," Kvass says. "I wasn't really thinking of it. So you think I should just check out people carefully and find out by appearance."

"Yeah, well sure. Bobby thinks that I'm promiscuous, but he just doesn't understand me. I can't feel sure of myself yet in a one-to-one relationship and I want to keep all my options open for the time being. I have so much to do before I can settle in. It isn't being promiscuous, though, the thing has to be meaningful to me."

"The point is that the alien looks exactly like anyone else. In fact, he *is* anyone else. You see, what they did—"

"Of course," Laurette Coombs says, "if you just wanted me to sit on your lap for a few minutes and just sort of *neck,* I don't see how Bobby could possibly object to that. It would be a simple, harmless, friendly gesture and it's about time that he began to understand that he didn't *own* me yet or something like that."

One way or the other Kvass will get the issue out and presented to this girl; it is time that he told someone what was going on. He continues with a kind of monomania: "What they did was to abduct someone and substitute the alien for them and the alien looks exactly like this person, so it's very hard—"

"Oh, sure," Laurette Coombs says, coming over to Kvass and sitting on his lap. She is a thin girl but with a certain blocky muscularity around the thighs; her sudden pressure causes him to gasp and he has the feeling of being impaled upon the chair. "I dig that. There was a story about that once, wasn't there? There were these aliens, you see, who could imitate anyone and what they did was to go up to this place around the North Pole and then—"

She puts her mouth against his and begins to kiss Kvass very insistently. It is surprising how much energy she has left although, to be sure, women are constructed differently. "Oh your mouth drives me *wild,*" she mumbles. "I could tell right away when I saw you that you had this terrific mouth—"

"Umph," says Kvass and does his best to return the kiss in a manner which will indicate that he *is* sealed off. Business is business, after all; he still has to get to the center of the matter. He feels her tongue graze against his, feels breasts begin to rise toward his neck from the vicinity of his chest, mumbles, finds a small core of response hidden within him after all (although at some time in the past he would not have been surprised at, you are young). He puts his hands on her, his arms all around her, thrusts his thighs, begins to feel a tortuous connection; it is interesting what you can take for granted, impossible as this may be. Thoughts of the aliens depart from his mind, considerations of the convention and his own predicament begin to drift away. He exposes the thin but hanging breasts of Laurette Coombs and begins to work upon them and at that moment there is a sound at the door, creak of wood, turning of knob. He looks up from his disadvantageous position to find that he is being looked at by a thin ascetic looking man of forty or so, bright eyes glinting madly between enormous sideburns, a hint of dandruff on the shoulders of his double-breasted suit which he pulls more tightly around him.

"What is this?" the ascetic looking man says. "Is this what I *think* it is?"

"Oh Bobby," Laurette Coombs says and breaks the connection with Kvass to revolve on his lap. "Don't be ridiculous."

"What are you doing? Tell me what you are *doing?*" Bobby says and begins, clumsily, to remove his jacket, glaring at Kvass. "I know you," he says. "I've seen you around. You're that nut who walks around in medieval costume and waves a sword at everyone. I'm going to kill you for this."

"You don't understand," Kvass says. He *is* beginning to get a little mad. Nothing at this convention seems to be quite under his control; a certain fine sense of situation which has kept him going for decades has deserted him over this Labor Day weekend. "I'm not that person at all. You're thinking of my ex-collaborator, Marcus Stein. We look a little bit alike but we have nothing to do with one another."

"All right, Stein," Bobby says, tossing the jacket over a chair and beginning inexpertly to work on his cuff. "We'll just take care of that right now."

"Oh come on, Bobby," Laurette says, getting to her feet with some assistance from Kvass's lap which palpitates in the moment of release although in no sexual fashion. "I know that you've got this masculinity block and all this insecurity and so on but it's very immature to carry on this way, don't you think?"

"My name isn't Stein," Kvass points out "Stein is another guy. My name is Kvass. I don't have anything to do with him."

"Let's go, Stein," Bobby says and begins to dance in front of Kvass, weaving up and down on his heels, balancing precariously, moving a clumsy left jab in the vicinity of an eye, which breaks off to become a scratching gesture on the forehead. "Let's just settle this whole thing now, man to man."

"Get this man away from me, Laurette," Kvass says. He is in the act of looking for his shoes, which seem to be underneath the bed. As he bends over for them, Bobby lands a light tap in the area of his kidney and emits a scream of triumph. "I'm getting you, Stein!" he shrieks. "I'm going to even the score, now."

"What can I do?" Laurette says and shrugs. "I told you that we would have this. I warned you to keep away from me but you wouldn't listen."

"It's unfair," Kvass says, sticking a foot into a shoe, feeling a palm brush the back of his neck. "It's unfair."

"Well, there's nothing I can do, Sanford, you have to work it out yourself. I'm going to the bathroom."

"You didn't even listen to me," he says, putting on the other shoe, using his buttocks to bounce Bobby away from him. "You didn't hear a word I said."

"Sure I did. About the alien and all. I thought it was very interesting. I just don't know what I can tell you to do about it, though."

"No one listens," Kvass says angrily as Laurette takes a dress from the closet and, humming, goes into the bathroom. "No one at all. Goddamnit, isn't there any way to get control of the situation?" He turns reaches toward Bobby, seizes the man by the folds of his shirt and shakes him into attention. "Will you listen to me?" he says.

"I can't. I can't listen to you right now, I'm trying to fight you, Stein."

"Oh the hell with this," Kvass says with fury and hurls Bobby on the recently-used bed; he lands, buttocks-first, in a damp spot and bounces querulously, then subsides with a moan. Kvass takes his jacket from the closet, puts it on, finds his pipe, adjusts his tie. "You're not reasonable!" he says. "The trouble with you people is that you simply aren't reasonable and the whole thing is going to catch up with you soon. Don't you care? Don't you care at all?"

He leaves the room in a fury, not bothering to close the door. It is really too much for him; he does not understand how these people live. Halfway down the hall he recollects the plot of the story which Laurette had reminded him of, but it hardly seems to do him any good at all. In the story they had used a blood test and then a flaming drill to get rid of the aliens and this is one piece of equipment which he doubts he will be able to find at a world science fiction convention.

The alien pops out of a corridor and attempts to intercept him. Kvass cuts through without breaking a stride. "Oh for God's sake," he says. "You can see now that I'm willing to try but it isn't easy; you've got to let me do this my own way. You selected the wrong territory. Now if you want me to cooperate, you leave me alone and let me do it *my* way. Your way has gotten us in a mess, that's all, and it's your own goddamned administrative problem. You want me to handle this, let me handle it," Kvass says and strides away, leaving the alien for once nonplussed and without further comment. Kvass neatly cuts a corner into the service elevator and is gone.

XI

He spends the remainder of the afternoon walking alone through the garment district, returning to the hotel only in time for the gigantic masquerade ball which is the official high-point of the first part of the convention. Sunken within him is the glimmerings of an idea, but he does not want to touch it for the time being. His best ideas, when he used to be a writer, were always subconscious and spontaneously generated and there was no way to hurry them along without losing them.

The garment center, on a summer Saturday, is hot and deserted with a permeating smell of animal musk and cloth cutting the air. It is not what you would call an aesthetically provocative place, but then it is away from the hotel while being within walking distance and Kvass has always had a moderate interest in cloaks and suits. He feels that his whole life might have turned out differently if he had followed upon his instincts in adolescence and become a coat cutter.

A few prostitutes, walking the district on a Saturday afternoon for no reasons which Kvass can understand, peep at him shy from the alcoves of closed luncheonettes and occasionally offer him forthright speculation. He pushes by all of this; he has nothing against prostitutes who strike him as being forthright people doing a difficult social service well within their limited ability, but he has, for the moment, had all the sex he can handle and perhaps a little more than that and he can complicate his life at this instant with a further stab at a Mature Relationship. One, or possibly two of the prostitutes, have a resemblance to Katie Elizabeth Templeton and in the instants before his mind can make the adjustment he finds this perfectly reasonable as well; why should she not? What would be bizarre about Katie Elizabeth Templeton hitting the outside of the hotel for a few hours in the interests of a little action and some extra royalty rates? It would certainly be as sane an act as that of writing books about rockets for consumption by adolescents; probably even more sane than that. One thing which distinguishes the prostitute is realism or at least a certain simulated sense of realism and this is all, Kvass decides, that science fiction could use at the present time. The moon landing has complicated the affair; it is time that the field got down to issues and told them what rockets could do to their lives. But there is a very small hope that this will work out and, strictly speaking, Kvass is a pulp writer himself and not really allied with that segment of the field which believes that science fiction must be self-destructive in order to survive. This does not seem to make too much sense either.

"No thank you," the most promising new writer of 1963, now somewhat gnarled and confused, says to a particularly insistent prostitute (a rather matronly woman in furs and jewels who looks as if she has unwittingly stayed overtime for the Friday bookkeeping rush and is now quite sure exactly how she is going to pass the time through Monday) and goes into an open coffee shop, one of the few in the district that exists between Friday and Monday. It is time for some coffee after his very brisk walk and perhaps some more thought. Seated at the counter, however, is V. V. Vivaldi, staring at an empty water glass with a peculiar look of contemplation upon his face. Kvass turns rapidly to leave the coffee shop, unspotted by Vivaldi in mid-vault. So much for good intentions.

"Hey," says the dean of the rocketry school, churning his spoon in the coffee cup so violently that liquid oozes out over the counter. "Hey you, come here! Come here, boy! I know who you are! Here!" Vivaldi says in a quavering voice and Kvass goes. He has seen V. V. Vivaldi, off and on in his latter stage for many years and finds avoidance the only real way to deal with him…. But there was another time, not many years before then, when Vivaldi was in Stage I and an eleven-year-old Sanford Kvass would have gone several miles or at least across the room to perform any service for the grand old man. This is not the kind of thing which one can shake easily. The trouble with science fiction, as a matter of fact, is that it is still a one-generation field; virtually everybody who ever wrote or edited it is still writing or editing the stuff today. This unique feeling of compression makes the principles unable to maintain any kind of dignified distance, although more often or not they carry on then only like cats in a barrel.

"All right," Kvass says, and sits next to the dean of programming therapy. "What can I do for you?"

"You can have a cup of coffee and keep an old man company," Vivaldi says. He leans over the counter, distends an elbow and gives Kvass a full, foul whiff of his breath: it occurs to him that V. V. Vivaldi is drunk. Thick fumes of gin mingle with the steam from the coffee cup and assault Kvass mightily; he shakes his head and grapples with the counter for support. "Go on," Vivaldi says to the counterman who has appeared to glare malevolently at both of them. "Give this young man a cup of coffee. What's your problem, son? You don't look well."

"I'm not feeling so hot," Kvass says. "It's nothing personal, but I'm just not feeling so good." He fumbles for his pipe which he finds is already in his jaws and bites down on it hard enough to sever the already weakened stem. The bowl falls with an ominous *plop!* to the counter and then into Kvass's lap. "Goddamnit anyway," he says.

"You too," Vivaldi says with utmost understanding as the counterman, groaning, puts a cup of coffee with a crash before them. "I haven't been feeling so well for two days, son. You were on the panel with me, weren't you? I remember you."

"That's right."

"You were the only one who talked any goddamned sense there. Pack of fools and liars. They used to come around in nineteen-forty and ask me for my autograph; now they don't have a thing to say to the old man. Go on, stir your coffee, son; you don't want it to get cold. Drink it while it's hot, that acts as a sealant for the gastric humors and blocks the bad charge out. The charge doesn't get into your central nervous system that way."

"All right," Kvass says, lifting the cup with a shaking hand and taking it to his lips. He does not seem to be entirely present at this meeting; his mind, wildly abstracted, is instead concerned with prostitutes. Prostitutes, Kvass finds himself thinking, are paperback while affairs are hardcover. There's little future in paperback, but on the other hand you can take a quick deal without any of the complications. Of course, you can wind up in paperback and then, where has love gone? All of the paperback prostitutes on West Thirty-seventh Street, being angled for a fast deal.

"Going to tell you something," Vivaldi says. "Got to talk to someone; I can't take the suspense anymore. No man is an island, that's the truth of it, you've got to make contact sooner or later, you got to talk to your fellow man. Drink your coffee, son, you're trembling."

But then, of course, if you take the fast deal with the paperback prostitute you're just filling in time, just going from month to month. There are no royalties or increment with paperback. On the other hand, who has the time to angle for hardcover? Then too, hardcover can be a worse deal than paperback unless you get some kind of an edge or a break in the reviews. Most affairs end dismally and are more expensive than simple relationships with prostitutes. "Paperback prostitutes," Kvass mumbles and then, embarrassed, plunges his head into the coffee cup. The counterman looks at him and Vivaldi with great interest and decides at that moment that the counter needs a fast wiping with a dirty rag.

"Must tell you," Vivaldi says, "been having trouble with hallucinations. Hallucinations and aliens. Now, I don't believe in any of it. I just don't think that it exists, despite the business, but these aliens came to me just a few weeks ago and they said, 'Victor!' That happens to be my name, Victor, Victor Vance Vivaldi, but Steele wanted me to use the initials; it had an easier recall factor or something. 'Victor,' they said, 'you have been appointed on a mission of great importance, to save your home planet. It so happens that at the world science fiction convention we are going to infiltrate one of our number'—they meant an alien you see—'in human disguise and it will be your job, Victor, to deduce'—that means to figure out—'who the alien is. If you do not we will destroy your planet but, Victor, if you cooperate with us and do find out the identity of the alien who will look just like anyone else demanding great shrewdness and cunning on your part, if you do that, Victor, then we will be forced to conclude that you've got yourself a pretty shrewd and intelligent little race there and we won't bother you further. The fate of humanity lies in your hands!' they say to me and then they go away. Now I never heard of such foolishness in my life, but it kind of sticks in your mind, you know what I mean? I mean if you've been writing science fiction all your life you just can't push these things away as easily as you might want to otherwise. One way or the other it stays in the head. Well, I tried to program it out but that really didn't work; the point of programming therapy is fast serenity, you see, and I'm not serene. So you see, son, I've spent the last two days walking around trying to find an alien and at my age I just don't think that this kind of thing will work anymore. I'm beginning to feel ridiculous, as a matter of fact. Now you tell me where I could find an alien, how you're supposed to *tell* and maybe I could do something. I'm taking you into my confidence, of course. I wasn't supposed to tell anyone."

Kvass has been listening to this in a state of some suspension over the coffee cup. When Vivaldi has finished he notices that the counterman also has been plugged into the conversation although at some remove and now, jaw open, is very delicately trying to move away from proximity in such a way that he will attract as little attention as possible. "Oh," Kvass says, as one alternative in a series of responses. "Oh. I see."

"You have any ideas, son?" Vivaldi asks and takes off his steel-frame glasses to wipe them. "Appreciate anything you might have on your mind."

"Not exactly," says Kvass. "You say that they told you you had to find the alien and that the whole fate of mankind depended upon your ability to pass this test and that you would carry the responsibility?"

"Something like that. They had a very good way of phrasing it I forget now, but it was effective. It was very much like some of the dialogue I used to write as a matter of fact. Of course, I don't believe in that anymore, I'm trying to do a newer, more serious kind of fiction, but so few people care about being given things the hard way. They just want to hear the same things from you they heard thirty years ago. Isn't that the truth? Of course, you're not really a writer so you wouldn't understand that. It's a writer's problem."

"I've got to leave now," says Kvass.

"I didn't mean to insult you. Hey, son, listen to me, what am I going to do about that alien?"

"No, really," Kvass says, consumed by an urgency moving through all of the interstices; beginning with warmth in the soles of his feet and then moving out madly to embrace all sections. "No, it has nothing to do with that. My feelings aren't hurt or anything. I just have to go."

"Stay and listen to me."

"I can't," Kvass says. He beckons to the counterman, finds a dollar bill in his pocket and hurls it on the counter. "This should take care of everything," he says. "Shouldn't it?"

"Get a net," the counterman says, taking the dollar bill with a twisted move of the arm, looking at him with some terror as he holds his body away from proximity. "That's what I say, get a net."

"You're really not going to stop and help me, son? Here I am, drunk as a coot, and you won't even help an old man to bed. Help me to bed, son, forget about the aliens. I really need some help."

"No," Kvass says, trembling with the responsibility of giving refusal to a Grand Master for the first time in his life. "No, I can't help you, I have things to do. You'll be all right. Just hold your head in your hands for a while with your eyes closed and when things stop spinning you'll be in shape to stand and walk. Take it from me, I've gone through it hundreds of times."

"A net," the counterman says, retreating, "or maybe I'm thinking of some kind of a truck. Yeah, a truck would be better; you can put bars on it and that way they would have a lot of trouble getting outside. That's what I vote for, a big truck with bars on it, just like the movies."

"*Hundreds* of times," Kvass says frantically. He retrieves his broken pipe; places the two pieces in his right pocket. Vivaldi slumps over with an expression so woebegone that Kvass feels moved, genuinely moved for the very first time under the auspices of this world science fiction convention. "Listen," he says, leaning over the old man and taking his thin shoulders in his palm. "Listen to me. It's not only your responsibility. I heard from them too."

"Heard from them?"

"The aliens. I heard from the aliens with the same proposal that you did. They must have spoken to a lot of us that weekend. There must be a lot of people with exactly the problem you have. Listen, I'll take care of it from here on in. It's not your worry anymore."

"Oh thank you, son," V. V. Vivaldi says and begins to cry, very neatly, into the speckled backs of his hands. "Oh, you don't know what this means to me. I just appreciate so much—"

"It's okay. There are others behind you. We will carry the burden. Relax. Be of good cheer."

"That's my vote," the counterman says with some satisfaction, as if he has resolved a matter of great difficulty and duration in a way which will irrevocably change his life. "That would solve the situation. First a net with big stripes to catch them and then the truck with bars. And after the truck with bars I think a nice thick room somewhere with padding on the walls and so on, so that when they get violent they can't hurt anyone, not even themselves. That would be the best way of handling it. Of course, you got to think of drugs too; they done wonders with this modern drug therapy. I think they're entitled to the same chance that we are."

Kvass turns and flees the luncheonette. The door closes behind him with a thump. Three prostitutes spot him and come from all angles to surround and proposition him. A driverless taxi, abandoned by its owner with the motor running, engages suddenly into gear and lurches toward him, seeking to run him down. Three strands of smoke, wafted from three separate building incinerators, converge at a point somewhere near his nose and force their foul vapors cruelly into his nasal passages. A malevolent beggar with a long iron cane waves the implement in his face and demands all of his money. A crone in a flowered hat hurls herself at his feet to solicit contributions to the Mother of Mercy Shrine in Denver, Colorado. A plank of wood from a burning building across the street sails through the air on a collision course with his goatee.

None of this deters Kvass. He is, for the first time in months, seized by purpose. Unconscious of all obstacles, he dodges to his left, strides to his right, gestures toward the center and proceeds. The taxicab, prostitutes, beggar, crone and plank of wood fall away from him as if ash. Only the threads of smoke remain, lodged now in his lungs, causing him to cough slightly with exertion as he propels himself forward. The pollution problem is omnipresent, of course, and has nothing to do with the effectuation of our daily lives, not to say the major crises.

XII

Armed with the knowledge of the aliens' treachery, Kvass returns to the hotel full of determination, but at the hotel itself he realizes that the true outlines of his problem have still evaded him. In the first place, the aliens seem to make appointments only at their own choosing and then in a rather peremptory fashion and he is in a poor position to summon the leader and have it out. In the second place, the hotel is now sealed off by a cordon of armed police who brandish clubs and demand full identification when he returns (he passes, although just barely; one of the policemen makes a suggestive comment), meaning that the convention is now somewhat limited in scope. The influx of people has now stopped and there is a certain staticity about affairs now that the seventeen thousand have gotten to know one another rather all too well. In the third place, the attention of almost everyone is now engaged by the massive Masquerade and Costume Ball which is being held in the master ballroom on the third tier above the hotel's lobby.

It is to the masquerade that Kvass feels himself drawn—the only people who do not attend it are embittered losers from last year or uncomprehending professionals like V. V. Vivaldi. There at least he will be able to deal with some people and obtain some direct answers. By the time he manages to work his way past the Committee on Credentials some of the purposefulness has washed off him. It is so difficult, after all, to accomplish any raising of the consciousness of science fiction people and never more difficult than when they are about to engage in the gigantic masquerade-and-costume party which is for so many of them the highlight of the year. Outside the door hundreds of contestants are arrayed in full costume, waiting for the masquerade to begin so that they can enter one by one, move down the aisle and display themselves on stage for a period of twenty seconds. They look at Kvass and any other normally-attired person who enters the room with fury; the Committee on Credentials has been particularly difficult, refusing Kvass admission for lack of proper identification. He raises the issue of the Boilerplate Award and even invokes some of his other credentials and successes in the field, but the committee, four or five adolescents in white robes with bedazzled eyes, seem dissatisfied and tell Kvass that he will have to check the question of his admission upstairs. They cannot randomly admit people unknown to them who might be harmless and then again might be equipped with flamethrowers to incinerate the dress of contestants (this has never happened but there have been a few mailed and telephone threats received on this order, mostly from disgruntled losers in the past).

He is saved and admitted to the masquerade as a matter of fact only through coincidence. The convention chairman appears at the table while Kvass is arguing, now hopelessly, and recognizing him says, "Sanford, we need a judge. Would you fill in?"

"Fill in?"

"Bill Culp quit. He said that he had other things to do and we're out a member of the committee. Will you fill in?"

"I've never judged a masquerade before," Kvass says hesitantly. "I don't know whether or not I could do a fair job."

"No one's got any experience," the chairman says. Excitation causes a stammer to flood into his voice; he gesticulates rather unsteadily. "Look, Mr. Kvass," he says, "you've got to help. I can't carry all the responsibility for this alone. I haven't had a moment's rest since this whole thing started. We've got the hotel under cordon, the entire treasury's been stolen, the hotel is going to sue and is trying to evict already and the least you can do, goddamnit, is to judge a goddamned masquerade. I've got enough trouble as it is; I've got to get some cooperation."

"I had plans," Kvass says. "I just wanted to *look*—" but before he can say anything more he finds himself in the grip of the chairman, who in turn has signaled a small group of fan marshals. Kvass is being transported to the platform rapidly, his heels hardly seeming to hit the floor as he is shoved panting into a seat "I really appreciate this," the chairman says. "I appreciate everything you're doing for us. It will only take an hour or so anyway; we're going to rush them right through this year. Some of the costumes are flammable and they're trying to get an ordinance against us."

Kvass sits uneasily, looking at the tumult in front of him. In any event being put on the judges' platform has given him a small enclosed cave of space, probably more space than he could have negotiated otherwise. He sighs, stretches his legs, decides that he will do what he can to get through the next hour. In any event, he will be thinking all the time. He turns to his right, sees Stanley Lupowitz, who with enormous concentration and a great deal of facility is drawing an obscene picture upon a sheet of notebook paper given for the judging. The doodle appears to be feminine but just as Kvass decides that he understands the root basis of the Lupowitz obsession, Stanley adds an enormous genital in the dead center of his drawing, turning it into something else.

Turning to Kvass, beaming, he whispers the name of Michael Foote, then pencils in that name above the drawing. "That's what I think of *him,*" Lupowitz says with a flashing grin. Then his expression turns vague; his mouth seems to turn down at the corners and he says, "Haven't I seen you around somewhere before?"

"I'm a judge," Kvass says.

"Yes, I know that, but I have the feeling that I've seen you somewhere *else,*" Lupowitz says and then turns over his sheet of paper, shakes his head and returns to doodling. This time he begins matters with a rocket ship which, except for portholes and some lettering on the sides, appears strikingly close to the genital which he has just drawn.

Kvass feels that he has taken the relationship with Lupowitz, perhaps, as far as it can go at the present time and turns to his left, where he sees Katie Elizabeth Templeton looking at him fixedly. A glaze in her eyes suggests the fact that she has been looking at him for quite a while. "I wondered if you'd ever notice," she says, "or if you were going to make believe I didn't exist."

"Look, Katie—" Kvass says.

"I've found out a number of interesting things about you, Kvass. I've heard a lot about you in the last day. Everybody seems to know something. All I can say is that I have no idea why I was associating with a person like you—"

"Look, Katie," Kvass tries again. "I'm just here to judge the contest. There really isn't any point in rehashing—"

"Oh, there's nothing to rehash," she says with enormous satisfaction. "There is absolutely *nothing* to discuss. I've heard some very interesting things about you, Kvass, and I've managed to tell a few interesting things about you, too. A lot of people were very interested in what I had to say. I don't know if you understand or care but it so happens that I command a lot more respect and audience in this field than you do at the present time. People pay a great deal more attention to me than they do to you. You thought that you could take advantage of me, but you were absolutely wrong because the fact is—"

"Katie," Kvass says, somewhat desperately. "Katie, I've got to *think.* I'm sorry if I did anything to hurt your feelings and I'll certainly make it up to you somehow, some way, if I can later, but there isn't anything to discuss now because what I've got to do—"

"Don't you worry about that," she says somewhat ominously. "You'll have all the time in the world to think, Kvass. You'll have nothing *but* time. Nobody gets away with doing to me what you did. I told you that I would get even with you and I have."

"How?"

"Never mind," says Katie Elizabeth Templeton and leans over him, begins to engage Stanley Lupowitz in animated conversation.

It seems that Lupowitz will be doing a chapter on Katie for his proposed volume *Diaries of the Modern Masters* and Katie is making sure that the magazine serial rights will be protected for her own use. This is agreeable to Lupowitz, or so it appears, but in return Katie must guarantee that she will hold off from all other interviews to competitors until the first paperback edition of his book is published. This will guarantee the exclusivity of his material and enable him to tap the British market which, as everyone knows, is presently very hungry for intimate biographies of the major science fiction writers of America.

"Do you want to interview me?" Kvass asks on impulse, while watching the scurrying of the marshals around the doors, trying to close off further entrances. He identifies himself carefully to Lupowitz until he sees connection made. There seems to be much excitement in the vicinity of the panels; the closed doors bulge from the pressure of bodies. The hotel, apparently, is not very well constructed.

"Of course not," Katie Elizabeth Templeton says. "Stanley is doing a book on current major writers."

"I really don't think so," Lupowitz says. "You really don't have much of a reputation nowadays. You've tailed off, you really have."

"I'll say he has."

"No, let me handle this, Katie. The thing is, Sanford, you made quite an impressive debut and a lot of us have been looking forward to good things from you. It's quite clear now that you're never going to live up to your promise. Your stuff is getting quite repetitious and dull."

"I've been exploring my themes in greater depth," Kvass says sullenly. "Of course, you wouldn't understand that."

"You've been repeating yourself, Sanford. And a lot of the stuff has been terribly weak and imitative. Of course, I'm just trying to help you in saying this. If you're going to take offense—"

"Michael Foote is the only real critic of science fiction," Kvass says somewhat artlessly. "You're not a critic. You're not even a biographer. You're just a grown-up fan. You have no standing whatsoever within our field."

"That's sour grapes, Sanford."

"Besides that," says Michael Foote, who has, sometime during this discussion, insinuated himself among them and is now standing to the rear of the table, a sardonic twinkling expression in his somewhat maddened eyes, "Sanford, the fact is that your stuff is really lousy. You haven't done any work worth mentioning for *so* long that it's very difficult to take you seriously."

"You tell them, Michael," Katie Templeton says. "You tell him what he is."

"You see what I mean?" says Stanley Lupowitz with a sad expression.

"I'm only telling you this for your own good, Sanford," Michael Foote points out.

"As far as I'm concerned, they *should* put the whole thing out of business, the sooner the better," Sanford Kvass exclaims.

"You've got to get hold of yourself, Kvass," says Stanley Lupowitz.

"It's too late for you to get hold of yourself," says Katie Templeton.

"I don't think that you've *ever* gotten hold of yourself," says Michael Foote.

"I don't think I can stand much more of this," says Sanford Kvass.

The convention chairman hoarsely calls the assemblage to order and demands that the festivities begin.

XIII

In the darkness, the stage lit only by strobes and the occasional beams of flashlights to help the contestants find their way, the masquerade assumes a different aspect. Ominous atonal music plays through a loudspeaker; the noise in the room slides toward a dull rumble. One by one, as their names and roles are announced, the participants in the grand masquerade slide through the doors and down the aisle, holding themselves in a stately dignity that seems to render them impervious to air currents, floor paneling or the gasps from the audience.

There are fans dressed like spaceships, fans dressed like monsters, fans dressed like trolls from *The Wizard of Izzinius,* fans dressed like fans in *Dwellers of the Deep,* fans ambulating themselves while holding small vehicles which are meant to be mock-ups of the proto-cars in the famous *Sands of Mars* series. It is an awesome spectacle and, even in his present difficulties, Kvass, as judge, would like to pay attention to it and render a disinterested, compassionate, professional judgment. It seems that he will have a bit of difficulty in doing this because between his opened calves underneath the table he feels a strange throbbing. When he looks down to swat the source of it, he finds that he is looking into the eyes of the alien who is crouched uncomfortably at his feet, trying to get his attention.

"Ah," the alien whispers hoarsely. "There you are, Kvass. I thought I'd never get your attention."

"You son of a bitch, everybody will see us," Kvass whispers harshly. "Get out of here."

"Don't worry about it, Sanford, nobody's paying attention. They're all watching the spectacle. Besides, we've really got to talk."

"Drop dead."

"No, Sanford," the alien mumbles with a whining appeal. "No, please, Sanford, we really *do*. We've got to settle this. Listen to me. I promise you, nobody will hear us. This is just between the two of us. Look, I'm being uncomfortable for you. Isn't that proof of some sincerity?"

"Traitor," Kvass says. "Miserable, lying son of a bitch. Double-dealer. Hypocritical bastard."

"I thought you'd take that attitude, Sanford," the alien says mournfully. "I knew that you were going to react that way. I admit that I had hopes, but all the time I knew that this would happen."

"Get away from me, you bastard," Kvass says and makes a slapping motion with his hand. Beside him, Stanley Lupowitz, seemingly somnolent, emits a tremendous belch and quivers, causing his obscene doodle to fall to the floor. The alien picks it up quickly and begins to smooth it with a nervous gesture, his tentacle covering the indelicate parts.

"I don't blame you, Sanford," he says. "Really, I'm quite sorry about the whole thing. It wasn't our intent to mislead you."

"You lied to me, you bastard. Now listen, I'm through with you. Get away from here or I'll kick you."

"I'm all shrunken and reduced, Sanford. You'd only hurt me very badly and it wouldn't change the situation at all. Besides, I can only suspend time a little bit more; my powers are ebbing. Don't you want to be reasonable?"

"You bastard," Kvass says again. He realizes that his speech has reached a certain level of low monomania, but it is not unsatisfying. He begins to fear that a good deal of his anger is feigned and that like a petulant child he is carrying things a bit past their purposes.

"We had to protect ourselves, Sanford," the alien says. "Of course we had to have other contacts. Just in case there was illness or a decision on the part of some of you not to participate in the test. You can't put all your eggs in the same kennel, you know. Is that the expression? But all along, you were our primary contact. You were the one we really counted on. The others were just back-up people, so to speak. You shouldn't doubt us, Sanford."

"How many others?"

"It doesn't matter."

"How many?"

"Maybe fifteen. That's all."

"Fifteen?"

"Or sixteen. Twenty at the tops. You were the one we had faith in."

"You did this to fifteen or twenty people? You mean, there are fifteen or twenty others and all of them have been through the same thing that I have?"

"Not all of them. Some of them haven't come. Quite a few lack sensitivity or any sense of altruism. It's surprising how high a percentage of you people simply don't care. In fact, I think that most of you *do* want the world to end. You're an exception, Sanford. You have a life-force."

"I'll get you for this," Kvass says. "I'll get you."

"It's too late for that now; don't you see that? It's too late in the game. Listen, Sanford, everyone else has quit or never got started to begin with. You see what happened to Vivaldi. Now, you're our last hope. If you don't try, then nobody will. Everything rests on you."

"You told me that already."

"But now it's the *truth,*" the alien says frantically and wiggles a bit between his calves, mottles in a rather disgusting way to distort the normally healthy green of its complexion. "It really is the truth, Sanford, and you've got to *do* something. I don't think you know the predicament we're in; we're a very small part of the sector. If we screw this thing up we'll be in a lot of trouble. You can't just wipe a planet out of the universe; you've got to have a clean report. If we don't we're going to have some serious complications; we may even get blacklisted. Who knows what may happen to us? A test, a fair test, Sanford, *please.* I'm *begging* you now. It's just me, just you, just the two of us. Can't we creature to creature come to terms? I think that I can guarantee you safe passage after the test. When you fail, I mean. The world will be destroyed but I think that we can take you in tow and get you into a Terran environment somewhere. There are lots of atmospheres in which you could live very happily and we can control the climate as well. And a lot of humanoid females. Try. You've got to try."

"You disgust me," Kvass says, and reaches below the table to give the alien a good yank. His exterior is rather slimy, but it is satisfying nevertheless. It feels something like inserting one's hand into the belly of a raw fish and seizing hold of some entrails. The alien emits a high squeal, then flops submissively under his hand.

"All right," it says. "I deserved that. I can understand that. You're upset. Of course. You have a perfect right—"

"You disgust me," Kvass says. "Furthermore, you've ruined my convention. I used to love these things; I haven't been able to think straight for three days. As a matter of fact, I haven't felt like myself since you came into my room the first time. You've wrecked everything, you've made me a different person and now you appeal to me. You're a lousy son of a bitch. What happens if I passed your test, huh? Aren't you afraid of that?"

"The test is insoluble, Sanford," the alien says quietly. "You know that. It is supposed to be. But we need the appearance of effort in order to remain clear with Headquarters. Headquarters does not really understand the nature of imperial conquest at all. They, uh, aren't that way. All that they want is some confirmation of a fair test. They have no way of knowing how the test is slanted or what the chances are. There, I've told you everything now. We're totally at your mercy."

"But what if I *did* pass your test? What if I found the alien for you? What then?"

"No one ever has, Sanford. No one."

"How many times have you done it?"

"Many," the alien says. "I can't continue. I can't hold back time. It's in your hands. I beg—"

"But what if I *did?* What if I *did?*"

"Well," the alien whispers unhappily, "if you did and of course you couldn't, then by the terms of the test *précis* we send to Headquarters, *we* would be destroyed, of course. A fair test and so on. An even chance either way. Win and we get you; you win and you get us. Of course that's all on paper. But Headquarters has orders to destroy our planet if that ever happened."

"All right," Kvass says, "enough of this. Get the hell out of here. I'll find your goddamned alien."

"Will you, Sanford? Will you try?"

"I didn't say I'd *try,* you stupid bastard," Kvass screams. "I said I'd *find* him!"

The lights flicker on and faces begin to turn toward him and voices start in the room again because the alien has vanished, leaving only a sweaty place on the floor underneath as evidence of his calling card. Kvass finds that he is being watched closely by many contestants, Stanley Lupowitz, Katie Templeton and the convention chairman. All of them are turning toward him and all of them are looking menacingly, but Kvass no longer cares. He has had enough of defensiveness. He has been defensive for too long and to no purpose and now, at last, the secret in his hands, the real Sanford Kvass can emerge. He understand everything.

He says to Katie Elizabeth Templeton, "Give me your compact."

"What?"

"I said give me your compact. Get into your goddamned handbag and take out your compact and give it to me."

"Sanford—"

"This is a masquerade ball," Stanley Lupowitz booms. "The high-point of the convention thus far. Sanford, have you gone out of your mind?"

"Give me your compact," Kvass says to Katie Elizabeth Templeton, "or I'll punch you in the teeth."

Her lip trembles. He has found the sweltering core of her. She reaches into her handbag which has been lying sprawled before her on the table and hands him a small silver case, marked with small scratches and recent sweat.

"I hate you," she says for no particular reason. "You've made my life miserable. I hate you."

"It's too late for that, Katie," Kvass says. "It's too late; we'll have to pick up the score in some other way." He takes the compact, holds it, weighs it, examines it carefully and then opens it to regard a small mirror which twinkles within, gathering the lights of the strobe and hurling them back into his eyes.

"Fine," Kvass says. He raises the compact. Stanley Lupowitz, afflicted by an insane impulse, attempts to deter him with a clumsy chop but Kvass ducks it, swings at Lupowitz himself and sends the dean of modern fandom with a crash to the floor. Contestants in glittering costume mill in the aisles, screaming. The chairman reaches for a gavel. Two sergeants at arms, their faces white and frightened, begin to advance upon him from the aisle.

"No," Kvass says and lifts a majestic hand. "No, stop," and they stop, sensing the power in him, although maybe he is merely self-absorbed or he misses the situation. That does not matter either. He hoists the compact, lifts it toward his face, looks at himself in the mirror.

In the mirror he sees the familiar Kvass face, the face he has known and dwelt with for some thirty-five years, still solemn, a bit gross, sad-eyed for pain and the lack of a pipe and with a strange gleam in the back of the eyes which he should have seen and understood a long time ago if he hadn't been so damned self-absorbed, if he had kept some mirrors in his apartment.

"All right," Kvass says. He takes a deep breath. *"Ave atque vale."* He looks at himself for an instant longer, seeing everything in the mirror then: his block, his pain, his confusion, his loss of control, his misunderstanding, his manipulation, his failure with Katie Templeton, his failure with Laurie Coombs, his failure with Michael Foote; seeing all of it and seeing in his revealed eyes that on whatever level he not only asks but grants forgiveness. All is forgiven. All is understood.

"Okay," Kvass says and steels himself. "Okay. *Unmask.*"

The alien unmasks.

There is a great deal of tumult in the masquerade hall and the convention comes to a stricken if sensational end. Of the exact nature of the end of the convention, or what role it will play eventually in the lexicon of conventions, or what the histories will write of this convention, or what happens to Katie Elizabeth Templeton and Stanley Lupowitz at this convention, or any other part of it … of all this, Kvass will know nothing. Considering the way that things were going in his career when the whole goddamned thing broke open over him, this is probably for the very best.

THE END

THE PRESENT ETERNAL
By Barry N. Malzberg

Wollheim never said a kind word about *Dwellers of the Deep* but kind words were not his specialty. ("You think you had a tough time with him?" his daughter said to me after a memorial panel in 1991, "Think of what it was like to *live* with him.") A kind of weary silence was about the peak encouragement and a few days or weeks (all time blurs when you are writing a dozen novels a year) he said, "There has never been a novel set at a science fiction convention. Why don't you try that?"

"I spent an hour and a half at the 1967 Worldcon in Manhattan" I said. "That's it. Do you think I can do this?"

"Of course you can do it" he said. "You're a science fiction writer."

Actually, this seemed plausible. The scene at the McAlpin Hotel (I may be misremembering the name; it was on 34th Street and Broadway) had been briskly informative: Sitting at a banquet table in the restaurant with Michael Moorcock, Judith Merril and a turnover parade of Big Name Fans had exposed me to stunning gossip and Moorcock's *je ne sais quoi* in classic form, had exposed me to the Merril conjoined contempt and passion for science fiction, compressed me to the some of the finest personal technique going when Merril decided to leave and Moorcock who had come late to the festivities jumped from his chair and escorted her out, leaving the rest of us to split the bill and all managed like a virtuoso.

I had gotten the waves of the lonely crowd there and of course I had read *The Immortal Storm* and some other fannish classics; I was a rookie at the Scott Meredith Agency still but already a minor bench player on the team with a heavy adolescent reader's background and on the verge of selling "Final War" to F&SF, with "Death to the Keeper" coming on its heels... knew what the field was really about, sort of, and I had an invaluable, irreplaceable adolescent background in the canon. GALAXY was soaring; Wyman Guin's *Beyond Bedlam* which still haunts me was at the time the great work of fiction extant. Like Mike Nichols taken by a friend to watch a play rehearsal while trying to figure what the rest of his life might be, I thought "I can do this". (It took me a while but both of us were right, on shockingly different levels.)

Gather in the Hall was then, remains a true roman a clef and for the truefen at that time every character was recognizable. I knew of them almost completely by reputation but science fiction was the kind of cathouse where all of us shared the customers, the wardrobe, the lingo and a savagely warped but powerful community and most, maybe all of this, was transferred into the novel which was written very quickly (even by my standard) and in savage passion for a field I both embraced and simultaneously fled. That pushpin studio exercise persists, six decades later.

The savage accuracy of a work coming from a writer utterly unknown to, unknowing first hand almost nothing of the field astonishes me. As some novelist wrote of her own imitation of *Valley of the Dolls*, "I made it all up and was shocked to realize how accurate I was." Over the years to follow I had similar aftershocks.

Probably the second novel set wholly at a science fiction Convention was Sharyn (sic) McCrumb's *Bimbos of the Death Sun* published close to two decades later; that roman a clef was wrapped around a murder mystery and its author won the Edgar for best paperback novel, an astonishing development I thought. (The novel is wise, funny, neatly handled.) I met the author only once at the MWA annual banquet at which her award was announced and could not resist seeking her to say "It's a remarkable work and I have to ask you if *Gather in the Hall* was an inspiration or influence." Furiously, reflexively, she absolutely denied. Properly put in place, I skulked my way to the outer partitions of the banquet where after a while I was briefly joined by Ms. McCrumb. "We're all influenced," she said, "And your novel might have been part of that." Not the most handsome of concessions but I took it anyway. There was a sequel a few years later which scouted the same plantation and went nowhere but the McAlpin Hotel was approaching (if not completing) demolition by then.

It is a savage little narrative and along with *Dwellers*, along with *Beyond Apollo* made me a shambling target for a while in some quarters. More than half a century since publication *Gather* is still breathing faintly.

April 2024: New Jersey

Barry N. Malzberg Bibliography

FICTION (as either Barry or Barry N. Malzberg)

Oracle of the Thousand Hands (1968)
Screen (1968)
Confessions of Westchester County (1970)
The Spread (1971)
In My Parents' Bedroom (1971)
The Falling Astronauts (1971)
The Masochist (1972, reprinted as Everything Happened to Susan, 1975; as Cinema, 2020)
Horizontal Woman (1972; reprinted as The Social Worker, 1973)
Beyond Apollo (1972)
Overlay (1972)
Revelations (1972)
Herovit's World (1973)
In the Enclosure (1973)
The Men Inside (1973)
Phase IV (1973; novelization based on a story & screenplay by Mayo Simon)
The Day of the Burning (1974)
The Tactics of Conquest (1974)
Underlay (1974)
The Destruction of the Temple (1974)
Guernica Night (1974)
On a Planet Alien (1974)
Out from Ganymede (1974; stories)
The Sodom and Gomorrah Business (1974)
The Best of Barry N. Malzberg (1975; stories)
The Many Worlds of Barry Malzberg (1975; stories)
Galaxies (1975)
The Gamesman (1975)
Down Here in the Dream Quarter (1976; stories)
Scop (1976)
The Last Transaction (1977)
Chorale (1978)
Malzberg at Large (1979; stories)
The Man Who Loved the Midnight Lady (1980; stories)
The Cross of Fire (1982)
The Remaking of Sigmund Freud (1985)
In the Stone House (2000; stories)
Shiva and Other Stories (2001; stories)
The Passage of the Light: The Recursive Science Fiction of Barry N. Malzberg (2004; ed. by Tony Lewis & Mike Resnick; stories)
The Very Best of Barry N. Malzberg (2013; stories)
Ready When You Are and Other Stories (2023; stories)

With Bill Pronzini

The Running of the Beasts (1976)
Acts of Mercy (1977)
Night Screams (1979)
Prose Bowl (1980)
Problems Solved (2003; stories)
On Account of Darkness and Other SF Stories (2004; stories)

As Mike Barry

Lone Wolf series:
Night Raider (1973)
Bay Prowler (1973)
Boston Avenger (1973)
Desert Stalker (1974)
Havana Hit (1974)
Chicago Slaughter (1974)
Peruvian Nightmare (1974)
Los Angeles Holocaust (1974)
Miami Marauder (1974)

Harlem Showdown (1975)
Detroit Massacre (1975)
Phoenix Inferno (1975)
The Killing Run (1975)
Philadelphia Blowup (1975)

As Francine di Natale

The Circle (1969)

As Claudine Dumas

The Confessions of a Parisian
　　Chambermaid (1969)

As Mel Johnson/M. L. Johnson

Love Doll (1967; with The Sex Pros
　　by Orrie Hitt)
I, Lesbian (1968; as M. L. Johnson)
Just Ask (1968; with Playgirl by Lou
　　Craig)
Instant Sex (1968)
Chained (1968; with Master of
　　Women by March Hastings & Love
　　Captive by Dallas Mayo)
Kiss and Run (1968; with Sex on the
　　Sand by Sheldon Lord & Odd Girl
　　by March Hastings)
Nympho Nurse (1969; with Young
　　and Eager by Jim Conroy &
　　Quickie by Gene Evans)
The Sadist (1969; with Flesh by Max
　　Collier)
The Box (1969)
Do It To Me (1969; with Hot Blonde
　　by Jim Conroy)
Born to Give (1969; with Swap Club
　　by Greg Hamilton & Wild in Bed
　　by Dirk Malloy)
Campus Doll (1969; with High
　　School Stud by Robert Hadley)
A Way With All Maidens (1969)

As Howard Lee

Kung Fu #1: The Way of the Tiger,
　　the Sign of the Dragon (1973)

As Lee W. Mason

Lady of a Thousand Sorrows (1977)

As K. M. O'Donnell

Empty People (1969)
The Final War and Other Fantasies
　　(1969; stories)
Dwellers of the Deep (1970)
Gather at the Hall of the Planets
　　(1971)
In the Pocket and Other S-F Stories
　　(1971; stories)
Universe Day (1971; stories)

As Eliot B. Reston

The Womanizer (1972)

As Gerrold Watkins

Southern Comfort (1969)
A Bed of Money (1970)
A Satyr's Romance (1970)
Giving It Away (1970)
Art of the Fugue (1970)

NON-FICTION/ESSAYS

The Engines of the Night: Science
　　Fiction in the Eighties (1982;
　　essays)
Breakfast in the Ruins (2007;
　　essays: expansion of Engines of the
　　Night)
The Business of Science Fiction: Two
　　Insiders Discuss Writing and
　　Publishing (2010; with Mike
　　Resnick)

The Bend at the End of the Road
(2018; essays)

EDITED ANTHOLOGIES

Final Stage (1974; with Edward L.
Ferman)
Arena (1976; with Edward L.
Ferman)
Graven Images (1977; with Edward
L. Ferman)
Dark Sins, Dark Dreams (1978; with
Bill Pronzini)
The End of Summer: SF in the
Fifties (1979; with Bill Pronzini)
Shared Tomorrows: Science Fiction
in Collaboration (1979; with Bill
Pronzini)
Neglected Visions (1979; with
Martin H. Greenberg & Joseph D.
Olander)

Bug-Eyed Monsters (1980; with Bill
Pronzini)
The Science Fiction of Mark Clifton
(1980; with Martin H. Greenberg)
The Arbor House Treasury of Horror
& the Supernatural (1981; with
Bill Pronzini & Martin H.
Greenberg)
The Science Fiction of Kris Neville
(1984; with Martin H. Greenberg)
Mystery in the Mainstream (1986;
with Bill Pronzini & Martin H.
Greenberg)
Uncollected Stars (1986; with Piers
Anthony, Martin H. Greenberg &
Charles G. Waugh)
The Best Time Travel Stories of All
Time (2003)

www.ingramcontent.com/pod-product-compliance
Lightning Source LLC
Chambersburg PA
CBHW050345160726
48002CB00001B/463